D0741897

DOGSBODY, INC.

A Mystery

By
L. L. THRASHER

A Write Way Publishing Book

Copyright © 1999, by Linda Thrasher Baty

Write Way Publishing
10555 E. Dartmouth, Ste 210
Aurora, CO 80014

First Edition; 1999

All rights reserved. No part of this book may be reproduced in any form, except by a newspaper or magazine reviewer who wishes to quote brief passages in connection with a review.

Queries regarding rights and permissions should be addressed to Write Way Publishing, 10555 E. Dartmouth, Ste. 210, Aurora, CO, 80014

ISBN 1-885173-65-2

1 2 3 4 5 6 7 8 9 10

For
Bert Baty
Nathan Baty
Susan Baty

Chapter One

I watched myself get shot three times.

A lot of other people were in sight, but I was hard to miss: when you're six foot four, you're always head and shoulders above the crowd. I walked into view from the right, ducking under a tree branch and saying something over my shoulder to someone out of sight. I was dressed in faded jeans, scuffed hiking boots, and a light blue down jacket, unzipped, a darker blue shirt showing beneath it. Concealed beneath the jacket was a thirty-eight caliber Smith & Wesson in a shoulder holster. A lot of good that had done.

Walking forward, I looked straight ahead for a moment and gave a little self-conscious wave, then I headed off to the left, looking back once and grinning, deep vertical creases appearing in my cheeks.

Coming into view from the left, identical creases appearing in her cheeks as she smiled, was my twin sister Carrie, only five foot eight but equally hard to miss in a crowd. Men's heads swiveled as she passed by.

Carrie was also wearing faded jeans, but hers came that way. Her boots were knee-high gleaming black leather, her jacket maroon, the white pile lining of the hood framing thick black hair, shoulder length and almost straight, her last perm having faded away. Her eyes were the same bright blue as the cloudless sky. We were making our way toward each other, but slowly because of all the people milling around.

In the background, a slender, gray-haired woman in a white blouse, dark green skirt, and white oxford shoes was striding purposefully through the crowd. Carrie was still a few feet from me when the gray-haired woman touched my arm. I reacted to her touch by taking a half-step backward and turning toward her, which put me right in front of her, my body concealing hers.

At that instant, I lurched forward and turned to my left, my right hand going out toward Carrie as she ran the last few steps to me and threw her arms around me. The gray-haired woman was in sight again, falling gracelessly to the ground. I fell to my knees, dragging Carrie down with me, a dark stain spreading across the shoulder of my jacket as I pitched forward and lay still, legs sprawled out, face turned away, head on Carrie's thighs. She was sitting back on her heels, her face blood-spattered. She bent over me, leaning down until her forehead was against my back, black hair spilling out of the hood and hiding her face. The gray-haired woman in the white blouse was on her back, one arm flung above her head, legs apart, sensible white oxfords pointing obliquely at the sky. Her face was obscured by dark, glistening blood.

We made a stark tableau, the three of us absolutely still while around us the crowd was in frantic motion, a human wave surging past us and out of sight.

The police chief strode into view, dressed in old jeans, cowboy boots, and a navy blue ski jacket. Sandy curls showed beneath a western-style hat shoved back on his head. He dropped to one knee beside the gray-haired woman, one hand holding a radio handset to his mouth, the other hand moving toward the woman's throat.

That was the end because the woman with the video camera had dropped it as her mind finally comprehended what her eyes were seeing through the lens. Her scream was the only distinct sound on the tape. A cold winter wind blowing against the microphone had muffled the rest of the soundtrack. The gunshot was barely audible, a faint pop like a champagne cork going off in the distance.

After watching the scene for the third time, I hit the rewind button on the remote control for the VCR. For a moment, I stared at the snow pattern on the screen of the television, which was mounted on the wall beyond the foot of the bed, then I turned it off, using a control that was strapped to the bed rail. I closed my eyes, forcing them open again when I felt myself falling asleep. I turned the television back on and started the VCR. I had fast-forwarded through the first ten minutes to find the shooting scene, but it was the beginning of the tape Phil Pauling had asked me to watch. He had been able to identify everyone on the tape except a man who appeared briefly in the background before glancing at his watch and walking away quickly.

I noticed the man immediately, dismissed him as a suspect, and watched the rest of the tape. As soon as I appeared on the screen, I started counting off seconds out loud, saying "One thousand twenty-two" just as Mary Jo Collins screamed and dropped the camera. I shut both machines off.

Twenty-two seconds. The last ten would make a moderately interesting clip for the evening news. Twenty-two seconds of my life, captured in a rapid sequence of pictures, which may not lie but sure as hell don't tell the whole truth. It hadn't been like that at all. It hadn't even started there. It had started forty minutes earlier when five telephones woke me up.

Chapter Two

The phone by the bed and three of the others had electronic warbles that were easy to ignore, but the kitchen phone rang the old-fashioned way, a loud, clangorous ring, urgent and demanding, a sound that evokes a Pavlovian response from anyone who's ever heard it.

I stubbornly refused to respond to the stimulus, clenching my teeth and counting the rings instead. I'd have to get up and listen to the message but I'd be damned if I'd actually talk to anyone who had the colossal gall to call me at–I rolled over and squinted at the clock–ten minutes after eleven on a Monday morning.

After the fourth ring, I heard the distant rumble of my own voice coming from the answering machine's speaker. It was followed, not by the indistinct murmur of someone leaving a message, but by a loud, shrill whistle–the kind you can only make with two fingers stuck in your mouth. I muttered "Shit!" and picked up the phone on the nightstand and said "What?" into it.

With a gratingly cheerful east Texas twang, the Chief of Police said, "O.S.I.M., Bucky. Sandhoff's office had another bomb threat. Just another crank call but I figured you'd want to know. I'm hanging around for a while. The whole damn town managed to hear about it, and we got about two hundred rubberneckers out here."

"Shit!" I hung up and dragged myself out of bed. After scraping some whiskers off and taking a quick shower, I felt a little better, more like I'd had, oh, maybe four hours of sleep instead of three.

The six-mile drive to town was one I could make in my sleep, which was just as well since I hadn't had any coffee yet. I took care of that first, making a quick stop at a drive-up window, then I turned north at the corner of First and Main and made a series of turns that would get me to Belle Foret, which is properly spelled Belle Forêt and pronounced Belle Foh-reh. In French, it means "beautiful forest." In Mackie, it's the name of a street and everyone pronounces it Bell For It.

Whoever named it must have known some French. Belle Foret is less than a mile long and marks the western boundary of Mackie Woods, six hundred acres of undeniably beautiful forest in a wedge shape, its narrow end coming within a few blocks of downtown. Belle Foret is one of the prettiest streets in town, a winding road with a steep, rocky hill almost sheer enough to be called a cliff rising thirty feet above the pavement on the east side and a row of tall cottonwood trees on the west side. In the spring and summer, the cottonwoods shade the narrow road with a canopy of green highlighted by the silvery underside of the leaves; in the fall, the canopy turns to gold; in winter, the branches form a skeletal arch against the sky.

For reasons that were probably explained in great legalistic detail in old records at City Hall, Belle Foret, with woods on one side and an upper-income residential area on the other, was zoned for limited commercial use, medical offices to be precise. There were no buildings at all on the southern end of Belle

Foret, the land being the back of huge lots on the next street over.

Spaced far apart on the north end of the road were six bungalows, which currently housed four dentists, three Family Practice doctors, one pediatrician, one ophthalmologist, one orthodontist, and one obstetrician/gynecologist. Anyone going to Belle Foret was going to a doctor's office. Or to an abortion rights demonstration, which was where I was going.

When Irene Sandhoff opened her practice two years ago, it had been at least a decade since there had been an obstetrician in town. Family Practice physicians had delivered most of the babies, while women with complicated pregnancies had to go out of town to see a specialist. Since Sandhoff was an outspoken advocate of women's rights, it shouldn't have taken a genius to figure out she performed abortions, strictly in compliance with the laws of the state of Oregon. She didn't advertise her services and women having abortions tend not to make public announcements of their decisions, so the anti-abortion activists in town feigned ignorance of her sideline and concentrated their efforts on collecting signatures on petitions to send to Salem and Washington, D. C. After all, Mackie really needed an obstetrician and you can't be held accountable for what you pretend you don't know.

Then, on a snowy morning three weeks ago, a nineteen-year-old named Misty Connors arrived at the doctor's office, accompanied by the man who had inflicted an inconvenient pregnancy on her, a chronically unemployed roofer named Howard Delwin, who also happened to be Misty's mother's live-in boyfriend. Karen Connors had somehow found out what was going on and had also shown up at Sandhoff's office where she engaged her treacherous daughter and her cheating lover in a hair-pulling, eye-gouging, name-calling free-for-all. The police arrived; the press followed.

When the reason for Misty's presence at the doctor's office

became public knowledge, the town's anti-abortion contingent was forced to pull its head out of the sand. A small group of protesters with pictures of bloody fetuses on posterboard placards appeared in front of Sandhoff's office that same afternoon. By the next morning, the pro-choice advocates had mounted a counterattack. One of the pro-choicers was Carolina O'Brien Smith Harry, my twin sister and my reason for driving down Belle Foret on a cold, clear Monday in December with my stomach churning its complaint against black coffee for breakfast and my eyes gritty from lack of sleep.

I squinted against the strobe-like flashes of sunlight flickering between bare branches. Sandhoff's office was in the next to last building. She was the only doctor who wasn't sharing space with a colleague. Her building was designed to accommodate two separate medical offices but the other half had been empty for months, ever since my brother-in-law closed his private practice and went to work for Mackie General Hospital. Today, there were enough cars lining both sides of the street to suggest that an entire convention of doctors was in attendance.

I backed the Camaro in at an angle between a rusted-out Chevy pickup and a brand new Lexus and checked out the crowd while I finished my coffee. Two hundred was a fair estimate. I couldn't for the life of me figure out why a bomb threat would draw a crowd, especially since it was the fifth one in two weeks and nothing had blown up yet. Both groups of demonstrators were hard-pressed to come up with a handful of participants on a daily basis. People had jobs to go to or children to care for or appointments to keep or soap operas to watch and, besides, it was cold. Apparently there was nothing like the possibility of a big bang to spark people's interest.

Carrie had attempted to enlist my services in her battle, but I declined, although I sided with the pro-choicers. The abortion issue was one I had difficulty coping with because it was linked in my mind—illogically but apparently permanently—with the day I made history at Mackie High as the only junior ever called out of gym class because his wife was having a miscarriage in the nurse's office.

My public opinion, when I was forced to express it, was a purely pragmatic one: Outlawing any product or service for which a strong demand exists results only in putting money in the pockets of the people who step in to provide the product or service illegally. Guns, drugs, alcohol, prostitutes, abortions—outlaw any of them and people who want them will get them anyway. Outlaw cauliflower and people will buy it from their friendly dealer at twenty bucks a head and it will probably be coated with carcinogenic pesticides. Legalization, at the very least, provides some control over quality and cost.

Carrie denounced my opinion as simplistic—or maybe she said simple-minded—and Typical of a Man. I didn't care. It was an opinion I could express in public without flashing back to Patricia Ann Flynn, who had been Patricia Ann Smith for a mere three weeks, standing in the nurse's office, wrapped in a bloody sheet, glistening clots of blood the size of my fist quivering like mounds of translucent cherry gelatin on the floor at her feet.

I swallowed the last of the coffee and got out of the car, wishing I were back in bed, wishing even harder that my sister would develop a serious case of apathy and stay home so I didn't have to worry about her.

I walked across the street, looking for cops. The only ones I saw were Patrolman Dan Fogel, who was trying to convince people the excitement was over, and Chief of Police Phil Pauling, who nodded at me. He was standing on the steps to the building, looking like he wasn't doing much of anything but his eyes never stopped scanning the crowd. He had called me because Carrie was there and he knew I'd want to come keep an eye on her, but it also didn't hurt to have a man my size on his side, especially one who's licensed to carry a gun and has a reputation–completely unfounded–for being quick with his fists, and who doesn't have to waste time explaining people's rights to them. We'd worked together when I was a cop and we both knew that it didn't take much—one voice raised a little too high, one fist shaken in the wrong face—and any crowd can turn into a mob. Even in Mackie.

Chapter Three

Carrie's radar was working. She was on the far side of the crowd, engaged in what appeared to be a heated argument with Reverend William Sloan. I had no sooner caught sight of her than she spun around to face me, her eyes meeting mine instantly. She gave me a look I had no trouble interpreting: *Stay out of this, Zachariah. I can take care of myself.* I responded with a message of my own: *At the first sign of trouble I'm getting you out of here if I have to hogtie you to do it.* She had no trouble interpreting my look either. Rolling her eyes heavenward in mute appeal to a far higher intelligence than mine, she turned back to face her adversary. I strolled through the crowd, looking for potential trouble.

I knew most of the people by sight if not by name. Mackie's Catholic population was represented on both sides of the battle line: pro-lifers following the dictates of their church; pro-choicers who had made the difficult decision that on this issue their church was wrong. Father Daniel Thomas, tall, angular, prematurely gray, and stooped as if he carried a heavy load on his narrow shoulders, moved between the two groups, torn by his duty to his church and his responsibility for his flock.

The right-wingers were the largest and most vocal segment

of the pro-lifers. They were the same people who had fought and lost a heated battle against sex education in the public schools. The contradiction inherent in their beliefs was puzzling: Don't teach our children about sex and contraception and when their lack of knowledge results in unwanted pregnancies, don't let them have access to safe abortions. They would consign poor women, uneducated women, desperate women, and frightened teenagers to the machinations of back-alley abortionists, knowing very well that women with money would have safe abortions in foreign countries. Restrictive laws had never stopped abortion; they just made it more dangerous for some women and more expensive for others.

Technically on the same side as the right-wingers, but careful to keep a safe distance from them, was a group of young women who had brought their children, infants in arms and toddlers as round as snowmen in their colorful snowsuits. I knew most of the women well enough to know that their objection to abortion was based less on political or religious beliefs than on their inability to understand how any woman could choose abortion over childbirth and their more fundamental inability to understand anyone different from themselves. These were women who had never experienced poverty or mental illness or brutality, whose lives were blessed with a sane security into which they could bring their children. For some of them the security was a fragile façade, delicately balanced on a man's goodwill, that would eventually tumble down, taking their smug righteousness with it.

That had already happened to some of them, a few of whom were now aligned with the radical feminists, another group that had turned out in force this morning, bearing signs: IF MEN GOT PREGNANT, ABORTION WOULD BE A GOD-GIVEN, INALIENABLE, CONSTITUTIONAL RIGHT; KEEP YOUR LAWS OFF MY BODY; RU-486—THE

PILL THAT WILL TRULY SET US FREE. The abortion pill seemed to be the primary topic of conversation, with men's shortcomings coming in second. I managed to get past the group without giving in to the temptation to say *Excuse me, honey* to any of them.

My tenants were on the fringe of the group, figuratively as well as literally. Myrna and Rosie co-owned Fanciful Flowers, which occupied half the building where my office was. Rosie was a dead ringer for Marilyn Monroe, which meant she also looked a lot like Madonna. She was making the most of it today, visibly shivering in something black and lacy and thigh-high. I wondered whose eye she was trying to catch. Myrna's tolerance of her partner's affairs had been wearing thin lately. I foresaw endless squabbles over the flower shop if they split up. As landlord and friend, I'd end up refereeing between two warring lesbians. Just thinking about it made me tired.

I said hello to Myrna, a distant cousin of mine, and got a cool smile in response. Rosie fluttered spiky eyelashes at me and cooed a greeting in her little-girl voice. She slithered against me, saying, "Ooh, it's so cold, Zacky."

"Maybe you should go home and put some clothes on." Since Rosie was coming on to me, she was putting on her act for the benefit of the men who were watching her like starving cats at a mouse hole. I had once suggested to Myrna that half her problems with Rosie would be eliminated if they came out of the closet. Myrna had said tersely, "She doesn't fuck guys to maintain her cover, Zack. She *likes* it. All the women in the world and I fall for one who's bi."

Myrna was frowning at Rosie, who was rubbing her right breast against my arm. I disentangled myself from her and left them quickly.

Three bikers had stopped by to check out the action. Their jeans, wrung out, would have provided enough grease for a lube job, but their choppers were immaculate, sunlight flashing off the chrome. The bikers looked mean and tough and they were, but unless an outsider deliberately provoked them, any trouble they caused would be to one another. All three of them were hunkered down by their bikes, the best vantage point for looking up Rosie's skirt.

Near the bikers, but oblivious to Rosie, were the local gay activists, all four of them. I assumed their interest in abortion rights was purely theoretical. I responded to their greetings, then continued my stroll.

The rest of the crowd seemed to be more interested in socializing than in demonstrating. Some were unemployed, some unemployable, some employed but conveniently possessed of social consciences that could be activated just in time to take a long break on a Monday morning. There were also several homemakers, a handful of drunks, four men of God, three truant teenagers, two druggies, and one dealer in a camel's hair coat. I watched a transaction that involved the exchange of cash for white powder, then continued working my way around the edge of the crowd and back to the steps at the front of the building, where the chief of police was still standing.

"Well?" he asked.

"Looks like a peaceful, law-abiding crowd to me."

"Remind me to bust that asshole in the eight-hundred-dollar coat as soon as I'm through here. You look like hell. What time'd you get back last night?"

"This morning."

He laughed, then, scowling suddenly, said, "Those goddamn stupid women bringing those little babies out here oughtta be jailed for reckless endangerment of minors."

I shrugged. "You're the cop. Arrest them. Where are the rest of your men?"

"Burglary in progress, missing three-year-old, and an injury accident. Never rains but it pours. Well, it's about *time.*" I turned to follow his gaze. Several people were heading toward their cars, apparently a spontaneous group migration since none of them seemed to be together.

Phil said, "I got no complaint with peaceable assembly, but goddammit, there were only five people here Friday, two on one side and three on the other, then some jackass decides to play with the phone and people come crawling out of the woodwork hoping to watch something blow sky high. I oughtta confiscate every goddamn scanner in this town. People oughtta have something better to do than sit around monitoring police calls and fucking up my day."

"And mine," I said and yawned. Phil's radio crackled with static and I left him issuing orders into it. I stood under a towering evergreen, catching bits and pieces of conversations as people moved past me.

". . . frigging transmission went out on me and that sumbitch down at the dealership says . . ."

". . . at conception. What do they think it is? A vegetable? A human being is what it is and anyone who . . ."

"I don't really know. Something about a bomb . . ."

". . . aces and I was sitting there with three kings and . . . "

". . . about Tina? You *didn't?* Well, I heard she . . ."

". . . not even viable until about twenty-six weeks and then it's iffy. Abortion in the first trimester . . ."

". . . get the abortion pill and then *finally* our reproductive choices won't be subject to public scrutiny and the Supreme Court can go . . ."

"I can get the affidavit by Wednesday and we . . ."

". . . kill me if I got rid of it and now it's too late and he's never around and, god, I could just kill him."

Two death threats in one sentence caught my attention

and I turned to look at the speaker. Angela Billingsly had been head cheerleader our senior year at Mackie High. I had vivid memories of her body arching in mid-air, the curve of her breasts playing hell with the straight lines of the gold M on the front of her navy blue sweater. She had lived out her fantasy, marrying the captain of the football team after graduation, although a maternity wedding gown probably hadn't been part of the fantasy. A few years later, she was divorced with two children to raise alone. From what I'd just overheard, her second marriage wasn't working out any better, no surprise since she'd been scraping bottom when she dredged up Joe Knox, whose only talent was emptying six-packs in record time. Angela appeared to be about twelve months pregnant. Another baby, another twenty pounds, the cheerleader figure existing only in my memory.

I didn't know the woman Angela was talking to or I might have walked over to say hello. Instead I turned the other way. A mistake: I came face to face with Reverend William Sloan. Or rather, his face to my chest.

"Ah, Zachariah," he said, "I was just speaking to our dear Carolina. Such a lovely young woman, even if our views in this matter are sadly at variance." What Sloan lacked in stature, he made up in pomposity.

"Hi, Willie. How's the salvation business going? All those sinners sending in their pledges in a timely manner?"

His sincere smile faltered momentarily. He didn't like being called Willie and he didn't like having emphasis placed on the financial side of his Sunday-morning radio show. He also didn't particularly like me. Among other things, I had committed the unpardonable sin of correcting his Biblical quotations on a few occasions.

Maybe he'd forgotten about that. Gesturing toward a group of women holding pro-choice signs, he said, "So misguided of them to feel they are doing their sisters a service by supporting them in their sins. As the Lord told us, 'Let her have the child and in no wise slay it.'"

"The Lord didn't say that, Willie. It was when Solomon was going to divvy up that kid the two women were fighting over. The real mother was speaking to Solomon: 'Oh, my Lord, give her the living child, and in no wise slay it.' Doesn't have a damn thing to do with abortion."

Sloan drew himself up to his full five feet, seven inches and smoothed back his John Kennedy hairdo. "I consider the Bible in its entirety to be the Word of God. Much of it, like the Constitution, must be interpreted within the context of our own times. Surely the moral of the story is clear: A true, loving mother does not destroy her own child. Before or after its birth."

"I guess that depends on when an embryo qualifies as a child and I'm not going to argue that point with you because I don't know the answer. I do know that women have been having abortions since the beginning of time and making it against the law just sends them back to wormwood and knitting needles and back-alley butchers."

"Men have been committing murder since Cain slew Abel, Zachariah. Shall we legalize it so murderers can carry out their foul deeds in a more convenient manner?"

Christ! Why couldn't I learn to keep my mouth shut? I was over my head and out of my depth. "That argument only works if you consider abortion murder."

"And is it not? What better definition of murder is there than the willful destruction of a human life?"

"You're back to the question of when life begins and I already said I don't know the answer. I can't see why your opinion on that is any better than anyone else's though." I started backing away. "Nice talking to you. I need to see if

Carrie's ready to leave." Adding "See you around," I turned away quickly, almost decapitating myself on a low branch.

Sloan responded, "In church, perhaps?"

I ducked under the branch as I looked back at him and said, "I doubt it, but you can pray for me if you want to."

I looked around, hoping Carrie hadn't been close enough to overhear my feeble defense of her Cause. I caught sight of her where she'd been earlier. She smiled when she caught my eye. I headed toward her, maneuvering around people in my way.

Mary Jo Collins, vice-president of my senior class, was pointing a video camera at me. I waved, feeling stupid and thinking there should be a law against unauthorized video-taping. I didn't want to star in anyone's home movies.

Mary Jo called, "An Academy Award performance, Zack." I looked back at her and smiled.

A ripple of excited murmurs ran through the crowd. Dr. Sandhoff had come out of her office. I hoped she wasn't planning to make a speech. It was almost noon and I wanted to talk Carrie into going home. Enough of this activist shit. She had two children to take care of and a business to run. If I could get her to leave now, she'd nurse the baby, play with Melissa, have some lunch, and by then all the excitement here would have died down. And I could take a nap.

Someone touched my arm. I turned and looked down into Irene Sandhoff's brown eyes, then a rifle cracked and something sharp jabbed me in the left shoulder, hard enough to make me stagger forward, and one of Irene Sandhoff's brown eyes turned to dark red liquid and blood streaked down her face. *Oh, Jesus, someone's shooting! Carrie!* Where was she? I turned, aware of pain in my shoulder, a dull pain with undertones of worse to come. People were running, screaming, jostling me, and I couldn't find Carrie, then suddenly she was right in front of me, bright blue frightened eyes, blood splashed like scarlet rain across her face. I felt her arms go around me and heard her saying my name—not *Zachariah* but my name way back when we were "the twins" and spoke a language of our own invention. "Dabby!" she said and "Dabby!" again. I tried to say *Get inside, someone's shooting,* but my voice wouldn't work. I didn't realize I was falling until my knees hit the ground.

My vision was going, light fading in and out, a strange threatening darkness closing in on me. For a moment I saw Carrie's face clearly then I felt myself falling forward against her, my face sliding on padded fabric, then denim, cold beneath my cheek. I felt a heartbeat, mine or Carrie's or maybe both of ours beating in unison. Darkness engulfed me, but I could hear people in panicky flight and—overriding it all— Phil Pauling in a cold rage, commanding order out of chaos. My last thought was a memory: *O.S.I.M., Bucky.* O.S.I.M.: Oh, Shit, It's Monday.

Chapter Four

I lived.

I regained consciousness briefly in the ambulance, long enough to know that Carrie was with me and was unharmed. She was clutching my hand and sobbing. I wanted to tell her everything was okay, but I thought of Irene Sandhoff's face and didn't try to talk.

I came to again in the emergency room and saw Carrie's husband Tom leaning over me, stethoscope dangling, blue eyes not quite serious enough to scare me, saying, "A mere flesh wound. Rambo would stitch it up himself." I thought I heard myself laugh then I was gone again.

Sometime later I descended from a Demerol cloud long enough to roll onto a bed without assistance. I felt Carrie's hand in mine and I held on tight and drifted away.

When I finally woke up, her hand was gone and mine felt cold and empty. I was aware of a thick wad of bandaging on my left shoulder and a hint of pain beneath it. The chief of police was there, chair tilted back, boots crossed on the foot of the bed. "Where's Carrie?" I asked.

"She went home to feed the baby. The babysitter couldn't get him to take formula. Can't say as I blame him. You ever smell that stuff?"

"What time is it?"

"Three-fifteen."

"Same day, right?"

"Yep. Still Monday. It's been one hell of a long day so far and it ain't over yet."

"You didn't get him."

He swung his feet off the bed and the front legs of the chair hit the floor with a sharp smack. "Didn't even come close. The shot was fired from the hill across the street. No way to get up there to go after him and he could take his pick of where he wanted to go. Almost a square mile of woods and streets dead-ending into them all over the place. He could've had a car parked on any of them. We found a trampled down place where he probably fired from and we could follow his trail for maybe fifty feet but the damn ground's frozen. Too bad we didn't have snow last night."

The longer I was awake the more aware I became of an ache in my left shoulder. "So what's wrong with me?"

"Nothing much. You got hit on the top of your shoulder. Bullet went straight through. You'd think all that muscle you're packing would've slowed it down, but it went through slicker'n a whistle."

"And hit Irene Sandhoff."

"Yeah. I wasn't sure you knew about that. I was going to break it to you gently."

"I saw her face."

"Right through the eye and into her brain. She was dead before she hit the ground."

"He only fired once?"

"Yeah. One shot. What does that tell you?"

"He's a good shot."

"One shot, one target is what it tells me. This wasn't some fruitcake who thought firing into a crowd would be fun. One shot, one target. He hit what he was aiming at and packed it up."

"What's your point?"

"Which one of you was the target?"

The question stunned me. I hadn't even considered the possibility that I had been shot deliberately. I had just been in the wrong place at the wrong time, stepping in front of a bullet meant for Irene Sandhoff. "She was," I said.

"Okay. Why?"

"What do you mean, why? Because it's the only way it makes sense. I could've been shot any place. It happened at her office. I wouldn't even have been there if you hadn't called me."

"Yeah, I've been thinking about that. Makes me feel kinda bad. But the thing is, anyone who knows anything about you could figure out that you'd show up there."

"Oh, come on, Phil, what are you suggesting? Someone made a bomb threat on the off-chance I'd hear about it and be worried about Carrie and go down there so he could shoot me? That's pretty far-fetched."

"Except for one thing: If I wanted to shoot someone in Mackie and not get caught, I'd sure as hell try to do it from that hill across from her office. And there's another thing."

"What?"

"Anyone who was after Sandhoff couldn't't've been expecting her to come outside. She never did. She made one statement to the newspaper the first day the protesters showed up. After that, her policy was business as usual. If people got there early enough or stayed late enough, they'd catch a glimpse of her as she was coming or going, but that's it. She never came out of the office during working hours."

"She did today."

"Yeah, and that was pretty damned funny. She made a beeline right for you."

"Now what are you saying? Someone figured out how to get me there then figured out how to get her to come outside so he could shoot us both? You're fishing, Phil. Some anti-abortion fanatic shot her. I don't know why she came over to me. I didn't even know her. The only time I ever talked to her was at the drug abuse prevention program at the high school."

"Well, I'd sure like to know why she came outside. Sure looked to me like she wanted to talk to you."

I shrugged, not a wise thing to do with a bullet wound in your shoulder. After I finished moaning and groaning and swearing, Phil said, "All I'm saying is I need to know for sure which one of you was the intended victim. So which one, Bucky? Am I looking for someone who wanted Sandhoff dead or someone who wanted you dead?"

The impact of his suggestion was starting to hit me. If I was the target and Irene Sandhoff was killed by mistake . . . I didn't want to think about that. "Nobody's out to kill me."

"If you were just Joe Citizen, I wouldn't even be wondering, but you aren't. You're a private investigator and an ex-cop and you've been mixed up with some pretty bad types over the years. You've had death threats. You've managed to piss off a lot of people and some of them wouldn't bat an eye at murder if they thought they could get away with it. Soon as you're feeling up to it, make me a list."

"A list. Of what?"

"People who'd like to dance on your grave. I know some of them and I've already started checking."

"You're wasting your time. He was after Sandhoff."

Phil stood up and stretched, then pulled a remote control from his pocket and handed it to me. "I hooked up a VCR. Mary Jo's tape's in it. There's a guy I can't ID right at the beginning, looks at his watch and walks away like he's in one hell of a big hurry. See if you know him. You can't miss him: cowboy clothes and a full beard. I'll be back later." He picked up his jacket and walked to the door. Turning back to me, he said, "Look, I think you're right. I hope you are. But if you're not . . . try to remember you didn't pull the trigger."

Chapter Five

I watched the videotape after Phil left, then slept, not waking up until the phone rang at six-thirty. Tom told me Carrie was sleeping. "You want me to come down and hold your hand?"

"No, thanks. Carrie didn't call Mom and Dad, did she?"

"They would have heard about it from someone else if she hadn't. She downplayed it nicely. They aren't coming."

"Thank god. What did they say?"

"I talked to your dad."

"And?"

"I got a lecture on gun control laws."

"Jesus, they never change. Am I going to have any trouble with my shoulder?"

"Not permanently, but you won't want to move your arm or turn your head for a while. I did a great job. The scars won't be too bad. You need to take it easy, and absolutely—"

"—no sex for six months." It was the advice he gave me every time he patched me up. We talked a while longer, then I hung up and buzzed a nurse to see if they planned to feed me. My efforts were rewarded when a nurse's aide appeared with a tray of something that smelled fairly edible. "Visiting hours in fifteen minutes," she said cheerily as she left.

I wasn't expecting any visitors. I underestimated the good people of Mackie or maybe it was their curiosity I underestimated. I had a steady stream of visitors, some of them people I hadn't talked to in years. Most only stayed a few minutes. Too many brought flowers. The room began to smell like a funeral chapel.

The only visitor I was glad to see was Phil's wife Patsy, who brought me a homemade get-well card from Philip the Second and gave me a kiss that had more restorative power than all Tom's medicine. Phil showed up while she was there. I told him the man on the videotape was a patient of Dr. Halsey. I didn't know his name but I'd seen him several times in the fall when I was having a lot of dental work done and he had complained that he'd be having work done for months. "If you check with Halsey's office, you'll probably find out he had an appointment and was sitting in the dentist's chair when the shot was fired," I told Phil. He took his wife with him when he left.

By nine o'clock, I thought I'd seen the last well-wisher and was thinking bitterly that the one person who hadn't shown up was Mattie Hagen, whose bed I'd been sharing on an occasional basis for over a year. I was in the mood to resent her absence, although I wasn't surprised by it, the congruence of our lives being limited to an area roughly the size and shape of Mattie's brass four-poster.

I was trying to find a comfortable position for sleeping when a plump woman with curly blond hair poked her head in the doorway and said, "Are you decent?"

I smiled and told her to come in.

Dora, whose last name I'd lost track of through her several marriages and divorces, worked for Main Street Answering Service. I'd known her since high school, when her bad reputation had piqued my interest briefly.

"How are you feeling, sweetie?"

"Not too bad, thanks."

"I brought your messages. Didn't know if you felt up to it but I figured they might be important. I'd've got 'em over here sooner but I called and they said you were sleeping and then I got busy at home and forgot about it. Sorry."

"No problem, Dora."

"You had a couple others but I called back and they said no hurry, they'll call you later. That was Jorgensen and Barr Law Offices and some insurance guy. So there's just these two." She pulled two yellow message slips from her coat pocket. "One's a guy named Clausen, says his kid ran away. Other one's just a phone number. It was a woman but she wouldn't leave her name."

"Did you take that call?"

"Yeah. She called at . . . let's see . . . eleven twenty-five this morning. She seemed to know she reached an answering service. I asked for her name but she said just give you the number. Her voice was kinda familiar, like maybe I talked to her before, but I couldn't place it."

"Did she ask for me by name?"

"Yeah. Mr. Smith, not Zachariah."

"Okay. Thanks, Dora."

She tucked the edge of the message slips under the phone on the nightstand. "I stopped by the office before I came over here. You haven't had any other calls except people wanting to know how you're doing. I guess I'd better go now. You're tired, huh?"

"Yeah, a little."

She bent and kissed my forehead. "Everyone at work, they say get well quick, okay?"

"Tell them thanks for me."

After she left, I set the phone on my chest then propped

the receiver on the pillow by my left ear and called Clausen's number. When a man answered, I said, "This is Zachariah Smith from Arrow Investigations."

"Oh. Yeah. I didn't expect you'd be calling, what with getting shot and everything. How're you doing?"

"Pretty good. I understand you have a missing child."

"Child, ha! Kid's fifteen and taller'n me already. Thinks he's all grown up. Got a real mouth on him, you know what I mean?"

"Yeah. How long's he been gone?"

"Friday night. We kinda got into it. Nothing major, he was pissed because I told him to go help his mama with the dinner dishes and he started going on and on about how he was sick of all the hassle, school and me getting on his case all the time." Clausen sighed. "I don't know, the wife says I'm too hard on him. Shit, is it so bad I want him to get a normal haircut and maybe wear something besides jeans with the butt ripped out? Christ, he looks like some kind of bum most of the time. And a little help around the house, is that too much to expect? What would it hurt him to carry out the trash once in a while without me telling him to a hundred times first? We get into it pretty good sometimes. I don't mean physical stuff, I never lay a hand on the kid, but, tell you the truth, I think a good whipping might straighten him out. Anyway, Friday night we had a big argument and he went to his room and later on I heard him go out the front door. I waited up 'cause I was going to give him holy hell when he came back, but he never did."

"Did he take anything with him?"

"Uh . . . don't really know. I was at the kitchen table having coffee with the wife when we heard him leave. He was around the corner and way the hell down the block by the time I went to look."

"Do you think he'd leave town?"

"No, I don't think so. Where would he go? He's lived here his whole life, all his friends are here, most of the relatives, too, not that he's got much use for any of them. That's another thing—his grandma, that's the wife's mama, she's over in Willowhaven Convalescent Center, not doing too good, and probably not going to be around much longer and all the time she's asking when's Jordy coming to see her and the wife says she'll get him over there but he won't go, says he can't stand the way the place smells. Hell, I don't like it much either—that hospital smell, you know, but, shit, it ain't the old woman's fault she's dying. Family's got to stick together is what I always say. Jordy, he could give a shit."

Jordy. Jordan Clausen. The name rang a bell, not a melodious one, either. Jordan Clausen was a sullen kid with an attitude problem who spent his spare time slouching around downtown, trying to look tough and succeeding only in looking like he needed a swift kick in the seat of the pants. His running away didn't surprise me. The fact that his father was thinking about paying someone to bring him back did.

"I've seen your son around town, Mr. Clausen. I didn't make the connection until now. He looks like he's pretty capable of taking care of himself. The best I can suggest right now is for you to tell a lot of people you're looking for him. If he's in town, you'll hear about it sooner or later. I know it's hard sometimes, letting people know there's a family problem, but if I look for him, people will know about it soon enough anyway. I can make a few phone calls for you, just informally, no charge, and if he doesn't show up in a few days and you still want me to look for him, we'll talk it over."

"Yeah, I guess that's best. Lot of people already know anyway. The wife called around looking for him. Listen, I know you guys aren't cheap. I got some money set aside, supposed

to be for college, but, hell, I don't think Jordy's college material, if you know what I mean. Be better if he'd enlist, maybe
the service would straighten him out but I don't think they
take them now unless they finish high school, so mostly what
I want is to keep him from really screwing up school, you
know? The wife's been telling them he's sick but she can't
keep that up for long."

"Winter break's coming up soon."

"Yeah, Friday's the last day. I'd sure like to get him back
on track by New Year's, get him back in school, at least. The
wife's having a regular fit about it, too. She was going on and
on last night about that serial killer out in the midwest, got
all those young guys to come to his apartment then cut 'em
up in little pieces. I said, Judy, honey, those guys were all gay.
Jordy isn't going to follow some faggot home, for chrissake.
More likely he's holed up with some chick, you know what I
mean?"

"Yeah, look, I'll make some calls, okay? Did you file a
report with the cops?"

"Oh, yeah, figured I better. I mean, if something happened, not that I'm worrying, you know, but if something
did, well, he's a minor and we're responsible. Figured I better
let the authorities know, you know?"

"Yeah, that's good. I'll get back to you."

Chapter Six

I managed to get the receiver back in the cradle. My hand was shaking and I was drenched with sweat. A three-minute phone call and I was exhausted. A couple days in the hospital doing nothing but lying in bed letting nurses spoon-feed me sounded good all of a sudden. I closed my eyes and rested for a few minutes. The weight of the phone on my chest kept me from drifting off. In fact, it seemed to be gaining weight, pressing down, making it hard to breathe. I forced myself to make the second call just so I could get rid of the phone. The woman with no name wasn't home. I hung up after the twelfth ring, glad no one had answered. Getting the phone back on the nightstand took all my strength and I fell asleep immediately, but not for long. Boot heels striking the tile floor dragged me toward consciousness.

"Wake up, Bucky," Phil said.

I mumbled something at him and tried to roll onto my side, wanting to burrow down into the covers and sleep for a week or two. The movement made my shoulder hurt. "Jesus Christ! Don't they believe in pain killers in this place?"

"Tom's got you on a real low dose."

"Sadistic bastard."

"Well, he doesn't want you to get to liking it too much."

"A little Demerol isn't going to turn me into a raging drug addict."

"How about if I said a little shot of whiskey wouldn't turn me into a drunk again."

"That's different."

"Bullshit. An addict's an addict. Doesn't matter what your choice of poison is. A little pain won't hurt you." He laughed and added, "Well, I guess it'll *hurt* you, but it won't hurt you if you get my meaning. Did you make that list for me?"

"No."

"Didn't think you would, so I made one myself. Tell me if I left anyone out." He read off several names. The only ones who were even remotely possible were a woman named Virginia Marley and the parents of a dead boy named Johnny Dale.

I'd tangled with Virginia Marley while I was searching for a runaway teenager in Portland last August. "Virginia didn't make bail, did she?"

"Nope. Tons of money rolling into a kiddie porn operation and she managed to end up without a pot to piss in. That court-appointed attorney of hers is dicking around with a bunch of delays but she'll do a year or so at least. Once she gets out though—Hell hath no fury like a woman doing felony time on account of some guy whose cock she sucked. She gets out and your ass is grass, Bucky."

"Well, I don't have to worry about that for a while, do I? Even if she had the money, she wouldn't pay someone to do it for her. She wants to be there and make sure I die real slow." I hitched myself up a little, scrunching the pillow up to support my head better. "All you really have is Johnny Dale's family." The Dales had hated me steadily ever since the day I shot and killed Johnny, the firstborn son. I was a cop then; he was an armed robber. That didn't lessen their grief for him, or their anger at me.

"They're accounted for except for Kevin being home alone watching TV. Did you get your birthday card last month?"

"Yeah, it came." My birthday's in September, not November, but every November for the past seven years I've received a birthday card, unsigned but with a note scrawled at the bottom, the same message each time with only the number changing. This year's said: *He would have been twenty-one years old today.* "Isn't Kevin still in school?"

"Should be but he turned eighteen the first of the month and dropped out. Spends his time sitting in front of the television and whining about how he can't get a job."

Time flies. It seemed like only yesterday that Kevin Dale was a scrawny eleven-year-old, small bony hands in tight fists, saying, "You killed Johnny. You killed my brother." Now he was eighteen. After seven years of listening to his parents call me a cold-blooded murderer and with a lot of time on his hands, maybe he decided to be a vigilante since he couldn't get any other work. I didn't think so, though. Kevin Dale didn't have the initiative to wipe his own butt. I couldn't see him getting organized enough to try to kill me.

"You know for sure Kevin was home?"

"Nope. Says he was. He was watching a rented video. No point in asking him the plot, he'd seen it a dozen times."

"So he knows he's a suspect?"

"Well, he isn't exactly a suspect. He can't shoot that good for one thing, but, don't worry, I handled it with my usual finesse. He doesn't know there's any connection between the shooting and me wanting to know where he was Monday morning. He's been hanging out around the high school with some other drop-outs and I told him I was checking into some vandalism at the school. So far, no one seems to be questioning whether Sandhoff was the one the killer was after and I'd just as soon keep it that way."

"I was wondering why no reporters had shown up."

"No one's interested in you right now. You're just an innocent bystander." He snickered, *innocent* not being a word he felt applied to me under any circumstances.

"Did they recover the bullet?"

"Yeah, it was lodged in her skull, flattened out pretty good so they aren't going to get any ballistics information from it."

"What about a casing?"

"Nope. He either took the time to pick it up or he had a brass-catcher on the gun. Probably did. Lotta people around here use them so they can save a few bucks by reloading the casings themselves."

"You don't have much, do you?"

"Not much at all. A motive would help."

"Rabid anti-abortion beliefs seems like a reasonable motive to me."

"Well, most of the pro-lifers in town were on the scene and the ones who weren't . . . Hell, Bucky. In Mackie? We just don't have a lot of homicidal types running around."

"Is this getting a lot of coverage?"

"Are you kidding?" He blocked out headlines with his hand: "'Sniper Slays Abortionist.' It's tailor-made for the media."

"You're going to take some heat if you don't come up with something soon."

Phil grinned. "The Fourth Estate can go fuck itself. I was hired, not elected. I don't owe anybody anything except for doing the best job I can and if this town doesn't think I'm earning my pay, they can put some pressure on the mayor to fire me. You know I don't get along real good with reporters. Nosy sons of bitches."

Actually, reporters loved Phil. He was colorful and garrulous, without ever giving anything away, and he was unpredictable. He had achieved minor fame in October when the body of a missing woman was found in a vacant lot. It was the middle of the night so Phil was wearing his glasses instead of his contact lenses. When a television reporter asked if he had any suspects, Phil said, "Until I get it narrowed down, everybody's a suspect. Where were you between eight and midnight last night?" The reporter laughed and, still grinning broadly, asked if the woman had been sexually assaulted. Phil said "No comment" and slowly pushed his glasses up on the bridge of his nose—using his middle finger. The tape—with the reporter's smile edited out—was shown repeatedly, the television station gleefully innocent about his gesture. Just a man adjusting his glasses, nothing obscene about it.

I told him about Clausen calling me. "You're kidding," he said. "You better get some money up front 'cause I don't think he can afford you."

"What's he do?"

"Works down at Buddy's Auto Body. Me and him got off on the wrong foot first time we talked. He musta figured anybody with a southern accent's a bigot. Started telling me nigger jokes."

"I'm almost afraid to ask what you did."

"I was real nice about it. You know me, Bucky, the original nice guy. I was going to tell him the only reason I'm alive today is because some black marine whose name I never even got carried me through the fucking jungle for about three hours 'til he found a medic to leave me with, but somehow I didn't think Clausen would get the message, so I just told him Billy Haynes is a *real* good friend of mine."

I laughed, which hurt. Aside from being black, a definite minority in eastern Oregon, Bill Haynes was about six-eight, weighed close to three hundred pounds, and looked mean enough to melt iron with a glance. He wasn't, but few people got to know him well enough to find that out. The cops always knew which nights Haynes was bouncing at the Honky Tonk because they never had to drop by to break up fights.

"What do you think about Jordan running off?"

He shrugged. "I saw Clausen when he came in to make the report. I told him not to worry, bad pennies always turn up. Jordy needs someone to take him down a peg or two. I've thought about doing it myself but he's smart enough. He treads real close to the line but he doesn't step over it." He walked to the door, turned and said, "I gotta go." Then, abruptly: "Patsy's pregnant."

Oh, my Lord, give her the living child, and in no wise slay it. Out of context, but it seemed appropriate, unlike any of the standard responses to such an announcement.

"How far along is she?"

"Not very. Three days late and she pees in a bottle at home and you know for sure."

"Well," I said, and Phil said, "See you around," and left.

Later, I woke to the silence of a hospital in the middle of the night, a silence with an odd muffled quality, as if, at a decibel level just below the threshold of hearing, there were sounds no one wanted to hear—weeping and death rales and whispered goodbyes.

My watch wasn't on the nightstand, but it felt like three AM. I called my house. When the answering machine picked up the line, I tapped in some numbers, listened to some beeps, then smiled to myself when Allison Vanzetti's recorded voice said, "Hi, it's me." I had met Allison in August and befriended her, unaware at first that she was on the run after fleeing the scene of a murder in Mackie. After things were sorted out to the satisfaction of the police, she returned to the private school in Connecticut where she had lived most of her life.

Hearing her voice now made me realize that Connecticut was way too far away. After a pause while she had waited to see if I would pick up the phone, she said, "Phooey. It's Monday, four in the afternoon. Well, I wouldn't call you at four in the morning, would I? Call me if you can."

After another beep, there was a sigh, then Allison again, saying, "Are you there?" Pause. Another sigh. "It's eight o'clock now. At night. I wish you were there." She laughed lightly and said, "Actually I wish you were *here*. Or I were there. Or we were somewhere in the middle together. 'Bye."

There were no more messages. I repeated the entire procedure so I could listen to Allison's voice again.

Chapter Seven

Like any good PI, I have informants everywhere. When I woke up in the morning, I called Ellen Finch, a former English teacher who was now a counselor at Mackie High.

It was just past seven-thirty and she responded to my greeting by saying, "Good lord, Zack, I just walked in the door. Aren't you supposed to be in the hospital? Don't keep me in suspense, who is it this time?"

"Jordan Clausen."

"Well, there's a surprise." From her tone, it obviously wasn't a surprise at all. "Outwardly belligerent, which generally means inwardly defensive. Surly, bad-mannered, and foul-mouthed, all of which some of the girls unfortunately interpret as a sort of macho sexuality. Nice-looking if he ever wiped that smirk off his face. Academically, he's hanging in there. C's are fine, but he's capable of doing better. With an ounce of effort, he could bring his grades up considerably, but making that effort would destroy his image of himself as a latter-day James Dean. Not, I am sure, that he has any idea who James Dean was. His role model is undoubtedly one of those rock singers who smashes guitars on the stage. Do I sound cynical? It's been a long week and it's only Tuesday."

"You sound sensible, as always. What about drugs?"

"God, do you have some? Sorry. Just joking. I did consider a stiff drink for breakfast this morning, but my better nature prevailed. Drugs. I don't think so. Maybe on a strictly recreational level, but nothing more. I'm pretty good at picking up on the signs."

"I know you are. So what's his problem, besides being fifteen years old?"

"I've been flipping through the attendance reports. Excused absences since Friday afternoon. I assume he ran away and his parents are covering for him?"

"Yeah."

She sighed. "His problem. Well, let's see. His mother is so submissive as to be almost nonexistent as an individual. I don't believe I have ever heard her use the word *I*. It's always *we*. *We* think this, *we* did that. She's her husband's wife, period. I suspect her parenting skills are minimal, although she probably did quite well with Jordan when he was a baby. But now, well, he's close enough to being a man for her to feel totally intimidated by him. Had she had a daughter, she probably would have been an extremely overprotective and domineering mother. With a son, she's simply unable to assume a dominant role or even an equal role with any male who's out of diapers."

"What about his dad?"

"In his own mind, he's a Real Man, does all those things Real Men do—football and beer and dirty jokes and patting the little woman on the head when she's being silly, meaning emotional. *His* emotions are well in check. Real Men don't, of course, express their emotions, except the acceptable ones—anger and lust, primarily."

"You're pretty rough on us Real Men, Miss Finch."

She laughed. "Sorry, Zack, you simply don't fit the mold."

"Damn."

"And I wish you'd call me Ellen. 'Miss Finch' from you makes me feel like a little old gray-haired spinster. Which I am well on the way to becoming, but you needn't keep reminding me."

"*You* don't fit *that* role, Ellen."

"Much better. Did Mr. Clausen say what precipitated Jordan's departure?"

"Problems at home, problems at school. Nothing specific."

"Well, the only real problem he has at school, aside from his overall smartass attitude, is excessive absences, although he does make up the work."

"He's absent a lot?"

"Twelve days in . . . let's see, it's the fourteenth week of school. That's why I've been in contact with his parents. They insist he's only absent when he isn't well. It's always something minor—upset stomach, headache. My guess is he simply doesn't want to come to school and his mother feels powerless to make him do it. I know his father leaves for work early, so she's in charge of seeing that Jordan gets up and goes to school. By the time his father finds out he skipped school, it's too late for him to do anything about it, although I suspect his wife pays for her inadequacies. Of course, when I speak to him, he backs up her story. Doing anything else would indicate he's not completely in control of her."

"What about friends and girlfriends?"

"I'll have to ask around. I can't recall seeing him with any particular girl often enough for me to take notice. Other friends . . . Well, he's always lived here so he knows everyone. My impression is that he's *accepted,* but not necessarily well liked, if that makes sense."

"I know what you mean. Let me know if you come up with anything else. Clausen hasn't actually hired me yet. I just told him I'd make some phone calls, see if I could come up with anything."

"How are you feeling? I spoke with Carrie and she assured me there was nothing to worry about."

"I'm feeling okay and there's no permanent damage. I'll be out of here as soon as I can talk Tom into releasing me."

"Well, you take it easy, Zack, and I'll get back to you as soon as I can."

"Thanks, Miss—I mean Ellen."

I had lied to her. I wasn't feeling okay. I was feeling like hell. However, I'd managed to eat breakfast, take a shower with my left shoulder wrapped in plastic, and walk down the hall to the nurses' station without falling on my face, so I figured I could suffer somewhere else just as easily as I could suffer in a hospital.

I called Tom and he agreed to release me in the afternoon. I asked about my gun, my watch, my wallet, my keys, and my car. They were at his house. I called the answering service but I didn't have any messages. I called my house and listened to the same two messages from Allison. I tried to think of something else I needed to do. Anything. Anything at all that would give me an excuse to postpone calling Allison.

I couldn't think of anything but I waited until nine o'clock, when it was noon in Connecticut, lunch time at the Fanhaven Academy. Allison would be in a hurry because she had a watercolor lesson Tuesdays at one and she had to go across town to get to it. She sounded breathless when she came on the line. "Zachariah?"

"Yeah, hi. I got your messages, but this is the first chance I've had to call. How is everything?"

"Fine. Have you been busy working?"

"No, not really. There was some excitement here yesterday, though."

"What happened?"

"You remember I told you about Carrie being involved in an abortion rights demonstration?"

"Uh-huh."

"Well, the doctor was shot to death."

"Oh, no. How awful. Who shot him?"

"Her. Phil's still working on it. The shot was fired from the woods across from her office."

"Carrie wasn't there when it happened, was she?"

"Yeah, as a matter of fact, both of us were."

"You were?"

"Yeah, but we're fine. I was shot, actually, but I'm getting out of the hospital in a couple hours."

There was silence on the other end of the line. "Allison? Don't panic, babe. I sound fine, don't I? I was hit in the shoulder, the bullet went straight through and I'm almost back to normal already."

She started crying. I listened, feeling helpless. Finally, I said, "Allison, I'm fine. I was hit by accident. It was just a fluke that I was even there. It didn't have anything to do with me at all. I was just in the way."

I heard a voice in the background, then Allison's voice, muffled, saying, "No, I'm okay." To me, she said, "I'm sorry, I'm all right. I just . . . I don't want you to be hurt."

"I know, babe. I'm fine, honest."

She sniffled for a moment or two, then asked exactly what had happened. I told her the whole story and then we talked about other things for a few minutes until Phil walked into the room and made a *hurry-up* gesture. I reminded Allison of her one o'clock class. "Are you going home," she asked, "or will you be staying at Carrie's?"

"Home, but I picked up a runaway case last night, so I'll be in and out. Don't try to call, you'll just run up your phone bill. I'll call you soon, okay?"

"Okay. Don't forget. Oh, I've sent for applications to some colleges. For next fall. I'll write you about it." She paused, then added, "Two of them are in Oregon." There was a questioning tone to her statement.

I said, "Good. You shouldn't have any trouble being accepted anywhere. You'll be able to take your pick."

"I'll pick Oregon."

"I hope so."

"I will. I'd better go. I love you."

"I love you, too."

"Don't forget to call," she said and made a kissing sound before she hung up.

I replaced the receiver, saying "Just shut up" to Phil.

"I didn't say a word."

"You were thinking it." After a moment, I said, "What do you want?"

"You getting out today?"

"This afternoon."

"Are you planning to go by your office?"

"I don't know. Depends on how I feel. Why?"

"Jackson and Daughter's sending someone over this afternoon to put a new window in front. There's a piece of plywood over it right now."

I stared at him, my mind still on Allison, his words taking a moment to register. "What happened to the window?"

"It broke. Probably had something to do with the hunk of concrete that was on the floor."

"Someone threw a rock through my office window?"

"Not a rock, a hunk of concrete, looked like maybe a piece of broken curb."

"I don't give a shit what it looked like. When did it happen?"

"Middle of the night. Three-fifteen. Patrol car got there a

couple minutes after the alarm went off and no one was in sight."

"Shit."

"Yeah. I gotta go." He turned at the door and said, "It could've just been a kid or a drunk, picking a window at random."

I didn't answer and after a moment he left.

Chapter Eight

Carrie picked me up at one and took me home—her home, not mine. I spent a few minutes convincing Melissa that I wasn't in any shape to play games with an exuberant two-year-old. She brought me a stack of books and we settled in the recliner in the family room. Somewhere in the middle of *Goodnight, Moon* I fell asleep. When I woke, it was late afternoon and the room was lit only by weak sunshine. Carrie was curled up at one end of the couch, nursing Matthew. Judging from the noise, Melissa was in the kitchen putting dents in the pots and pans.

I pushed the recliner to its upright position and got up, moving slowly, my shoulder throbbing. I sat on the couch beside Carrie, giving Matthew a finger to hold. He smiled at me around his mother's nipple.

"Jim's quitting," Carrie said. "Friday's his last day. He could have given me a little more notice." She started crying, not noisily, just a silent stream of tears that she wiped at angrily. "I'm already short-handed because of Doug being on vacation 'til after the first."

Jim and Doug were two of the four paperhangers employed by C and Z Paperhanging, a business Carrie and I co-owned but she ran. Paperhangers came and paperhangers went and Carrie never cried over them. "Well, hell," I said, "I'd help you out but isn't a one-armed paperhanger an old joke?" She leaned her head against my shoulder. "Witnessing violence hits everyone hard, angel. All of a sudden you're aware of how vulnerable you are, of how quickly something can happen, with no warning, and you realize it really could happen to you."

"I know all that. Here." She handed me the baby and went out of the room, returning with a box of tissues. "Irene was . . . well, we weren't close friends. It was horrible, but . . . actually, I think I was so glad you weren't killed . . ." She wiped at her eyes. "I was going to go out to your house this morning and pick up some more clothes for you."

"But you were afraid to."

She nodded. "I've been there hundreds of times by myself. It never bothered me. But this morning . . . I thought of how isolated the house is . . . and I just couldn't. It's stupid, I know. It's not as if someone tried to hurt me. Even here at home, this morning after Tom left . . . Zachariah, I thought about loading the gun."

"Don't let him win, Carrie. That's the best I can tell you. If you let it get to you, if you change your life, if you let it keep you from doing the things you need to do and want to do, then you're letting him win. Never let the bastards win."

"Words of wisdom from Zachariah Smith." She blew her nose, then said, "See if you can find me a paperhanger, will you?"

Tom came home a few minutes later. He looked tired and seemed to make an effort to smile when he joined us in the family room. We talked for a while about the shooting. The reaction around town was shock and outrage and a fairly naive certainty that the killer had to be an outsider—no one in Mackie would have done it. That assumption seemed a little ludicrous to me since the town had made the national news just last August when I brought Allison back to Mackie, against her will, to clear up the homicide case she was mixed up in.

After dinner, while Carrie was bathing the children and Tom was reading a medical journal in the family room, I used the phone in the kitchen to call Clausen to see if Jordan had shown up. He hadn't.

"Look," Clausen said, "the wife and I were talking and we pretty much decided not to hire you to look for him. The cops are supposed to do that, aren't they?"

"They'll get the information out, but runaway teenagers aren't high priority. Especially when they're working on a homicide."

"Well, still, it's not like we don't know he left on his own steam. He didn't just disappear so . . ."

"You don't have to hire me, Clausen. I did make some calls this morning. If I get any feedback, I'll let you know." When he didn't say anything, I added. "No charge."

"Goddammit, it isn't the money,"

"I'll get back to you if I hear anything," I said and told him goodbye.

I tried the number for the woman with no name again, but there was no answer, so I called the library to have someone check the reverse phone directory for me. All I found out was that the number was unlisted. As I was folding the two message slips to put them in my wallet, the time written above Clausen's name and phone number caught my eye.

I called the answering service. Dora had left for the day but I reached her at home.

"I was looking at this message from Clausen. It says the call came in at one o'clock Monday afternoon."

"Yeah, that's right. I just got back from lunch. It was the

first call I took. I remember because everyone was talking about the shooting and it kind of spooked me. I mean, we were talking about you getting shot and we didn't know what shape you were in and I sat down and your line rang right away."

"Okay. I just wanted to check the time."

"It was one o'clock. The only call you had before that was the woman. About eleven-thirty, I think. I was about to track you down when we heard about the shooting."

"Yeah. Thanks, Dora."

I hung up and stared out the window into the darkness, not realizing Carrie had come into the room until she said, "What is it?"

"What? Nothing. I was just thinking."

"Melissa's in bed. She wants you to read her a story."

"How long do you think it took for the news about the shooting to get out?"

"In *Mackie?* Five minutes."

"By one o'clock just about everyone in town would have known about it, right?"

"Sure. Long before that."

"Would you call a private detective right after you heard he'd been shot?"

"To hire him? No."

"A man called at one o'clock yesterday. His son ran away Friday. Seems funny, doesn't it?"

"I guess so. Unless . . . Maybe hiring a detective hadn't occurred to him and when he heard about you being shot, he realized it was a possibility."

"Yeah, that makes sense."

"Still, I think I'd at least wait a while. The first news reports said you were in stable condition, which could mean just about anything. Of course, you are the only detective in town, so . . ." She shrugged. "Are you staying here tonight? The bed in the spare room's made up."

"Yeah, I think I will. See if you can talk your husband into giving me something so I can sleep. My shoulder's killing me. I think the prescription he gave me's baby aspirin."

She left the room, returning a moment later and handing me a pill. "Darvon, okay?"

"One of my favorites." I went upstairs, read a story to Melissa, then went to bed. It was nine o'clock. Early to bed, early to rise. I didn't wake up until noon.

Chapter Nine

I was at my office by two. The new window looked just like the old one. Myrna and Rosie saw me arrive and came out of the flower shop to see how I was and also to complain about having to get out of bed at three-thirty in the morning when the alarm company called them. I told them to send themselves some flowers as a thank-you gift from me, which made Rosie giggle hysterically.

A piece of concrete about the size of a baseball was on my desk, serving as a paperweight for a bill from Jackson and Daughter Glass Company. The mini-blinds had suffered minor damage, but not enough for me to consider replacing them. Whoever had cleaned up the broken glass had shoved all three chairs against the wall. I put the swivel chair behind the desk and arranged the two captain's chairs in front of it. Plants in hanging pots completed the decor. I unlocked the metal fire door behind the desk and went into the back room, sitting down at a long table under a barred, opaque window.

Clausen was listed in the phone book as Robert W., with an address on South 27th Street. I ran a routine credit check on him. When I finished, I propped my head up with my right hand and closed my eyes. If Clausen had money set aside for college, he had it stuffed in his mattress. I didn't think the money existed. If it did, surely he'd use it to get caught up on his bills or at least make the payments on time.

I thought back to my conversation with Ellen Finch. She hadn't known Jordan was missing. The cops should have contacted the high school as a matter of routine. I called the police department to find out when Clausen filed a report on his missing son. Four-fifteen Monday afternoon—after he called my office, but before I talked to him. He hadn't lied about reporting Jordan missing, but he hadn't mentioned he'd waited three days, either.

Something else Ellen had said came back to me. I called the high school and asked to speak to her. After the hellos and how-are-you's, I said, "You said something about Jordan being absent last Friday. Is that right?"

"Hold on." After a moment she came back on the line and said, "Excused absences since Friday afternoon, Zack."

"Friday afternoon. What does that mean?"

"He attended school Friday morning, left on the lunch break, and didn't return. His mother—or his father, it just says parent—informed the office he was staying home the rest of the day."

"Did they give a reason?"

"Illness."

"Jordan lives on the east side of town. He'd ride the school bus. He wouldn't ordinarily go home for lunch, would he?"

"Well, no. Let me check into this, Zack. I hadn't thought about it, but it does seem a little strange, doesn't it? I suppose he might have called his mother and asked her to pick him up if he wasn't feeling well. No, that wouldn't work. She doesn't drive. One of the parents definitely called, though. I mean they didn't come into the office to sign him out. It was logged as a phone call."

"Get back to me as soon as you can. If I'm not in, leave a

message and I'll call you. Incidentally, I'm not working for Clausen. He decided to let the cops handle it. I don't have any authorization for access to Jordan's school records."

"*Now* you tell me," she said and laughed. "You know I don't worry about that, Zack, not with you. You're always on the right side when children are involved."

Johnny Dale was fourteen years old when I killed him. I said, "I try to be, Ellen."

The phone rang as soon as I hung up. Carrie said, "Hi, the funeral's tomorrow at ten. Will you go with me? Tom's scheduled to work and he doesn't want to ask any of the other doctors to cover for him. They'll all want to go."

"Sure, I'll go."

"I don't suppose you've found me a paperhanger yet?"

"Haven't even thought about it. Sorry."

I took a pain pill and left the office on foot, headed for Buddy's Auto Body Shop. It was only fourteen blocks but halfway there, I started wishing I'd driven. Every step I took jarred my shoulder. Driving a stick-shift one-handed had been awkward but not painful.

The front office of the shop was staffed by a tall, thin young woman, not more than nineteen, whose mouth dropped open when I walked in. When I asked if I could get a glass of water, she pressed a hand to her heart and looked frantically around, apparently hoping a crystal goblet filled with ice water would appear on the cluttered counter. "I'm sorry," she said. She appeared to be on the verge of tears. Blinking rapidly, she added, "There's a drinking fountain," and gestured to a doorway. It led to a drab waiting room. I found the fountain down a short hall next to it.

I took the bottle of pain pills out of my jacket pocket. Only a fool would take medication without reading the instructions. I read them: Take one every four hours for pain. It had been at least ten minutes since I took the last one. I popped one in my mouth and bent over the fountain. The water was so cold it made my teeth ache.

I continued down the hall, ending up in a cold, cavernous room that had an oily, metallic smell. The far side was a big open entrance. Three cars and a pickup truck took up most of the space. It was almost four, apparently quitting time. Both men in the room were tossing tools and greasy rags onto a long table against one wall. They turned toward the doorway as I walked into the room.

One was a red-haired man in his twenties. The other said, "Yeah?" when I asked for Robert Clausen. He was older than I'd expected, mid-forties I thought, and average height but heavy, a broad-shouldered, barrel-chested man, with a good-sized beer-belly adding to his bulk. The redhead finished wiping his hands on a ragged towel, tossed it on the counter, picked up a big lunch pail, and said, "I'm outta here. See you tomorrow, Bob." He left through the big open bay.

I walked over to Clausen and said, "Zachariah Smith," extending my hand. He held his hands out palms up, indicating they were too grimy for him to shake hands. "Any sign of Jordan?" I asked.

"Uh, no. No, he hasn't shown up. I expect he will though." He settled a Trailblazers cap on his thinning brown hair. The knuckles of his right hand were swollen and bruised. Noticing my glance, he said, "Banged it up Monday taking the tailgate off a 'eighty-nine Ford pickup. Thought I mighta broke something, but it's just bruises." He flexed his fingers a few times. "Stiff as hell, though," he said. "Look, the wife was all shook up. That's why I called you. Didn't really think it through first and after I did, well, I don't see any reason to hire a detective. Hell, the kid'll come home on his own sooner or later, if the cops don't pick him up first." He took a jacket off a hook on the wall and pulled it on, saying, "So what is it you want? I gotta get going. The wife gets nervous if I'm late."

"I told you I made some phone calls. I just wanted to let you know nothing much came of them so far."

He nodded and picked up a black lunch pail. "Look, if I owe you something for your time . . ."

"You don't owe me anything, Clausen. I just made some phone calls like I told you I would."

"Well, uh, yeah, I appreciate it, you taking the time to do that. And coming by to tell me."

He seemed to hesitate. When I didn't say anything, he shrugged, turned off the overhead lights, and hit a switch that controlled the big door. Noisily, it began to descend. He ducked under it saying, "Nice to meetcha," as he turned to walk away. The door continued its descent. When it clanged against the cement floor, I was left in the dark, not an unusual experience for me. I retraced my steps to the front office.

The young woman managed a weak smile at my return. She had combed her lank brown hair and applied fresh lipstick. She had also sprayed the room—and herself, I assumed—with a cloyingly sweet cologne that tickled my gag reflex.

"I was talking to Bob," I said. "His hand sure looks sore. I meant to ask him how he hurt it but we got to talking about something else and I forgot."

She was hanging on my every word, nodding her head, gazing raptly at me. But the words didn't seem to be sinking in. Subtlety wasn't going to work. "Do you know how he hurt his hand?"

"What? Bob? Oh. Um, I noticed it was kind of bruised. I'm sorry, I don't really go in the shop much. I mean, I don't talk to the men much. I just work here in the office and . . . I'm sorry."

"That's okay. I was just curious. I'm interested in an 'eighty-nine Ford pickup you had in here Monday. Bob said the owner might be interested in selling it but he couldn't remember the guy's name. You happen to have it handy?"

"Um . . . um . . ." She grabbed a stack of forms from a desk tray and looked through them. "Here it is." She started to hand me a form then stopped, glancing toward a closed door with MANAGER on it. "Um . . . I'm not really supposed to give out information about the customers?" It was definitely a question, almost a plea, whether for my permission to break the rules or my forgiveness for her inability to show me the form, I wasn't sure.

"I guess I don't need his name. I know where he works. What I'd really like to know is what was wrong with the truck."

"Oh. Well, that's okay, I guess." She looked at the form, brushing back a strand of hair that fell forward as she bent her head. "Damage to the rear end. I think he said he backed into a tree."

"Thanks."

I was turning toward the door when she said, "You were shot," in a tone that implied getting shot ranked right up there with getting knighted.

"Yeah. I'm fine now."

"I remember you from high school." She blushed bright red and stammered out, "I mean, of course *you* weren't in school. A student, I mean. I mean, you were giving a speech."

"The drug abuse prevention program."

She nodded, her left hand at her throat. A thin gold band with a tiny diamond was on her ring finger. "When's the wedding?" I asked.

"Wedding?" She held her hand out and looked at the ring as if she'd never noticed it before. "Oh. June. June seventeenth."

"He's a lucky guy."

I was closing the door behind me when she called out, "Thank you."

Outside, I took a deep breath of air that smelled of nothing worse than exhaust fumes. I walked south to Seventh and Main where the police station was located.

Phil was in his office, chair tilted back, boots on his desk, telephone at his ear. While I was waiting for him to finish his call, I read the front page of the *Oregonian,* which I found tossed in his wastebasket. Already the focus was shifting away from Sandhoff's murder and onto the broader issues of abortion rights and violence directed against abortion clinics. I searched through the wastebasket for the editorial section and was reading a diatribe against the pro-choice movement when Phil hung up the phone and said, "What's up?"

"Making any progress?"

"On what? The homicide or your window? Answer's no to both."

"I'm going to the funeral with Carrie. Are you going to be there?"

"Sure. Everybody knows the killer always shows up at the funeral. Maybe I'll get lucky and he'll throw himself on the coffin and confess in a fit of remorse."

"Are you expecting trouble?"

He ran both hands through his sandy curls, leaving them standing up all over his head. "Not at the funeral. Graveside service. No body to gawk at. I figure there'll be a good-sized turn-out but I think they'll behave themselves. Everybody'll be busy staring at Sandhoff's sister anyway."

"How come?"

"She looks like she's maybe ten years younger, but other than that, they could be twins. She flew in from San Francisco yesterday."

"Are a lot of relatives coming?"

"Hunh-unh. She's it, the only living relative. The parents have been dead for years and Sandhoff was widowed a few years back. She didn't have any children. Her sister's single."

"Are you expecting trouble somewhere else?"

"There's a lot of bad feelings. The anti-abortionists have been calling the pro-abortionists murderers and now the shoe's on the other foot as far as the pro-choicers are concerned. They're busy making posters with Sandhoff's picture on them and catchy little slogans like Anti-Abortion Equals Pro-Murder and We Don't Kill Doctors, You Do. They've asked City Hall for a permit for a memorial rally. I'm trying to convince the mayor to turn it down, but I don't think he will seeing as how his wife's one of the pro-choicers. Christ, I hate this whole abortion business."

"Me too. I wish Carrie'd stay out of it."

"I don't think we'll have any real trouble if it's just the local people. There aren't enough of them, for one thing. Most of the people there Monday just came by hoping for a little excitement. I'm worried that one of the big activist groups will decide to show up. Wouldn't matter which side they're on. I've seen pro-choicers cause as much trouble at clinics as pro-lifers. They're out there with their bullhorns and cheerleading squads, doing nothing but adding fuel to the fire. All they accomplish is swelling the crowd and upsetting the patients even more. Don't tell Carrie I said that."

"How's the investigation going?"

"Too damn slow. The Sheriff's office loaned me some men and we pretty much canvassed every street around the woods. Nobody saw anybody coming out of the woods, with or without a rifle or a bag big enough to carry one in. It seems to me if killing Sandhoff was someone's way to make a political statement, he'd want some publicity, call a radio or TV station anonymously and say he did it for all those butchered babies or something like that. Wouldn't you think so? What's the point otherwise?"

"I don't know. It could be personal. Maybe someone had a grudge against her for something that doesn't have anything to do with her job."

"She lived a real quiet life. Everybody liked her, no scandals in her past, respected by her medical colleagues, nothing suspicious at all."

"What about me? Are you still working on that angle?"

"You know me, Bucky. I work every angle there is until I figure it out. If he was after you, maybe he'll try again and then I'll at least know what I'm looking for."

A cheerful thought. I changed the subject, telling him about Clausen's decision not to hire me.

"I told you he can't afford you anyway," Phil said.

"Does it strike you as odd that he'd call my office at one Monday afternoon?"

"After you were shot." Phil clasped his hands behind his head and regarded me steadily. "Yeah, seems a little funny. But maybe hiring a detective never crossed his mind and then he heard about you getting shot and figured a detective was a good idea. Maybe he didn't know you work alone."

"He didn't even make a police report until later Monday afternoon."

"He came in after he got off work."

"Jordan's been gone since Friday."

"Lotta parents don't report missing teenagers right away. They figure the kid'll come home. They're also worried about getting the authorities involved. Makes them look bad and they don't know exactly what'll happen, if they'll suddenly have social workers knocking on their door, things like that."

I thought about mentioning Clausen's bruised knuckles. Clausen's attitude bothered me, but I didn't have anything solid, just my own suspicious nature and the fact that my knuckles had looked just like his on a few occasions and I wasn't taking off tailgates, I was busting jaws. I decided against saying anything to Phil unless something else off-key turned up. Which reminded me that Ellen Finch might be trying to contact me.

"How about giving me a ride to my office?"

"What the hell do I look like, a taxi?" Then he took a long look at me, sighed, and got his jacket. "If you can't walk twelve blocks, you oughta be home in bed."

Chapter Ten

I checked with the answering service as soon as I got back to the office, having been delayed briefly when Phil pulled over a gray Buick with California plates and a driver who couldn't read STOP. Everyone in Mackie kept an eye out for the police chief's unmarked police pickup truck, but he ticketed a lot of startled travelers.

I had a message to call Ellen Finch at home. She hadn't found out anything new. Jordan had attended school Friday until his lunch break at eleven-forty. Ten minutes after twelve, his mother called the school, saying Jordan had come home for lunch and was staying there because he didn't feel good. "He must have walked home, Zack. It isn't much over a mile and a half."

"Do me a favor, will you? Take a look at the attendance records tomorrow and see if there's any kind of pattern to his absences."

"I'm ahead of you. I brought a copy of them home with me."

"You don't remember him ever showing up at school with bruises or anything, do you?"

After a silence, she said, "I remember once, but it was weeks ago. He had a split lip, puffed up really bad. I suggested he see the nurse about it. He said he'd been in a fight. 'Kicked me some butt' is the way he put it. What a vulgar expression."

"But an excellent use of metonymy." I cleared my throat and intoned: "The use of an attribute in place of the whole; for example, 'the stage' to represent the theatrical profession. Or in this case, 'the butt' to represent the person."

"I don't believe it! I used to watch eyes glaze over whenever I mentioned figurative language. Do you mean someone was listening after all?"

"I remember everything you ever said."

"Goodness. I had no idea I was making any impression at all on any of you."

She had made quite an impression. She hadn't been more than twenty-five or -six when I was a senior and she was a hot topic of conversation in the boys' locker room. She might think of herself as being on the verge of gray-haired spinsterdom, but she was at least five years younger than Mattie Hagen, whose bed—now that I thought about it—I hadn't been near in weeks. Making a mental note to do something about that soon, I thanked Ellen for her help and told her goodbye.

I booted up the computer and spent a few minutes entering billing information into a file I'd named DICKHEAD, the endearment one of my clients used for her ex-husband. I'd tracked him down last weekend, completing my assigned task when I convinced him to hand over a check for eight thousand dollars, the first installment on his delinquent child support payments. I'd delivered the check to my client when I got back to Mackie at six Monday morning and she was going to deposit it as soon as the bank opened. If the check had bounced, I'd have heard about it by now.

I finished my entries and tapped a couple keys. The printer spewed out a professional-looking statement in seconds. It had only been two months since Carrie sat me down in front of the computer and said, "Step One: Turn it on." Already, I couldn't remember how I'd gotten along without it.

I brought up the directory on the screen and looked at my list of active cases. They were all at a standstill while I waited for information from various sources. Just for the hell of it, I opened a file for Clausen, naming it FREEBIE. I entered what little information I had, then stared at the screen for a while.

My gut feeling was that Clausen had beat the hell out of his son and hadn't reported him missing for three days because he was afraid the cops would spot him and ask some awkward questions. The thought crossed my mind that maybe Clausen had done more than beat him; maybe he'd killed him. I rubbed my hand across my face, thinking my imagination was running away with me. All I had was a delay in reporting a missing teenager, some bruised knuckles, and a history of absenteeism at school. None of which necessarily added up to child abuse, let alone murder.

Still, Clausen calling my office after I was shot seemed strange. What better way to look like a concerned parent than to appear willing to pay a private detective to search for your kid? I was the only private detective in town. Clausen probably assumed I would be in the hospital for several days. By then, Jordan might have returned home on his own. In the meantime, Clausen would look like Father Of The Year, telling everyone he was going to hire me to look for his son as soon as I was well. The thought of murder crossed my mind again. If Jordan turned up dead, any suspicion of Clausen would be lessened when he told the cops he contacted a detective agency. Which pretty much blew my whole murder theory: If Clausen had killed his son and called me to divert suspicion away from himself, he'd have gone ahead and hired me, even if he couldn't afford to. The thought cheered me up. I hate finding dead kids.

Feeling bored and restless, I paced around my office for a

while, trying to decide what to do next. Going home was the logical thing to do, but I didn't want to go home. I didn't need to either; I had clothes at the office and a choice of places to sleep in town. I thought about Mattie's brass four-poster, but without enthusiasm. Sex with Mattie was a lot like work and I didn't think I was up to it. Gradually I became aware that my shoulder was aching. Tom had said something about wanting to take a look at it today.

It was after six. He'd be home from work. I popped a pain pill and was ready to leave the office when I thought of the woman with no name. I found the yellow message slip in my jacket pocket and called the number. No answer.

Tom checked my wound and said he thought I'd live and Carrie told me if I expected dinner, I could either cook it myself or order out. I ordered pizza but left before it arrived, having worn out my welcome in a hurry when I tried to talk some sense into my pig-headed sister, who was painting anti-pro-life slogans on big sheets of posterboard at her kitchen table.

I drove back downtown and spent two hours sitting in the dark in my office. It was after nine when I locked up and left. I sat in the Camaro, considering my options.

Wednesday night in Mackie.

I could go to Sparky's and get something to eat, but I wasn't hungry anymore.

I could go to any of several bars and get something to drink, but the pill bottle said NO ALCOHOL and my days of playing Russian roulette with booze and drugs were a thing of the past.

I could go to Mattie's house, but she went to bed early and the last time she had to get up to open the door for me, she slammed it in my face.

I could go back to Carrie's but she'd want to talk and I didn't want to listen.

I could go home.

I went to the bowling alley, where I said, "Yeah, I did," to everyone who said, "I thought you got shot." I drank coffee while I exchanged pointlessly suggestive banter with the Honky Tonk Angels, who were getting their asses whipped by the GutterBelles from Gordon's Electric Supply. The Angels never managed to close a fifty-pin gap, but I gave them points for form, based strictly on bowling technique and not on their hot pink, too-tight T-shirts.

Declining an invitation to accompany the Angels to the Honky Tonk for a post-game drink, I slouched down in a chair near the bar and watched Mike Burrell clearing away glasses and emptying ashtrays. As the rest of the games were finished and the players left, the building grew quiet. Mike began to sweep up, the broom moving rhythmically back and forth, back and forth, back and forth . . .

Mike said my name quietly but I woke with a start anyway, straightening up in the chair too fast, pain shooting through my shoulder.

"Sorry, Zack. Time to go home soon. You're tired, huh?"

"Yeah, a little. Is everyone else gone?"

"Uh-huh. Mr. Fisher, he said let you sleep while I clean. You got shot. We saw it on TV. Becky, she got mad. Someone shooting you and that doctor, it made her mad."

"Kinda made me mad, too. You want a ride home? It's cold tonight." I stood up and eased my jacket on.

Mike shook his head. "I like to walk. Only three blocks."

I waited while he made a final check of the doors and turned off some more lights, leaving the building in partial darkness. He carried a clipboard with him and checked off each task as he completed it. I'd seen the checklist before. Each item was printed in big block capital letters and consisted of two or three simple words: BACK DOOR. OFFICE DOOR. POOL TABLE LIGHT. COFFEE POT.

Mike wasn't much of a reader. He'd been in special ed

classes at Mackie High, finishing up the year after I graduated. He was married, a fact that puzzled a lot of people, as if average intelligence was a requisite for love. Maybe it was the idea of a mentally retarded couple having sex that puzzled them. Mike and Becky had been married for over ten years and I'd never seen them together when they weren't holding hands. They were childless, something I figured one or both sets of parents had made sure of.

Watching Mike frowning over his list, I wondered if his mother had ever thought it would have been better if he'd never been born. I didn't know the answer to that but I did know his absence wouldn't make the world a better place. It might not change much of anything, but it wouldn't make it a better place.

He ran a finger down his checklist, making sure an X appeared in each box, then said "Okay" more to himself than to me, and hung the clipboard on a nail behind the counter and got his coat. As we left the building, he turned and gave the door a tug, making sure the lock had caught.

The wind had picked up as the temperature dropped. My breath puffed out in front of me as I told Mike goodbye. "Snow soon," he said. "Maybe tomorrow. 'Bye, Zack." He pulled a knit cap on, waved to me, and walked off into the night.

I went around the corner of the building, the wind like a cold knife against my wound. The lot had been full when I arrived but it was deserted now. I looked ahead to where the Camaro was illegally parked next to the dumpster at the far end of the building. The car looked funny, like it was squatting. As I got closer, I saw the reason.

Letting the air out of all four tires might have been someone's idea of a joke or maybe an indignant reaction to my disregard of the NO PARKING sign and it would have been inconvenient enough for me to get the message. Whoever'd gone to work on my tires had a much stronger message in mind. I'd slashed tires a time or two. Plunging a knife into thick rubber takes a lot of effort. Pulling the knife through again and again to leave the rubber in strips like flayed skin on the pavement not only takes a lot of effort but isn't necessary. Air only needs one escape route and one good slash ruins a tire. Whoever cut my tires to ribbons was either crazy or mad as hell.

I stood still and looked around, peering into the pools of darkness between the pale circles of illumination from the street lights. The dark hulk of the dumpster loomed behind the Camaro. I had my gun, having exchanged my shoulder holster for a hip holster, but I didn't want to get into a shootout over a set of tires.

The closest telephone was in the Camaro's dashbox. I tried to figure out where the second closest one was. Six blocks away, I thought, at the Blue Ribbon Bar. I thought of Mike's apartment, only three blocks away.

A little scenario played itself out in my mind: Myself, walking to Mike and Becky's place, a shadowy figure following me, stalking me. Mike and Becky hearing my voice through the door, opening it for me. The shadowy figure watching, waiting for me to leave, then knocking on the door. Mike and Becky, thinking I'd returned, opening the door again. A knife glinting in the light. I barred the next image from my mind. The thought that replaced it sent a jolt of panic through me: If someone really wanted to hurt me, he'd go after Carrie.

I walked quickly to the car, jabbed the key into the lock, and jerked the door open. Light flooded the interior. I glanced into the back seat then slid behind the wheel, slamming the door and locking it, feeling safe, as if the car were armor-plated and the windows bulletproof.

I punched the first four digits of Carrie's number, then

disconnected. It was after midnight. When she heard my voice she'd know something was wrong. Tom was home. They were together, safe in their bed, with Melissa and Matthew tucked into their cribs down the hall.

I called the police. While I waited, I tried to convince myself I was overreacting. The Camaro had been alone in the darkest part of the lot. Whoever slashed the tires might not even have known who the car belonged to. Maybe he was stoned out of his mind and thought he was attacking an alien spaceship from another galaxy. There was no reason to think the vandalism was directed at me personally.

I might have believed that if it hadn't been for the brand new window at my office.

Chapter Eleven

The cop dropped me at my office. I set up an army cot in the back room and tossed a sleeping bag on it. I must have slept, because I certainly dreamed, but I seemed to be suspended midway between sleep and wakefulness, dreams jumbling through my mind while I remained aware of my surroundings: the cramped cot, the sleeping bag rucking up beneath me as I moved restlessly, the click and hum of the furnace, wind seeking entry at the window, an occasional car passing by on the street outside, a distant siren wailing. Other sounds, too, sounds that roused me from my dreams for an instant: the creak of a ceiling joist, something wind-borne slapping against the window, the scurry of small feet—mice in the walls, I thought—and, once, a faint hissing sound like gas escaping that made me raise myself up on one arm and listen hard until the sound stopped.

I heard nothing else and lay down, drifting back into dreams: Myself, pushing through faceless crowds, pursuing a dark-haired woman in an emerald green dress—my ex-wife, April, fleeing from me, turning sometimes to look at me, suddenly close, almost within reach, but I could never reach her, the press of people around us was too great, then the distance between us increased suddenly and she was far away, out of reach, and I ran after her, a slow-motion run, all those people in the way, and I couldn't reach her, couldn't catch her, couldn't bring her back.

Suddenly I was standing before an open grave. *Dead,* I heard myself say. *She's dead.* But no, this was the grave of little Christina Pauling, Phil and Patsy's second child, who died in infancy. Phil was there—and Patsy, standing too close to the pit, perched on the edge as if she would step into it. Phil was standing alone at first, then I was beside him, gripping his arm, trying to hold him up, his weight dragging down on me, threatening to drag us both down to the ground, down into the grave, and Patsy was crying and someone kept saying *Too young to die, too young to die, too young to die,* and Phil's weight was pressing me down, down, my arm aching from the effort of supporting him. I woke from that dream, realizing I had rolled onto my left side and my shoulder was hurting. I turned over and fell into another dream.

I floated in tranquil darkness, sightless and weightless, peaceful and unafraid, knowing I wasn't alone in the blackness. Carrie was there, close to me, part of me. It was an old dream and one I shared with my sister. The sameness of our separate dreams had never seemed strange, not even when we first discovered we dreamed the same dream. The Womb Dream, Carrie called it. It came to me rarely, usually only when I was feverish, but it was so familiar, so comforting, that I always tried to hold on to it, willing myself to stay asleep, to let the dream go on and on.

Tonight it ended quickly, the darkness replaced by harsh light and blood: the nurse's office at Mackie High fourteen years ago, ugly green walls, ugly gray linoleum, blood on the floor, blood everywhere, splashed on the walls, dripping from the ceiling, blood on my hands. Some part of my mind, monitoring the dream, tried to change it, knowing this wasn't the way it had been. There was too much blood and I was alone, all alone, the blood without a source. The dream changed, shifting without motion, a change so sudden there was no sense of a change taking place, only an awareness that everything had changed. I was no longer alone. I was surrounded by people and Irene Sandhoff was standing in front of me. *You're dead,* I said and she answered *I stitched it up myself* and her face ran blood.

Panic jerked me awake and I tried to stand up, forgetting I was zipped into a sleeping bag. I rolled awkwardly off the cot, landing on my hands and knees, just awake enough to remember to keep my weight off my left arm. I struggled free of the bag and stood up. I had an uneasy sense of urgency, as if I'd forgotten to do something important. All I could think of was that no one knew where I was except the cop who had dropped me off and he'd been about to go off duty.

I used one of the phones on the long work table under the barred window to call my office. The phone in the front room rang once, then the line was picked up by Marilyn at the answering service. "Arrow Investigations."

"It's me. Do I have any messages?"

"Nope. All's quiet on the western front."

"Okay. I'm at my office."

"You're working late."

"Something like that. Talk to you later." I hung up and peered at my watch. Four-forty. Seven-forty in Connecticut. Allison would be awake. My hand hovered over the phone. But what would I say to her? *I was chasing April in my dreams.*

I moved away from the table and sat on the cot. Allison didn't need my troubles. I looked at the phone again, thinking I hadn't checked my answering machine lately. She might have called. No, I'd told her not to, I'd call her. But I hadn't. I also hadn't rewound the answering machine after listening to her messages at the hospital, which meant they'd still be on the tape. I called my house and pressed the receiver to my ear, listening to Allison's voice. Afterward, I lay down on the cot and fell into sleep like a rock into water.

I was barely aware of the phone ringing the first time, since it stopped right away. When it rang again almost immediately, I tried to stay asleep, knowing the answering service would take care of it. Eight or nine rings later, I was awake enough to understand why they weren't. I picked up the phone and said, "Yeah?"

"You *are* still there."

"Yeah, what's up?"

"I've got police dispatch on the other line."

I rubbed a hand hard across my eyes, then checked my watch: ten minutes after six. "What do they want?"

"Some cop wants you to meet him at your office."

"I'm at my office."

"So is he. Maybe you better open the door for him."

"Tell the dispatcher to tell him I'm here and I'm coming out. I don't want him shooting me."

Giggling wildly, Marilyn said okay and disconnected. I went to the bathroom and splashed cold water on my face, wasting enough time to be sure the message had been relayed. Just to be absolutely sure I didn't get shot by a trigger-happy cop waiting outside a dark building before dawn, I turned on all the lights on my way to the front door.

Andy Riggs was leaning against the hood of his patrol car, which was pulled into one of the diagonal parking spots in front of the building. As I stepped outside, he pointed at the front of the building. I turned and looked. Out of consideration for Andy, who was one of Reverend Willie Sloan's band of holier-than-thou born-againers, I limited my reaction to a single muttered *"Fuck!"*

My brand-new window was adorned with two words in

fluorescent orange: MOTHERFUCKER and COCKSUCKER. I almost laughed; they were possibly the only two accusations I could categorically deny with no fear of my nose growing. I remembered the faint hissing sound I'd heard in the night. If I had got up to see what it was, I would have caught him in the act.

Andy said, "Seems I heard something about your car being vandalized, Zachariah. Looks like you got someone mad at you. I wrote out a report while I was waiting for your service to track you down. I would've knocked but it never occurred to me you were inside. How about getting it cleaned off before the kids start heading to school."

"Yeah, sure."

As he drove away, I said all the things I hadn't said in front of him, then I got the key to Fanciful Flowers and rummaged around in the storeroom until I found an unlabeled jar of something that smelled caustic enough to eat through steel. Whatever it was, it made a good paint remover.

There's nothing like starting your day before dawn standing outside in below-freezing weather cleaning obscenities off your brand-new window. By the time I finished, I'd decided to go into another line of work. Flower-arranging sounded good. Myrna and Rosie would hire me.

Realizing that all I had to look forward to was a funeral did nothing to cheer me up. I tried to sleep for a while but the rest of the world had decided to get up and make as much noise as possible. I finally gave up and got up and shaved and showered. After calling a garage and explaining where and in what shape my car was, I checked the closet. My only choice was a medium gray suit but it seemed sufficiently funereal. I called Carrie to let her know she'd have to come pick me up because my car was temporarily out of commission.

Chapter Twelve

Carrie was also wearing medium gray, a tailored suit with a white silk blouse beneath it. We both had black coats, hers quilted, mine a wool overcoat. "People will think we coordinated our wardrobes," she said. "I had the Womb Dream last night."

"So did I."

"That's because you were so hateful to me yesterday."

I couldn't see much logic to that, but kept my mouth shut, glad we were on speaking terms. We dropped Melissa and Matthew off at Tom's mother's house on our way to the cemetery, which was located two miles south of town on a winding, hilly road. As Carrie negotiated the turns, I told her about the vandalism to my office and car.

"Quite poetic," she said, referring to the words painted on my window. "You don't have any idea who's doing it?"

"No," I said, and because I wasn't accustomed to guarding my thoughts around Carrie, I added, "I can't see how it could be connected to the shooting, though. Murder's in a different league from vandalism."

I swore under my breath as Carrie veered off the road and onto the shoulder, braking hard. "What the hell is that supposed to mean?" she demanded.

"Nothing."

She stared at me, her eyes wide. "Is there a chance he was shooting at you?"

"*I* don't think so."

"But Phil does?"

"Not really, he's just considering all the possibilities."

"But, Zachariah, that would mean . . . that Irene was shot by mistake."

"Look, I shouldn't have mentioned it. I didn't mean to. It makes a lot more sense that someone would shoot her in front of her office than me."

"You were only there because of me."

"Yeah, and I drove there straight from home. No one followed me and even if someone did, he wouldn't have had time to get into position after he found out where I was going."

She nodded and started to say something but glanced into the rearview mirror instead. I looked over my shoulder to see who had pulled off the road behind us. Phil got out of his black Ford pickup and walked to the driver's side window, leaning down and resting his arm on the sill after Carrie hit the button to open it. "Y'all stopping to admire the view or what?"

"Patsy didn't come?" Carrie asked.

Phil glanced past Carrie to me, then, speaking very evenly, said, "No, Carolina, Patsy didn't come. She didn't know Dr. Sandhoff and she thinks funerals are hard enough on the family without them having to be sociable to a bunch of strangers. I'm only going because it's my job."

Carrie clenched her hands on the wheel and stared straight ahead. Phil straightened up, slapped the roof of the car, and walked back to his truck. He drove past us, looking straight ahead.

"Christ, Carrie, you know how Patsy feels about abortion."

"Let her get pregnant by a rapist and see how she feels about it then."

I took a deep breath, held it for a moment, and let it out

slowly. "She doesn't want to see abortion outlawed, she just hates it being a political issue. She isn't your enemy just because she isn't out there carrying stupid signs. Your way isn't necessarily the best way, Carrie. What the hell do you accomplish anyway besides putting on a sideshow for people? If Sandhoff was shot by an anti-abortionist crackpot, maybe it wouldn't have happened if demonstrators hadn't been drawing attention to her for weeks."

She looked at me, her eyes bright with tears. "That isn't fair."

"All right. You're right. I'm sorry."

"The government doesn't force men to take responsibility for their children *after* they're born, let alone before. Look at all the women struggling to raise children and they can't even get the courts to enforce child support settlements. Men walk away from their responsibilities all the time. It isn't even a social stigma. They just tell everyone what a bitch their ex-wife is and everyone sympathizes."

"Don't lump all men together, Carrie. I know the system stinks. I spent last weekend tracking down a man who owes twenty thousand in child support. It didn't bother me a bit to threaten to tell his new wife about his girlfriend to get some money out of him."

She pressed her fingers to her temples. "That's your job. Don't make yourself sound so altruistic. You say the system stinks, but what are you doing to change it?"

I shrugged with my right shoulder only. I was almost as good now at one-shoulder shrugs as some teenagers I knew who used the gesture as their sole means of communication with adults. "I try to make an intelligent choice at the polls. If I can't decide, I vote for whoever you tell me to."

She sputtered with laughter and put the car in gear. "We'd better get going or we'll be late. Why on earth would anyone have a graveside service in December?"

"Must be what Sandhoff wanted. It's my favorite kind of

funeral. Next to burial at sea. It's not nearly as depressing as church services. Have you met her sister?"

"Irene's? No, but Tom met her when she was here in the summer. He warned me it'll be like seeing a ghost." She downshifted and turned into the narrow road leading to the cemetery. "I'll apologize to Phil, okay?"

"Just skip it. He knows how you feel and he knows how Patsy feels and he can't help but be on Patsy's side." After a moment, I added, "She's pregnant again."

"Oh, god."

"I don't think she wants anyone to know yet. Phil told me."

"I won't say anything. . . . Burial at sea?"

"I'd rather feed the fish than the worms."

"God, what an awful thought."

"The fish?"

"No, the worms. I try not to think about what's really happening at a funeral." She pulled off the road behind Phil's truck. A small crowd had already gathered at the top of a gently sloping hill. A canvas awning had been set up to provide some shelter from the cold.

There were only about fifty people, far fewer than had been present at Sandhoff's death. The curiosity-seekers must have been discouraged by the chill wind and the threatening clouds. One TV camera crew had lugged equipment up the hill. As we took our places toward the edge of the crowd, the cameraman aimed at Carrie and me: Yin and Yang in their matching outfits. How could he resist?

Sandhoff's sister was standing with the women who had worked in the doctor's office. Her hair was still predominately brown, only streaked with gray, but otherwise she looked just like her sister, same brown eyes, same slightly aquiline nose, slanted cheekbones, and pointed chin, same height and build. Judging from the stares she was getting, I wasn't the only one who found her appearance disturbing. I held Carrie's hand and kept my head bowed during the service, which was short and to the point, delivered by a man from the Hillside Memorial Chapel. I assumed Sandhoff hadn't been a church-goer.

As the service ended, I glanced around at the crowd: the Reverend Willie Sloan and his wife Bertie; Father Daniel Thomas; several doctors, some with and some without their spouses; some nurses from Mackie General; women who were active in various charitable organizations in town; Sandhoff's office staff; a sheriff's deputy in plainclothes—the cemetery was outside the city limits—and one other Mackie cop besides Phil. The rest were from the upper stratum of Mackie society, no doubt people Sandhoff had socialized with. They all looked cold. None of them looked guilty.

As the crowd started to move away from the grave, Marla Twill, Sandhoff's nurse, gestured to me. I walked over, grabbing Carrie by the hand and taking her with me. Sandhoff's sister's name was Nancy Johanssen. As Marla introduced us, I tried to push away an image of the face in front of me running with blood, one eye a deep red pool of viscous liquid. Carrie looked at me sharply and squeezed my hand, taking care of the condolences for both of us. Ms. Johanssen dabbed at her eyes, inquired about my condition, then spoke to Carrie about her sister's appreciation of people who were willing to put their time and energy into the fight to guarantee continued abortion rights for all women. Eventually, Marla took Nancy's arm, suggesting she needed to get out of the cold, and the two of them headed down the hill.

Carrie and I walked down with Phil. Halfway down the hill, we caught up to Dr. Fred Niles, who had stopped to blow his nose. Niles was tall and angular, with longish dark hair and a full beard and mustache. He glanced at us, looking embarrassed at being caught wiping his eyes. "Sorry. Funerals . . ." He completed the thought with a vague gesture toward the top of the hill.

Carrie had walked on, shooting a look over her shoulder that should have knocked Niles down with its force. I caught up with her, saying, "What was that all about?"

"How do you manage to miss all the gossip? The bastard walked out on Edie a few weeks ago. Twenty-seven years of marriage. She put him through medical school. They have three kids, all in college. Men and their stupid mid-life crisises. Crises."

I looked back at Niles. Phil was still with him, talking low. Niles shook his head abruptly and walked quickly down the hill, shoulders hunched, passing Carrie and me without a glance. We waited for Phil, who looked past us to the road. The limo carrying Sandhoff's sister drove off. Phil yanked off his tie and shoved it in his overcoat pocket. Undoing the top button of his shirt, he said, "I'm going to talk to the deputy for a minute. Are you going over to the hospital?"

I looked at Carrie for clarification. "The hospital auxiliary is serving coffee and pastries. Since Irene didn't have any family locally and the police"—she shot an accusing look at Phil—"couldn't decide whether or not her house would be available to her sister today, they thought it would be nice to have something at the hospital."

"I think I'll pass," I said. "You can drop me off at my office."

Carrie nodded, but when we reached the car, she handed me the keys. I waved goodbye to Phil as I got in the driver's side. Carrie cried quietly all the way back to town. I patted her knee absently, just like a Real Man. I was thinking about Fred Niles, who had been sitting behind the wheel of his blue Volvo when I drove past it on the way out of the cemetery. He was crying a lot harder than Carrie was.

Chapter Thirteen

In the hospital parking lot, we worked out a round of musical cars. I'd take Carrie's car and leave it at the garage when I picked mine up. She'd drive Tom's car home. Tom would get a ride to the garage after work and pick up Carrie's car. I wondered if anyone had ever done a study on the stress induced by the invention of the automobile.

The thought was reinforced when I stopped at Ernie's Garage. The car was ready to go. The bill made me blink. The Camaro was the latest of what Carrie called my "disposable cars"—old cars I picked up cheap and insured only against liability, the Blue Book value on them being too low to bother insuring the cars themselves. The last one, a Chevy Nova, had ended up at the bottom of a ravine in August. If I had insured the cars I'd totaled in the past few years, my insurance premiums would have rivaled the national debt.

I arranged to leave Carrie's car at the garage, then drove off in the Camaro, hoping it lasted awhile because I'd invested in a paint job after I bought it; instead of black with orange flames on the hood, it was now a sedate silver-blue. I had planned to go to my office, but decided to go to Carrie's house instead. I hadn't eaten all day and I was also dead-tired. Maybe some lunch and a nap would help.

As soon as I got there, I checked with the answering service, hoping I'd have a message from Ellen Finch. There wasn't one, so I suspected she hadn't discovered anything interesting about Jordan Clausen's absences. I did have one message: Judy Clausen wanted me to call her but only if I could do it before four o'clock. Interesting.

Her line was busy. I ate some leftover pizza, then tried again. Still busy. I wanted to meet her anyway, so I went to see her.

The Clausens lived in a neighborhood known as The Flats, one of the few residential areas where you could get by in the winter without chains or snow tires or four-wheel drive. The Flats was several square blocks of small houses that had been built right after World War II to provide affordable housing for the parents of the generation that was to become known as the baby boomers. The original owners and their offspring had long since moved on. Most of the houses were rentals now, the exceptions being easy to identify by their new siding and well-maintained yards and added-on decks and patios.

Clausen's house was obviously a rental, in need of paint and a new roof, the unfenced yard a combination of packed dirt and dead weeds. I parked in front and walked up the cracked sidewalk to the door. I had seen the flicker of light from a television screen through the sheer curtains and could hear a laugh track through the door, so when no one responded to the doorbell, I figured it was broken and knocked. After a moment, I rang the bell again, pressing my ear against the door. I heard a harsh buzz. Thinking Mrs. Clausen might be peeking out the window, afraid to open the door to a strange man, I backed away and stood in the yard, trying to look as non-threatening as possible.

Nothing happened so I rang the bell again, calling out, "Mrs. Clausen? It's Zachariah Smith."

I was about to leave, thinking she'd gone out and left the television on, when I remembered Ellen Finch saying she didn't drive. I walked out to the curb and looked around. There were two cars parked on the street, but they didn't look like they were in any shape to be driven. All the driveways were empty. The whole area had the lifeless look of a neighborhood that had emptied out by eight o'clock, the adults heading to work, the kids climbing on the school bus. Judy Clausen was probably the only person at home in the daytime.

The thought sent me back to the window. I leaned close to it, cupping my hands around my eyes to eliminate the reflective glare on the glass. The sheer curtains were easy enough to see through but the spreading branches of a Christmas tree blocked the view. The television was to the right. A couch was against the wall directly across from the window. Between tree branches and dangling ornaments I could see a woman face down on the couch, one arm hanging off the side. I rapped on the window with my knuckles. The woman didn't move.

I thought of the phone in the Camaro, but, hell, what if she was just a sound sleeper? She probably wouldn't appreciate knowing I'd been peeking in the window at her. Thinking the lock wouldn't be any problem—rentals are notorious for having cheap locks—I went back to the door. Having once wasted time trying to pick a lock on an unlocked door, I always try the doorknob first. It turned. I pushed it open and called, "Mrs. Clausen?" I waited a moment, then pulled my gun and walked into the house, keeping the thirty-eight down at my side.

The living room was to the right of the tiny entrance. I stepped to the doorway and looked in. The woman was still on the couch, arm still hanging off the side, but I could see her back rising and falling. She was also snoring softly. I put the gun back in my hip holster, looking around for the source of a high-pitched sound. A desk telephone, its receiver sitting crookedly atop it, was on an end table by the couch. I replaced the receiver, then picked up a tall blue plastic glass from the coffee table. It was empty except for 80-proof fumes.

I put the glass down and picked up the wind-up clock next to it. The alarm was set for three-thirty. She'd have thirty minutes to make coffee and splash some cold water on her face before her husband got off work and headed home. I wondered if the alarm would wake her when all my pounding on doors and windows hadn't. Maybe it would, since it was just past noon now and in three hours she'd have pretty much slept it off.

I leaned over, trying to see her face. Her brown hair was long and gathered loosely into a ponytail at the nape of her neck. Only a bit of her profile was visible—an unremarkable nose, round cheek, smooth forehead. I thought she was probably a few years younger than her husband. She was a large woman, big-boned and solid, her turquoise pants snug against full hips and thighs. The matching sweater looked hand-knitted.

I chewed on my lip for a minute, thinking how vulnerable she was, passed out drunk, the door unlocked, the neighbors all away. I shook my head, thinking I'd better leave in case she suddenly woke up and started screaming. I looked around the room again. The furniture was nothing special, mismatched and probably secondhand, but the room was clean and neat. Most of the decorative touches were handmade: multi-colored granny-square afghans on the couch and recliner, wicker baskets filled with straw flowers, throw pillows covered with colorful needlepoint, macramé wallhangings, fat Christmas candles standing in wreaths made of pine boughs. On the wall next to the entry were several framed photographs, all school pictures of Jordan at various ages. The earlier photos showed a chubby, freckle-faced boy with dark hair and a big, happy grin. In the recent pictures, the baby fat had melted away, the freckles had faded, and the happy grin had been replaced by a forced-looking smile.

I left, turning the button in the knob to lock the door behind me.

I went back to my office. Dora had two messages for me. "Ellen Finch wants you to drop by the school before four-thirty if you get a chance. And the chief called. He said—and I quote—tell him his boy's armed."

Chapter Fourteen

"Armed with what?"

Without looking up from his computer monitor, Phil said, "Rifle. Wait a sec."

It took him a lot longer than a second to find the file he was looking for. As the printer started, he spun his chair around to face me and tilted it back, swinging his feet up on the desk. "Clausen dropped by on his lunch hour today. Jordy was at the house last night, between seven and nine. Clausen and his wife visit her mother every Wednesday—she's got cancer or something and she's in Willowhaven—and when they got home, they found lights on they didn't leave on, and when they went in the kitchen, it looked like somebody'd been having a snack, so they figured Jordy'd been there. Clausen says he took a sleeping bag and a backpack, probably some clothes and food, and the Remington and a box of shells. Also a few bucks that Judy had stashed in her recipe box."

"Well, at least he's alive. Clausen doesn't want me to look for him."

"Which means nobody's looking for him. You know what kind of priority runaway kids get."

"So? Are you in a hurry to find him for some reason?"

"I'd kinda like to talk to the little shit, yeah. Last night—

two-thirty-seven this morning to be exact—three windows on the north side of the high school were shot out. Lot of people heard the noise but no one saw anything. Shots were probably fired through the chain link fence at the back of the school grounds. Seems a little coincidental to me, Jordy taking the rifle last night and next thing you know, someone's shooting out windows at the high school. I don't need some kid with a hard-on at the world running around with a gun."

"Did you mention it to Clausen?"

"Yeah, he says Jordy's been going to the rifle range with him for over a year and he knows guns aren't toys and he wouldn't do anything stupid like shooting out windows. Hell, he doesn't want to get stuck paying for the damn windows. There's damage to the inside walls, too, and an expensive globe took a hit."

"Did you see Clausen or just talk to him on the phone?"

"I saw him. Why?"

"You happen to notice his knuckles?"

"Yeah, as a matter of fact, I did. Says he banged 'em up at work. You got some reason to think he's lying?"

"It just bothers me that he called my office right after I was shot, almost like he was trying to make himself look good by pretending he was going to hire me to look for Jordan."

"Well, if he busted his knuckles knocking Jordy around, he must not've done too much damage. He isn't going to admit it to me if he did, so there's not much I can do about it until the kid turns up. So why don't you go find him for me?"

"You know anything about his wife?"

"Never met her."

I told him about Judy Clausen calling me and my discovery of her passed out drunk on the couch in the middle of the afternoon.

"There's a lady needs a little help. Seeing as how she wanted you to call before her husband got home, maybe you oughta drop by there earlier in the day tomorrow, catch her while she's still functioning."

"I don't suppose the police department is going to pay me for doing its work for it."

"You suppose right." He picked up the pages the printer had spewed out. "I got work to do, Bucky. Why don't you go do some sleuthing."

Ellen Finch was in a meeting when I got to the high school. It was almost two before she was finished. She motioned me into her office and closed the door. She sat behind her desk, grinning broadly. "I think I missed my calling. I should have been a private detective."

"What'd you find out?"

"Well, at first, I didn't think there was anything. I went over Jordan's records last night. There's no pattern. Nothing at all. He's been absent every day of the week, never more than one day in a row though, until this week, of course. It wasn't until I was in bed that it hit me. I checked first thing this morning and I was right."

"About what?"

"Rachel Harroldson."

"I'll bite. Who's Rachel Harroldson?"

"A student. She's a freshman. Last month I spoke with Mrs. Harroldson about Rachel's attendance record. She'd missed several days and I was concerned. Mrs. Harroldson is . . . a bit difficult. She rather forcefully told me that she is more qualified than I to determine when her daughter is too ill to attend school and she said that Rachel is a delicate child and she isn't going to send her to school when she isn't feeling well. In other words, she told me to mind my own business. I checked Rachel's records from grade school and middle school and she has always missed a lot of school. There is apparently no real health problem, just an overly protective mother who, I suspect, is easily duped by her daughter."

She sat back and folded her arms, smiling smugly. I smiled back at her. She was always easy to smile at, easy to look at—fair, freckled skin, pale blue eyes, dark blond hair, and muted pastel clothes, a light peach color today.

"What do you think?" she asked.

I thought the same thing I'd thought thirteen years ago when I was in her senior English class: I'd like to be in bed with her. The only thing that had changed was that now I felt guilty thinking it. I cleared my throat, making another mental note to go see Mattie Hagen sometime soon before I made a fool of myself. "Jordan and Rachel were absent the same days. Is that it?"

"Oh, damn. I didn't think you'd get it so quickly."

I laughed at her look of disappointment. "Sorry, Ellen. It's my job. Half of what I do is jumping to conclusions and hoping I'm right. How did they manage it? These were all excused absences, right? The parents have to send a note or call, don't they?"

"We ask parents to call in the morning, so the student's name can go on the absence list. Among other things, it helps us spot kids who are skipping classes. The absence list is distributed to the teachers before the end of first period. So if a student doesn't show up for, say, fourth period and his name isn't on the list, the teacher can let the office know he's missing. There's other information on the list, too. For example, if a student will be leaving school during the day to go to a doctor's appointment. Oh, you don't want to hear all this. The important thing is that every time Jordan and Rachel were absent, the school nurse received a phone call in the morning. Supposedly from the mothers."

"Would she recognize their voices?"

"Yes. That's the odd thing. Mrs. Clausen has a distinctive voice, low and, oh, breathy, I guess you'd say. There's no doubt in my mind that it was really Rachel's mother who called. The nurse knows her personally and, besides, I've discussed Rachel's absences with her. She works in Pendleton and so does her husband. It's unlikely that they come home for lunch. I'm sure Mrs. Harroldson calls Rachel to check on her when she's home alone, but as long as Rachel said everything was fine, she'd have no reason to suspect anything. Rachel, I should explain, is not only delicate but an absolutely *perfect* child. Her mother told me so."

I nodded my understanding. I had been a perfect child, too. And Carrie. Perfect children, the adorable little Smith twins, so cute and likable, good students, good citizens, good little troopers, taking it in stride every time Mommy and Daddy left the little darlings with whichever friend or relative was willing to take them so they could run off to save the world from nuclear power plants or famine or elephant poachers or whatever their Cause Of The Moment was. They never had to worry about us: We were perfect. They found out differently the hard way, when I was strapped to a bed in a drug detoxification center and Carrie was in a psych ward with her left wrist bandaged.

"What is it?" Ellen asked.

"Sorry. I was just thinking . . . it's going to be hard on the Harroldsons if Rachel was screwing around with Jordan when they thought she was sick. Which I guess is what's been going on."

"It would certainly be my guess. It's just too coincidental otherwise. Their absence records are identical, with one exception: Jordan was here last Thursday, but Rachel wasn't. Actually, she came to school but went to the nurse's office during first period and her mother came and picked her up."

"Jordan's mother would have to know something was going on. She called the school to say he was sick. Then what? He left the house and she didn't question it? She's home all day, isn't she?"

"Yes. She doesn't work and she doesn't drive. I suppose she might visit neighbors or something, but surely she wouldn't be gone all day. She would have to know Jordan had left the house."

Unless she was passed out drunk. I kept the thought to myself, thinking I'd tell Ellen only if it seemed necessary. It was possible that Judy was hitting the bottle because she was worried about Jordan. The alarm clock she'd set made me doubt that, but it was possible.

I was silent for a minute, working out the logistics. "Where does Rachel live? How far from Jordan?"

"It must be about a mile. The house is on Elm Street, one of those ancient mansions."

Not a long walk, but in Mackie a kid Jordan's age walking around during school hours would be reported by every busy-body in town. I mentioned that to Ellen, who agreed, and said, "But then how did they get together? He must have gone to her house."

"He'd leave home in the morning but instead of catching the school bus, he'd walk over to Rachel's. Anybody who noticed him would think he missed the bus and was walking to school. Then, he'd walk home again after school."

"But his mother would have to be condoning his behavior, wouldn't she?"

"Seems like it. What was her attitude when you called her about him being absent so much?"

"She was very flustered. I didn't think much of it. A lot of parents are uncomfortable dealing with the school. She told me she'd have her husband call me. He called the next day if I remember correctly. I set up an appointment. He came by himself."

"Was that after report cards went home?"

"Yes. Are you thinking Jordan somehow concealed his absences from his parents? I don't see how. The nurse is positive she spoke with Mrs. Clausen each time. But, yes, one grading period had already ended by the time I got in touch with them. And, of course, the number of absences is indicated on the report card. But report cards are computerized forms now. Frankly, they're a bit difficult to read, all those boxes and code numbers. I suspect a lot of parents don't look at anything but the grades. I had a case last year in which a student was having his grandmother, who has Alzheimer's, call the school and say he was sick. His parents had no idea. We'd completed two grading periods before I contacted the parents on another matter and went over his records with them. I happened to mention that his attendance could be better. As far as they knew, he'd never missed a day."

"Let's say someone else was making those calls and managed to convince the nurse she was Judy Clausen. What would the Clausens do when they found out?"

"My guess is they'd cover for him. Mr. Clausen was obviously uncomfortable having to come here. Admitting Jordan was skipping school without his knowledge would lead to more contact with me. I'm sure he'd want to avoid that. He also wouldn't want anyone to know he wasn't in control of his son."

"But the nurse is sure she was talking to Jordan's mother."

"Yes. Mrs. Richardson is quite diligent about these things. If the call strikes her as suspicious, she calls back to confirm it. She doesn't know Mrs. Clausen personally but, as I said, she has a distinctive voice. Actually, she sounds like Lauren Bacall."

I laughed. "Lauren Bacall. Everybody can do Lauren Bacall's voice. I bet you can."

"Oh, I don't think so." She pursed her lips, then in a low, husky voice said, "You know how to whistle, don't you?"

"Not bad. And people sound a little different over the phone anyway. I bet Rachel Harroldson does a great Lauren Bacall."

Ellen was silent for a moment, doodling circular squiggles on a notepad. "It seems a rather complex deception for kids their age."

"They probably tried it once, found out how easy it was and just kept it up. Rachel was squared away with her parents and Jordan probably figured his would never find out. He wouldn't expect anyone to question excused absences. I'm sure he didn't tell them what he was up to when they found out he'd been skipping school. Rachel went home Thursday because she got sick, right?"

"Yes."

"And Friday night Jordan ran away. I bet Thursday was the day the shit hit the fan at the Harroldson's."

"What do you—Oh, you think she's pregnant."

"Yeah, they've been at it long enough for her to have morning sickness. Her mother might have guessed or maybe Rachel confessed. They probably got the whole story out of her and called Clausen."

"And the shit—as you so eloquently put it—hit the fan at the Clausens'. And Jordan ran. Oh, that reminds me. I did find out something about last Friday. One of the boys Jordan usually eats with said his father picked him up Friday at lunch time. He said Jordan didn't seem to be expecting him."

"That fits. Rachel's parents talked to him and he picked Jordan up and took him home to face the music. There's one scene I'm glad I missed."

Ellen smiled sweetly. "Having been through it once yourself."

"Yeah, but my parents didn't even bother to act surprised. I think Clausen's reaction would be a little less controlled."

"It must have been, for Jordan to run away. Unless he simply didn't want to have to deal with Rachel's condition. Well, what do we do now? All this makes sense but it's pure conjecture. Although their absence records are certainly compelling evidence."

"I'm going to try to find Jordan. He's still in the area; he went home last night while his parents were out and took some camping gear."

"Lord, I hope he isn't spending the nights outside. He'll freeze to death. I'll talk to Rachel. She'll be hostile if she finds I already know what's going on, so I'll get her here on some pretext and do my I'm-always-here-if-you-ever-need-to-talk routine. Sometimes it works."

"Thanks, Ellen. You've been a big help."

Chapter Fifteen

The temperature had been dropping steadily all day. Judging from the clouds blowing in, the promised snow was on its way. I turned up my jacket collar and thrust my hands in my pockets as I hurried back to the car. I started the engine and turned the heater on, then leaned back and closed my eyes, trying to sort out my thoughts.

Jordan: If he took camping equipment and clothes, he might have decided to get out of Mackie. Most runaways headed to Portland, where they could get lost in the big city. They ended up lost in a lot more ways than one. Jordan wasn't old enough to drive, although he might know how. Unless he stole a car, he'd have to try to thumb a ride. With luck, the state troopers would pick him up.

Rachel Harroldson: Not my problem, thank god.

Clausen, Mr. and Mrs.: Jordan would have to be found before I could find out whether Clausen beat him. And then only if Jordan was willing to admit it. Clausen had lied about why his son ran off, so I considered anything else he told me suspect. Judy Clausen had wanted me to call before four. I'd call a few minutes after her alarm went off at three-thirty. With that in mind, I headed to my office, continuing my list en route.

Irene Sandhoff: Her murder was Phil's problem, not mine. But I wished he'd come up with some clear indication that the killer was after her, not me. The fact that I was still walking around alive wasn't proof but it made it likely at least. If someone wanted me dead, surely he would have tried again by now. I was a good-sized target.

Dr. Fred Niles: Crying in his car after Irene Sandhoff's funeral. Interesting. But Phil could leap to conclusions just as fast as I could and he seemed to be on top of the situation. It wasn't my business anyway.

The vandalism to my car and office: The timing had to be a coincidence. It couldn't have anything to do with Sandhoff's murder. Shoot two people and then resort to something as juvenile as painting dirty words on a window? No way. I hadn't pissed anybody off lately, except for my client's ex-husband over the weekend. But he lived in northern California and wasn't the type to slash tires. If he did anything, he'd sic a lawyer on me for my somewhat coercive method of collecting past-due support money.

Carrie: I didn't like her being afraid. I especially didn't like her thinking about keeping a loaded gun in the house. Post-Trauma Stress Syndrome. Well, Tom would handle it. Something else about Carrie . . . Oh, shit, a paperhanger! I kept forgetting about it.

Ellen Finch: Well, she wasn't a problem. I wondered if she realized she had automatically fallen into a seductive pose— eyes half closed, lips pouty—when she did her Lauren Bacall impression. A pretty woman, Ellen Finch, with all that dark blond hair and . . .

Mattie Hagen: I definitely needed to go see Mattie sometime soon. Hell, she might have replaced me by now and then what would I do? Sex with Mattie was trouble-free. She didn't want anything else from me, she couldn't get pregnant, and she didn't like men, so she was never involved with more than one at a time. Until recently, she hadn't even minded my occasional flings on the side. She knew I'd been practicing safe sex since long before it was a health issue, since the day Patricia Ann Flynn told me she was pregnant, in fact. Mattie had finally put her foot down, though. I had promised her I'd behave myself and I intended to, my last fling having been with Virginia Marley—the woman from last August's runaway case—who was no doubt spending her jail time carving likenesses of me out of soap bars and jabbing pins into them. Virginia was enough to make any man swear off strange women for good. One-night-stands always left me feeling depressed anyway. I could justify my relationship with Mattie—to myself anyway; no one else approved of it.

Which reminded me of Allison: I hadn't called her. Well, it was only Thursday, two days since I'd talked to her. I'd call her soon. Maybe tonight.

The first fat flakes drifted down as I pulled into a parking place. My office was intact: no broken windows; no graffiti; no bomb going off when I opened the door. I checked with the answering service first—no messages either—then called Clausen's house. Lauren Bacall answered immediately. After we established who I was, a point she seemed a little fuzzy on, I reminded her she had called me. The conversation went downhill from there.

"Oh. Well. I . . . I think . . . uh . . . my husband usually . . . you know . . . handles . . . uh . . . things. Um . . . I'll tell him you . . . uh . . . called." The hesitant speech didn't match the low, sexy voice.

"Mrs. Clausen, you asked me to call before four o'clock. I thought maybe you wanted to talk to me before he gets home."

"Oh . . . well, I don't think . . . why . . . why would I do that?"

"I don't know."

"Well, I'll . . . um . . . tell him you called." *Click.*

"Blackouts are a bad sign, Judy," I said as I hung up the phone. I decided to drop by her house in the morning. In the meantime, I had things to do. What? Go to the post office. I hadn't picked up the mail since Friday.

That killed ten minutes. Back at the office, I sorted through the mail quickly, hoping for a letter from Allison. There wasn't one. I unfolded the *Mackie Mirror,* fourteen pages of all the news that would fit between the advertisements.

The *Mirror* was published on Wednesdays and Saturdays. I had tossed the Saturday edition in the recycle bin since I'd already seen it at Carrie's house. Wednesday's front page was devoted to Monday's shooting: A large picture of Sandhoff, a small one of me taken when I was a cop, a long shot of her office, a detailed description of the shooting, a rehash of the demonstrations, and the first two paragraphs of an editorial which was continued on page eight where a formal obituary was also printed.

In keeping with its policy of not alienating advertisers, the newspaper's editorial stance was notoriously wishy-washy. Wednesday's editorial skimmed over the abortion issue but soundly denounced violence in general. A fairly safe position. Few people admit to being pro-violence.

I refolded the paper to the front page and shoved it to the corner of the desk. The only bit of information that was news to me was that there had been two telephoned bomb threats that morning. The first at ten o'clock, the second just before the shooting. That seemed to rule out the killer making the threats in an attempt to get Sandhoff to come out of the building.

Why had she come out? To talk to me apparently, but why? Because of the second bomb threat? That didn't make sense. Phil was there. She'd tell him, not me.

Suppose Sandhoff had answered the phone when the second threat was made. Suppose she had recognized the caller's voice. So what? She'd still tell the cops, not a private detective. Unless the caller was after her because of something she was involved in that she didn't want the cops to know about. Like what? Nothing came to mind. She was a reputable doctor, a prominent member of what passed for high society in Mackie, a member of several charitable organizations, a regular pillar of the community. And Dr. Fred Niles cried like a broken-hearted man at her funeral.

I called the police department, then Phil's house. "Did you find Jordan already?" he asked.

"I'm working on it. Who answered the phone Monday?"

"What phone?"

"Sandhoff's. The bomb threats."

"I don't need to remind you that you don't have any business messing around in police investigations, do I?"

"I don't have any business searching for runaway kids when no one's paying me to do it, either. Did Sandhoff answer the phone the second time?"

"Marla Twill answered it both times. The caller was whispering, but she's pretty sure it was a man. He didn't stay on the line to chat, just said his piece and hung up. Sandhoff never knew about the second call. Marla saw her walk out the door just as the phone rang. She'd barely hung up when the shot was fired. She didn't even tell me about the second bomb threat until the next day. Sandhoff getting killed kind of pushed it to the back of her mind."

"So there's probably no connection between the shooting and the bomb threats."

"Doesn't seem to be. Doesn't need to be, either. Everybody at Sandhoff's office was so shook up I had to wait 'til they calmed down a little to get much information out of them. Sandhoff usually ate at the office, but she was planning to take a long lunch break Monday. She was on the Holiday Ball committee and they were getting together at the Orange Mandarin at noon."

"So she would've been leaving in a few minutes anyway. That seems to narrow it down to someone who knew about the meeting."

"Might. Might not."

From his tone, I knew that was all the information I was going to get. I got even, though: I didn't tell him about Rachel Harroldson.

I was drifting off to sleep, one hand propping up my head, when the door opened and a local derelict named Eddie Paxton poked his head in. "Yo, Zack? You busy?"

"Depends on what you want."

Eddie walked in and closed the door behind him, his grin showing broken, tobacco-stained teeth. He was my height but fifty pounds lighter, his cadaverous physique not obvious now because he wore most of his wardrobe in the winter so he wouldn't freeze to death when he passed out in an alley or doorway. Four or five shirt collars showed under his army surplus parka.

"Don't want nothin'. Just stoppin' by to see if you was still around. Heard tell you got yourself shot up. Din't know but what you was dead."

"No, I'm not dead."

"Reckon not, less'n you're a ghost." Eddie lowered himself into the captain's chair across the desk from me, laughing at his own words, his laughter turning into a hacking smoker's cough. I was thinking about getting up and pounding him on the back, or maybe calling the paramedics, when he finally got it under control. "Goddamn," he said. "Them butts'll kill you, you know what I mean?"

"Yeah, I think I read something about it. A report from the Surgeon General, wasn't it?"

He pulled a pack of unfiltered Camels from his jacket pocket and lit up. I got my ashtray out of a drawer and slid it across the desk to him.

"You want something, Eddie?"

"I was down to the bus depot, musta been Monday, Tuesday evenin', something like that." He turned the *Mackie Mirror* around so the front page was right side up to him. "This the lady doctor got herself kilt?"

"She's the one who was murdered, yeah."

"Fast woman."

Fast? Wasn't that an outdated term for promiscuous? It hardly seemed to fit Irene Sandhoff. By all reports, her social life had consisted of an occasional dinner out with friends. And possibly an affair with a married man. On the off-chance the town drunk knew all the sordid details, I said, "What do you mean, Eddie?"

"Huh?"

"Fast, you said."

"You know, runnin'."

"Jogging, you mean?"

"Runnin', joggin', what's the difference?"

"You have to dress right to jog."

Eddie snorted with laughter. "Yeah, she had herself a fancy joggin' outfit. See 'em all over the place. Fat cats wearin' them sissy joggin' clothes an' runnin' in circles. Too fuckin' lazy to work so they gotta run 'round in circles to keep from gettin' fat as pigs. Lazy bastards. Me, I never had a ounce o' fat on me. You know why?"

Because people who put away a fifth or two a day year after year tend to be malnourished. I kept the thought to myself and said, "No, Eddie, why?"

"Worked hard all m' life that's why." He moved his hand forward slowly, tapping off an inch of ash into the ashtray.

"Come off it, when's the last time you held a job?"

He looked offended. "I'm retired now. Worked hard all m' life up 'til I retired. Retired now, don't hafta work no more."

Whatever he'd retired from hadn't had much of a pension plan. He'd been collecting welfare checks and handouts for at least fifteen years.

"He was up in them woods, huh? Shot her from them woods. Spooky. Don't think I'll go up there no more. People takin' guns up there and shootin' folks. Spooky."

"You go to the woods a lot?"

"Nah, not much now. Summertime, when it's warm. Sleep up there sometimes. Nice and quiet, not like down at the fuckin' shelter. Buncha drunks always snorin' and talkin' in their sleep like crazy people down there and all them Holy Joes wanting you to pray for your supper. Cop was down to the bus depot."

"So?"

"Lookin' for some kid, he was. Showed a pitcher around. Me, I was sittin' right there. Dumb bastard din't show me no pitcher so I din't tell'm shit."

"A picture of Jordan Clausen?"

"Hell, I don't know the kid's name. Got me a pitcher, though." He pulled a dirty folded paper from a pocket and handed it to me: a police department missing person handbill. I recognized the picture as one of the school photos of Jordan I'd seen at his house. "Thought maybe you was lookin' for him."

"Christ, Eddie, the cops must've been at the bus station Monday. This is Thursday."

"That so?" He took a final deep drag on his cigarette, sucking the burning tip to within a quarter-inch of his fingers.

"Have you seen him?"

"Mighta." He stubbed out what was left of the cigarette.

I took a ten-dollar bill out of my wallet and put it on the desk. Eddie plucked it up and stuck it in a pocket.

"Seen him down to the Quick Shop, musta been Sunday night."

"What time?"

"Early. Eight, nine, somewheres in there."

"Was he in the store? What was he doing?"

"He was inside all right. Doin' him some shopliftin's what he was doin'. Me, I never stole nothin' in my life."

Nothing that was firmly nailed down anyway. "Well, he was probably hungry."

"Wuddn't stealin' no food. Stole him some gee-lettes, is what he stole."

"Gillettes? Razor blades?"

"Yep. Seen him do it with my own eyes. Palmed 'em and slid 'em in his hip pocket and walked out 'thout payin' for 'em."

"You're talking about razor blades, right? Not a disposable razor."

"Reg'lar blades. Din't look to me like he's shavin' more'n once a week an' most folks use them disposable ones nowadays. Me, I like a ol'-fashion safety razor myself." He stroked a palm over five or six days' growth of gray stubble. "What you reckon he wanted with them gee-lettes?" He stood up, sidling toward the door and grinning slyly as he patted the pocket where he'd stashed the ten.

"Eddie, you see him again, you come and tell me. Right away."

He patted his pocket again and ambled out the door.

Chapter Sixteen

I left soon after Eddie did, and drove to Clausen's house. He invited me in, seeming more resigned than surprised by my visit. After introducing me to his wife, he gestured to the couch. I took a seat at one end of it. Judy was in a chair in the corner, poking green thread into fabric stretched tight in an embroidery hoop. Her work was illuminated by a small lamp but the rest of the room was in shadow, the Christmas tree lights twinkling holiday colors into the dimness.

Judy had acknowledged the introduction with a timid smile and returned to her needlework. Clausen turned off the television, saying, "This is about Jordy, I guess." He sat down in the recliner, leaving it in the upright position, leaning forward with his hands clasped between his knees.

"How upset was he when he left?"

"He was pretty pissed off. Look, I never should've called you but . . . I don't understand what you're doing. I already told you I wasn't hiring you."

"I'm not interested in being hired, Clausen, but I am interested in finding your son."

"Why?"

"Because I think he ran away after you beat the shit out of him and if I can get to him before you do, maybe I can convince him that keeping quiet about it isn't the best thing to do. And maybe then it won't keep happening."

Judy Clausen began crying quietly. Clausen didn't even turn to look at her. He held his right hand out in front of him, fingers spread. "Figured that was what you thought. Yeah, I was lying about banging up my hand at work, but I didn't hit Jordy. I never laid a hand on the kid in his whole life." He flexed his fingers slowly. "I hit the wall in the kitchen. You can go look if you want to. I haven't patched the hole yet."

He wouldn't have suggested it unless there really was a hole in the kitchen wall so I declined the invitation. "Why'd you do it?"

"Hit the wall? Because I was so fucking mad at Jordy and . . . like I said, I never laid hand on the kid. I guess . . . I guess I just needed to hit something."

I nodded, understanding far better than he probably thought I did: I had recently repaired the wall in the upstairs master bedroom at my house, patching a fist-sized hole I'd put there a couple years earlier, shortly after my wife April left me without a word of explanation. "You were mad about Rachel?"

Judy made a small sound of surprise. Clausen sighed heavily and said, "How'd you find out about Rachel? Her folks weren't going to tell anyone. They'll be pissed as hell if word gets out. This fucking town . . . Can't keep anything quiet."

"Nobody's spreading the story around. Did Jordan run away because you were mad or because he didn't want to face Rachel's pregnancy?"

"Hell, I don't know. Who the hell understands kids that age? Rachel . . . Well, her parents are taking her to a clinic in Portland next week. For an abortion. Jordy knew that so I guess it's me he's mad at."

"I'm trying to find out how upset he was. Someone saw him shoplifting—"

"*Shoplifting!* No way in hell. Who said that? Goddammit, Jordy's no thief. We raised that boy right."

"He was seen taking some razor blades—"

"*My boy's no thief, goddammit.*" He roared the words. His wife moaned and covered her ears with her hands for a moment.

"Clausen. He took razor blades. Good old-fashioned slit-your-wrist razor blades. How upset was he when he left?"

In the silence that followed, I heard the tick-tick-tick of a clock. I looked around for it, finally realizing the sound was coming from inside the drawer of the end table next to the couch. Judy's wake-up clock, hidden from sight. I was surprised when it was Judy who finally broke the silence.

"When?" she asked.

"When did he take the razor blades? Sunday evening."

"Sunday? But—"

Clausen interrupted. "Jordy wouldn't do that."

"The man who saw him has never lied to me."

"I mean he wouldn't . . . use them."

"Well, he apparently gave it some thought and didn't act on the spur of the moment, anyway."

"What do you mean?"

"He took them Sunday and he came home Wednesday evening, so obviously he didn't do anything rash Sunday night."

The Clausens exchanged a look I couldn't interpret, but fear seemed to be a major component. I looked from one to the other. Judy's eyes were reddened, but her tears had dried.

"What is it?" I asked.

Clausen shook his head—at his wife, not at me. Then he said, "It's just a lot to take in. You coming here saying maybe Jordy's thinking about . . . suicide. Look, I was bullshitting you the other day. I don't have any money. Hell, we're barely getting by. I can't hire you. Maybe I would if I could. You still want to try to find him, it's okay with me. But you gotta understand I can't pay you."

"Why'd you call me? You must've heard I'd been shot. It seems funny to me, you calling when you knew I was in the hospital, like maybe you wanted to make it look like you were serious about finding him and when you realized I was well enough to do it, you backed off in a hurry."

"I didn't know you'd been shot when I called your office."

I must have looked skeptical because he said, "Oh, I heard about the shooting, about the doctor, and I knew someone else had been shot, too, but I didn't know it was you. We had the radio on in the shop and we heard the news, but, hell, we were working. Didn't really pay much attention to the details. Maybe they mentioned your name, but, shit, I wasn't even sure what your name was when I called your office. I knew the name of your business. I drive by it every morning."

"That still doesn't explain why you called me if you knew you couldn't pay me."

He looked at his wife and that same look passed between them, some kind of message, laced with fear. Once again, Clausen shook his head at his wife. Judy put down her embroidery hoop and in that low, sultry voice said, "We were upset. We . . . I told him to do something, hire someone to find Jordy. I told him I didn't care how much it cost, we'd work it out some way. Later on, we talked some more and . . . well, things are bad enough without us spending money we don't have and what could you do anyway? We called everyone we know and the police are supposed to be looking for him. We just decided there wasn't much reason to hire you."

It was plausible, and yet that look bothered me. I let it go, asking Clausen whether Jordan was capable of surviving outside in below-freezing weather. He assured me he was. They spent a lot of weekends in Malheur County, where Judy had relatives, and did a lot of camping there. Jordan was a seasoned outdoorsman and he'd taken plenty of gear.

I was standing, ready to leave, when Clausen asked, "If you find him, do you have to take him to the cops?"

"If I find him, I won't take him anywhere he doesn't want to go, including here. Chief Pauling wants to talk to him about those windows at the high school though."

Clausen made an impatient gesture. "I told the chief Jordy wouldn't do anything like that. He's a good shot, Jordy is, but I made damn sure he learned gun safety and I drilled it into his head over and over again that guns aren't toys. He knows he'd never get to go to the rifle range or go hunting again if he pulled a stupid stunt like that. And besides, I been promising him his own rifle soon as I get the money together, maybe use the tax refund next year. He wouldn't go shooting out windows 'cause he knows damn well it'd be a cold day in hell before he gets a rifle of his own if he did."

"It was your rifle he took?"

"Yeah, we only have the one. We take turns using it down at the rifle range. We go every Tuesday after I get off work. Jordy and me and two or three other guys. Not like a gun club really, just a bunch of us got in the habit of going there once a week. I had to go by myself Tuesday. Looks like I won't be going again until Jordy brings the damn Remington back."

Another look passed between Clausen and his wife, but there was no fear in it this time. Instead, I had an impression of . . . I wasn't sure what. Relief maybe, or satisfaction. I thought back over what he'd said but couldn't see any significance in a weekly get-together at the rifle range. Maybe he was just trying to convince me Jordy wouldn't shoot out windows so I'd put in a good word with Phil. I left soon after that, not knowing much more than I'd known when I arrived.

The snow was coming down fast, faster than it seemed possible for something as light as snowflakes to fall. Some force other than gravity had to be at work. Wind, I supposed, although there was no wind, the flakes dropping arrow-straight from sky to earth.

I had been thinking all day that I should go home since the next target after my car and my office would logically be my house. I wasn't too worried though, since any major damage would set off the alarm. The snow made going home a necessity. I needed to change cars before the roads got bad.

I thought about Jordan while I was driving home. Where had he been sleeping? It had been below freezing at night for weeks now, with below-zero windchills, and he didn't even have a sleeping bag until Wednesday evening. I couldn't see him sleeping outside with the weather as bad as it was, so he must have been in town somewhere. But where?

Mackie isn't New York City. It isn't even Portland. Hell, it isn't even Eugene. There was no business or public building where a kid his age could spend the night without the cops showing up. He might have spent a night or two at a friend's house, but five or six nights? I wondered if Ellen had come up with any close friends. Clausen said they'd called around, but I wasn't sure I believed him. Besides, parents don't always know who their kid's real friends are.

I had planned to stay home, but the silence of the house got to me in a hurry. I was only there long enough to fix some dinner and change out of my suit and into a pair of jeans and a black turtleneck sweater. I got the cellular phone from the Camaro's dashbox, thinking for the hundredth time that I should just buy a second one so I didn't have to remember to move it when I changed cars. I seldom used it but having it with me in the car had become a compulsion. I headed back to Mackie in my Jeep Cherokee, blue, almost new, and insured to the max. If the vandal struck again, I could stick it to the insurance company.

Chapter Seventeen

I stopped by Carrie's house to see how she was doing. Also to see what she could tell me about Dr. Fred Niles. If she knew any juicy details, she wasn't sharing them with me, but Tom looked a little uncomfortable when I brought up the subject, so I cornered him in the upstairs hallway as he was coming out of the bathroom.

"Was Niles having an affair with Irene Sandhoff?"

"I don't know."

"Come on, Tom."

"Look, Pauling already talked to me. There was a rumor going around a couple months ago. That's all I know. I never saw them together. Edie Niles is going through a bad time. Fred hit her with a divorce right out of the blue, no warning, not even much of an explanation. I don't think she knows about Irene, assuming the rumors are true. Even if she did, she wouldn't kill her, for Christ's sake. Besides, as Pauling pointed out, she couldn't hit the broad side of a barn with a bazooka. That's a direct quote."

I grinned. "Sounds like him."

He frowned, running a hand through his blond hair. "Carrie got out of bed twice last night to check the locks and be sure the alarm was set. I'll be working nights next week. I don't know what to do. You think you can stay with her?"

"I can, but it won't help. It might even make it worse. She'll start feeling like she needs someone around to protect her all the time. She doesn't. She didn't before. She needs to remember how she felt before and having me hanging around isn't going to help her do that."

He sighed. "If I find out she's loading that damn gun when she's here alone . . ." He sighed again. "I don't like her being afraid. She said there's a chance the guy was shooting at you instead of Irene so now she's worried about that, too."

"I didn't mean to tell her. It kind of slipped out. I don't think he was after me. Why hasn't he tried again if he was?"

Tom shrugged. "Waiting for things to cool down or maybe killing Irene by mistake shook him up or, I don't know, maybe he only had one bullet."

"I'll mention that possibility to Phil. Look, if it happened somewhere else, I'd be worried, but no one knew I'd be at her office. Phil's just covering all the bases. He already checked up on everyone who has a grudge against me. The guy was after Sandhoff."

"What are you two doing up there?" Carrie was at the foot of the stairs.

"Men-talk, sweetie," Tom said.

"Oh, good. I was afraid I was missing something important."

Tom laughed and headed for the stairs.

"Tom."

He turned around. "Yeah?"

"Can you think of any reason Sandhoff would have wanted to talk to me?"

"Professionally, you mean? No."

I followed him downstairs, wondering if he was really lying or it just sounded that way to me. I didn't have time to talk to him again. The phone rang and it was for me.

"Hey, Bucky. I think your sex life just hit the skids."

"What's that supposed to mean?"

"I just got a call from Mathilda. She left her Mercedes parked in the driveway and someone keyed it. Scratched 'Z. Smith fucks me' on the rear quarter panel.

"Shit."

"She's pissed as hell and now if someone takes a shot at you I won't know if it's Sandhoff's killer or your easy lay."

"Shit. Well, maybe that narrows it down. It has to be someone who knows about me and Mattie."

"Narrows it down, hell. Half the town keeps track of how often the local private eye's car's parked in the local romance writer's driveway. They take bets on it down at the Honky Tonk. Winner's the one who comes closest to guessing how often you get laid."

"Oh, shut up, Phil. I'm not in the mood."

He snickered. "I don't think Mathilda is either."

I hung up on him and went to see Mattie.

Her house was old and elegant, with gingerbread trim and multi-paned windows. There were ten or twelve rooms, but she spent most of her time in front of a computer terminal in a small downstairs bedroom that she'd converted to an office. When she wasn't there, she was at the dining room table proofreading printed manuscript pages.

Mattie was, as usual, wearing a robe, dark blue with a wide belt cinched tight, emphasizing curves that she considered twenty excess pounds. They looked like curves to me. Her hair was dark and short and liberally sprinkled with silver. She said hello when she opened the door, which I took as a good sign. I followed her into the kitchen, where she poured herself a glass of white wine and failed to offer one to me.

"Did Phil call you?"

"Yeah. I'm sorry about your car. I'll take care of getting it fixed."

"That's the least of my concerns, Zachariah. He said your

office and car were vandalized, too. I assume there's some connection."

"Probably. Whoever's doing it seems more interested in irritating me than anything else. I don't think you're in any danger."

"But I don't suppose you can guarantee that."

"No." My office, my car, my whatever-Mattie-was. Not lover. Sex partner. What was next? My house. Or Carrie's house or car. "Look, if you're worried, I can get someone to stay with you until I find out who's doing it."

"A bodyguard?" She raised an eyebrow at me. I'd met her when she hired me as a bodyguard. It had taken us two days to make it to bed, but that was only because we spent most of the first day on airplanes, flying from Portland to Paris. Airlines tend to frown on in-flight sex, even in First Class.

I smiled at her. "Maybe that isn't a good idea."

She almost smiled back. "You haven't been here for a while. Are you feeling guilty?"

"About what? Not coming over? Your fingers aren't broken. You could pick up the phone if you wanted to see me that bad."

"That's not what I meant. The last time you were here was right after you got back from Connecticut. Did you make her a promise and break it with me?"

"No. I didn't make her any promises. I don't think she understands our relationship, but she knows—"

"That I don't really mean anything to you."

"You made the rules, Mattie. No strings. No commitment. No . . . emotional involvement. Do you want to change them now?"

She shook her head. "No. But I'd like . . . I don't know. Some consistency, I guess."

"You could have called. You've never seemed all that interested in whether I show up or not."

"You've never stayed away this long. Almost a month. I thought maybe it was your subtle way of telling me you wanted to end it."

"I'm never subtle, Mattie." Just to prove it, I added, "I'm here now. You wanna fuck?"

She covered her mouth with one hand to stifle a laugh. Then she crossed her arms, serious again. "I don't want your life, your *career*—such as it is—creating problems for me."

"Vandals are usually too chickenshit to go after a person. You're careful. Christ, you keep this place locked up like a fortress and you hardly ever leave. What was your car doing in the driveway anyway?"

"I should be able to leave my car in my own driveway without having someone ruin it. The Fosters"—she gestured vaguely to the north—"are giving their son a car for Christmas and they don't want him to know, so I'm letting them store it in my garage. The Mercedes is old anyway, what's wrong with leaving it out? This is a good neighborhood. I've never had to worry about it before."

"A Mercedes doesn't get old, Mattie, it ages. You should have an alarm installed in it. I'll take care of that when I see about getting the damage repaired, if you want. In the meantime, just keep the doors locked and set the house alarm."

She sighed. "All right. You're right, I suppose."

"You didn't answer my question."

"What question?"

"The un-subtle one."

"Oh, that." She gave me an appraising look. "A bullet wound, huh? I suppose it's possible that at some point in my writing career I might need to describe a bullet wound."

"Too bad it's not in a more interesting location." She smiled and I added, "So, you want to do some research?"

Chapter Eighteen

After the warmth of Mattie's bed, the temperature outside felt like forty below. A DJ on the car radio thoughtfully told me it was eighteen above with a wind-chill of five below. I'd have been happier not knowing. I stopped at Sparky's Restaurant for a late dinner so it was after ten when I got back to the office. Once there, I realized there was no reason for me to be there.

I sat behind my desk anyway, picking up the *Mirror* and looking at Irene Sandhoff's picture. She'd been fifty-two years old, an attractive woman, trim and fit. Eddie Paxton had seen her jogging. She probably ate right, too, and didn't smoke and drank in moderation and got plenty of sleep. A healthy lifestyle can add years to your life. Unless someone comes along and shoots you in the head.

I put the paper down and picked up the yellow message slip I'd dropped on the desk earlier: the woman with no name. I had considered asking Phil to find out whose number it was, mainly just to satisfy my curiosity, but I'd decided against it. Phil didn't mind doing me a favor now and then but I tried to keep them to a minimum. If it had been anything important, the woman would have called back.

I checked my watch. It was hard to believe it was still Thursday, that just this morning I'd been at Sandhoff's funeral. It had been one hell of a long day. I yawned a few times, thinking I should go home, then I picked up the message slip again. It was a little late to make a business call, but everyone's home at ten-twenty on Thursday night.

I got a hesitant "Hello?" after the first ring.

Breaking off in mid-yawn, I said, "Hello, this is Zachariah Smith from Arrow Investigations. Sorry if I woke you. I wouldn't've called so late but I've tried the number several times and never caught you in."

After a pause, the woman said, "Mr. Smith? It's quite all right. I wasn't asleep; I'm not staying here. I was just sorting through some papers and I didn't even notice how late it was getting. Goodness, it's almost ten-thirty; I'd planned to go back to the hotel long before this. I don't know where the time went."

I frowned, trying to place her voice, which was vaguely familiar. I couldn't attach a name to it and didn't have any idea what she was talking about. She seemed to be waiting for me to say something though so I said, "You wanted to talk to me?"

She made a small noise, a sociable pause-filler, sounding like she was racking her brain trying to figure out how to avoid making a major *faux pas*. "I'm returning your call," I said, helpfully, I hoped. "I got the message Monday but this is the first time I got an answer."

"Monday? But . . . I didn't get here until Tuesday morning. There was an evening flight but I didn't want to get here at night because I didn't know anyone so I waited until morning."

There was a brief silence which I broke by saying, "Who is this?"

"Nancy Johanssen."

Nancy Johanssen, Nancy Johanssen. Where had I heard that name before?

"Irene's sister," the woman added. "We met at the funeral this morning."

A little jolt of adrenaline hit me, making me feel slightly nauseated. "Sorry. I'd forgotten your name."

"Oh, it's all right. I probably wouldn't remember yours either if you hadn't been shot, too." Her voice broke and she sounded like she was trying not to cry as she said, "I'm sorry, it's all been so awful. She never hurt anyone in her life, always trying to help, and she truly believed women should have a right to safe abortions. She fought hard for it back before it was legal and, well, she never said so, but I think she performed abortions back then, too, because she didn't want those poor girls going to butchers. I just can't believe anyone would . . . She wasn't breaking the law now, it's legal, she wasn't . . . oh, god." She started crying softly.

I tried to think of something comforting to say, but she'd heard it all before and none of it helped anyway. I waited until she seemed to be calmer, then I said, "Ms. Johanssen, I'm sorry. I didn't mean to upset you. I'm a little confused. My answering service received a call Monday morning. A woman wanted me to call her at this number. You're at your sister's house, is that right?"

"Yes, but I haven't been staying here. The police were . . . I don't know what, searching for clues, I suppose. Besides, I didn't want to stay here. It's so sad . . . all her things. Just going through the papers is hard." She sighed, then said, "I'm sorry, I don't understand. Irene wanted to talk to you?"

"She didn't leave a name, just the number. If I'd known it was her number, I wouldn't have called."

"Oh, I see. Well . . ."

"Can you think of any reason she might have wanted to talk to me?"

"Well, I don't know. She was involved with some charities and they have fund-raising activities this time of year. Something like that perhaps?"

"I don't think so. Ms. Johanssen, your sister didn't give her name, even when the operator asked for it. Can you think of a reason why she'd need to talk to me? A problem in her private life maybe?"

"I . . . I don't understand. You're a private detective, aren't you? Why on earth . . . well, *no,* there's no reason Irene would . . . a private *detective?* What do you mean?"

"I'm sorry. I keep upsetting you. It was probably nothing important. Sometimes people ask me to do background checks on potential employees, things like that. Look, would it be all right if I came by and talked to you for a few minutes?"

"Now?"

"If you don't mind."

"Well, no, I don't mind. Do you have the address?"

She gave it to me and I told her I'd be there in fifteen minutes. After I hung up, I folded my arms on the desk and dropped my head onto them, feeling queasy. My shoulder, which hadn't been bothering me much, was suddenly throbbing; so was my head. I sat up straight and forced myself to think.

Irene Sandhoff called my office at eleven-twenty-five Monday morning, just about the time I left the house to drive to Belle Foret.

Less than thirty minutes after she called, I showed up in front of her office and she came out and walked up to me and touched my arm, and then she died.

If she needed to talk to me in a hurry, why didn't she leave her office number instead of her home number? Maybe that meant it wasn't anything important. Then why did she come out to talk to me? Phil said she never went outside when the demonstrators were there.

Why wouldn't she give the operator her name? One possibility occurred to me. I looked up her office number in the phone book and called it. The line was answered immediately by a woman with a high-pitched voice: Marilyn at the Main Street Answering Service. I started to tell her I had the wrong number but I just hung up instead. I took two pain pills and left the office.

Nancy Johanssen was watching at the window and opened the door while I was climbing up three steps that felt like Mount Everest. I followed her into the house, which was on a street of expensive, fairly new homes on large lots. Sandhoff's was a stately Colonial-style structure, with tall white pillars and a wide verandah across the front and down both sides. A big house for a single woman.

"This is a beautiful house," I said, as Nancy Johanssen led me into the living room and gestured toward a couch with elegant dark green upholstery. The furniture was Queen Anne, which always makes me nervous. Those spindly legs don't look as if they can support two hundred and twenty pounds. I lowered myself carefully onto the couch. The coffee table in front of me had several stacks of papers on it that she had apparently been going through when I called.

She sat on a delicate chair placed at a right angle to one end of the couch, saying, "Yes, it is, isn't it? Irene loved it. I was surprised when she moved here after living in San Francisco most of her life. Such a small town and out here in the middle of nowhere, but she was happy here. She said it was peaceful. And the house, well, she called it her *sanctum sanctorum*. She changed a lot after her husband died. When he was alive, they were always on the go, parties and traveling, and she had a very busy practice, both of them did. Some of the life seemed to go out of her when he died. She also had some health problems. That's when she closed her practice in the City. She simply didn't feel she had the energy anymore. She lived quietly here. I suppose that was part of the reason a small town appealed to her."

"She didn't have any children, did she?"

"No, she wasn't able to. I always wondered . . . I shouldn't say anything but . . ."

"If it helps you to talk, I don't mind listening. I keep a lot of secrets in my profession. And I don't think anyone could come up with anything that would surprise me anymore."

She laughed lightly. "No. There's really nothing new, is there? The same tawdry little secrets and foolish mistakes over and over again. There's something in the Bible, Ecclesiastes, I think . . ."

"'What has been is what will be, and what has been done is what will be done; and there is nothing new under the sun.'"

Her eyes widened with surprise and she grinned, looking younger, the sorrow leaving her face for a moment. "You surprise me, Mr. Smith." The smile faded as she grew serious again. "Irene is . . . was nine years older than I. I was just a child when she left home to go to college. She came home during her sophomore year. She was quite ill, almost bedridden, and missed an entire semester. I was too young for anyone to tell me what was wrong, but I remember overhearing my parents talking about her, saying things I didn't understand then, but years later . . . well, I think she had an abortion—it was illegal then, of course—and I think it was botched up. I never felt I could ask her. We were close in spite of the age difference, but she was reserved and . . . and a very private person. She told me she couldn't have children but never explained why."

"That could be part of the reason she was such a staunch advocate of abortion rights."

"Yes. She was a real fighter. I was always so proud of her. And a little envious, too, I'm afraid. She was so sure of herself, so confident. I've always been just the opposite, the original old-maid librarian." She paused a moment, frowning, then said, "I don't know what to do about these." She had picked up three manila file folders from the coffee table.

"What are they?"

"Medical files. I was surprised to find them in her desk. It was one of her rules—she never brought work home. She'd stay at the office until midnight if she had to, but she never brought work home. This was her place to get away from it all."

"Her *sanctum sanctorum*, you said."

"Exactly." She smiled slightly, then her forehead creased again. "I suppose I should return them to the office. Her nurse might need them. I don't really have time, though; I'm leaving tomorrow. I was just going through her papers to see if there's anything that needs to be taken care of immediately. I'm going to arrange a leave of absence from work and come back here after Christmas to finish getting her affairs in order."

Affairs. I thought of Dr. Fred Niles.

Ms. Johanssen continued, "My flight doesn't leave until noon but I understand it's a long drive to Portland so I'll be leaving early. It seems strange to be so far from an airport."

"You can get a connecting flight from Pendleton. It isn't far from here."

"I know; that's what I did when I came here. The thing is, those little airplanes—commuter flights, I think they call them— they just scare me to death. It's silly, I know. They're probably safer than the big ones, but you notice the movement so much more."

"Do you have a ride to the airport?"

"Yes, but thank you if you were going to offer. Reverend Sloan offered to take me. I felt a little funny accepting because . . . well, he's on the other side, isn't he? Pro-life. I hate that word. It sounds as if anyone who believes in legalized abortion is pro-death. Oh, well. I accepted his offer. Irene didn't like him but their differences were political, not personal, and he was so upset over her death. Tragedies always bring people together, don't they? Differences of opinion don't seem important now. He seems to be a very nice man."

I thought Willie Sloan was a pompous ass, but he'd be a fine escort for an old-maid librarian. "His followers think he's the best thing since peanut butter."

She laughed. I looked at the folders she was still holding. "I need to stop by Chief Pauling's house tonight. I can give those to him if you'd like. He'll be sure they get back to the office."

"Oh, would you do that? Thanks so much. One less thing to worry about." She touched her fingers lightly to her temples. "The police. I just remembered about Irene calling you. You made it sound as if she were being secretive, not giving her name."

"I don't think you should worry about it. I found out we both use the same answering service. She probably didn't want the operators gossiping about why she was trying to get hold of me. The woman who took the call knew her voice was familiar but couldn't place it. She'd probably talked to your sister dozens of times but didn't recognize her because she was calling in on my line and her voice was . . ."

"Out of context."

"Yeah, out of context. Whatever she wanted, it couldn't have been important or she'd have left her office number so I could get hold of her right away. She doesn't have an answering machine here, I guess, and she'd know I wouldn't be able to reach her until evening."

"Oh, she has a machine. It's hooked up to the phone in her study, but she only turned it on in the evenings. During the day she used call forwarding. I haven't turned the machine on. Her voice is on it and . . ." She waved a hand helplessly and dabbed at her eyes with a tissue.

"Call forwarding," I said. "So if I'd called her at home that morning . . ."

"The call would have gone to her private line at the office."

"I see."

"It does seem odd that she was trying to get hold of you and then you were both shot. A weird coincidence, isn't it?"

"Yeah, but I think that's all it is. My being there was pure chance. She probably happened to notice me outside and since I hadn't called, she decided to come out to talk to me. You know about her lunch appointment?" She nodded. "The man who . . . fired the shot probably knew about it, too, and was waiting for her to leave. The timing's right. She'd have been leaving in ten or fifteen minutes anyway. I think she came out early when she saw me and he was already in place."

"Yes, well, that would make sense, wouldn't it?" She glanced at her watch.

I stood up, saying, "I'd better go. Would you like me to drive you to the hotel?"

"I'd better drive. I have a rental car and I need to turn it in before I leave tomorrow. I don't know my way around very well, though. If you could lead the way, I'd really appreciate it. If it wouldn't be too much trouble."

"It's no trouble at all. I'm glad I had a chance to talk to you."

She followed me downtown. I waited until she entered the lobby of the Mackie Arms, then I parked around the corner and read through the three medical files. It took about ten seconds. Each file contained one standard medical form for recording information about office visits. There were only a few notations on them, all abbreviations that I couldn't make any sense of. Dr. Sandhoff's personal shorthand, I assumed.

I drove to the convenience store, fed three coins into the photocopy machine, tucked the originals back into the manila folders, and drove to Phil's house.

Chapter Nineteen

The house was dark, but Phil wasn't a sound sleeper. The porch light came on as I opened the front gate. The door opened and a big black Lab streaked out, took the steps in a single bound, and ran frenzied circles around me as I walked to the porch steps. No human had ever been that glad to see me.

Phil certainly wasn't. "This better be important," he said. He was barechested and barefoot, wearing jeans so faded they were almost white. As the dog and I jostled each other getting through the door, Phil pulled a limp gray sweatshirt over his head. Straightening his glasses, he said, "You come by to borrow a bullet to bite on? You look like shit."

"I feel like shit. You got anything cold to drink?"

"Sodas. Orange juice. Help yourself. I'll be down in a minute."

He headed upstairs and I went into the kitchen, the dog following me, his nails clicking on the tile. I popped the top on a root beer and sat at the table, dropping the three file folders onto the floor by my chair. The dog sat beside me, resting his chin on my thigh. I scratched behind his ears while he stared at me with soft brown eyes, his tail thumping against the floor.

Phil came into the room, socks and slippers on his feet now, and sat across from me, saying, "What's up?"

I handed him the message slip. "Irene Sandhoff's home phone number. I never got an answer until tonight. Her sister was there."

"Eleven-twenty-five Monday. So she did want to talk to you."

"Dora asked for her name but she wouldn't give it to her. She used call forwarding during the day, switching her home phone to a private line at the office."

Phil looked at me steadily, pale blue eyes giving nothing away, as usual. "That's interesting. That she called you."

"People like Irene Sandhoff don't hire private detectives, not personally. If they need my kind of help, their lawyers call me. Whatever she wanted, it was something she couldn't tell anyone else about, not her lawyer, not the cops."

"You're reading a lot into a phone call, Bucky."

"She wanted to talk to me badly enough to approach me in front of two hundred people. Something must have happened, something that shook her up."

"I haven't forgotten about her walking up to you. I don't know how the hell many people I questioned this week but not a damn one of them knew of any problems Sandhoff was having."

"Any of them mention Fred Niles to you?"

Phil gave me a long look. "Quite a few, as a matter of fact. Sandhoff's office staff knew her about as well as anyone and none of them noticed her acting upset or anything."

"She wasn't the type to show it, was she?"

"No. No, I don't guess she was. Still . . . I can't think of any way to find out now why she wanted to talk to you."

"I'd like to search her house."

"What for? There's nothing to find. No mysterious notes, no threatening letters, no nothing. Just a bunch of personal shit at the house and doctor shit at her office."

"You were looking for a motive for murder. I want to look for a reason she'd need a private detective. It's not necessarily the same thing, although it could lead to the same thing. If she wanted to hire me, she had some kind of trouble she couldn't handle. And maybe that's what got her killed."

"We would've noticed anything strange, Bucky."

"Who's 'we'?"

"Malcolm went through most of the papers."

Malcolm was a pretty good cop. That didn't mean he couldn't overlook something. "It doesn't have to be anything obvious, just something a little off-key, something that doesn't quite fit."

"Like what?"

"I don't know, but I'll know it when I see it."

Phil propped his elbows on the table and put his head in his hands. I left him alone, finishing my root beer then taking the can into the attached garage to put it in the recycle bin.

When I returned to the table, Phil raised his head and said, "Early tomorrow morning, okay? I have to be in at eight. Six o'clock, that'll give you two hours. You can sleep here if you want. Just shove all the shit off the other bed in Philip's room."

Two hours wasn't enough time and six o'clock was too early but it was more than I'd hoped for. "Thanks," I said. I leaned over and picked the file folders up from the floor. "I dropped by to see Nancy Johanssen after I talked to her on the phone. She asked me to give these to you. She wants them returned to the office and she's leaving too early in the morning to do it herself." I slid the folders across the table. Phil opened the top one, glanced at the contents, and closed it.

"Why'd you go see her?"

That wasn't a question I'd expected. "I don't know. I asked her on the phone if she knew of any reason her sister'd want to hire me and she got upset. I wanted to smooth that over. I told her Sandhoff probably just didn't want the women at the answering service gossiping."

"And she gave you these?"

"Yeah. What about it? She's not a doctor. She probably didn't think about medical reports being confidential. Besides, I glanced at them and they're nothing but notes. There isn't even a patient's name on them. The only thing interesting about them is that she said her sister had a rule about never bringing work home, so she was surprised to find them in the house."

"She was, huh?"

"Yeah." I rubbed the back of my neck, thinking I needed to get some sleep. I could usually follow Phil's train of thought, but this time he'd derailed me completely.

He stood up, his movement waking the dog, who had fallen asleep under the table. The Lab got up and stretched and yawned, then raised up on his hind legs, planting his front feet on Phil's chest. Phil patted his head absently. "Look, Bucky, I got a hunch about this murder. That's all it is right now and I don't have shit to back it up. Down, Thunder. Go to bed."

The Lab obediently dropped his front legs to the floor and trotted out of the room, tail wagging. From the sound, he took the steps about four at a time. Phil looked after him. "Not my bed, dammit, your own bed." He looked up, following the dog's progress in the upstairs hall. There was a loud thump: Thunder jumping in bed with Patsy. It was his favorite place to sleep. Phil's, too. They fought about it constantly. Patsy said she couldn't tell the difference once she was asleep. They both snored and they both kept her feet warm.

"Anyway," Phil continued, "don't go fucking up my investigation, okay?"

"Who, me?"

He grinned, a slightly buck-toothed, genuinely amused grin. When he's not mad at me, he tends to find me entertaining. He headed upstairs. I started to follow him, then returned to the kitchen to use the phone. I heard Phil speak sharply, then Thunder hit the floor running and galloped down the stairs. He skidded across the kitchen floor, and jumped into a large dog basket by the back door. I was laughing when Marilyn answered my line. "It's me," I said. "I'm spending the night at the chief's house. Don't call unless it's urgent."

"Okay," she said, "but Eddie Paxton came pounding on the door about ten minutes ago. Said he needs to see you. I couldn't tell whether it was important or not. You know what Eddie's like."

"Hell." I leaned my forehead against the wall by the phone and thought about it for a minute. "I'm going to my office. I'll be there the rest of the night."

"Okay. Talk to you later."

I went upstairs to tell Phil about the change in plans. The bedroom was dark, a narrow strip of light showing beneath the bathroom door on the far side of the room. I could hear the whir of an electric toothbrush.

I whispered Patsy's name. The bedside lamp came on and she sat up in bed, smiling, blinking a little against the light. Her red hair was mussed, curls all over the place. She was wearing an old-fashioned white flannel nightgown. With her face lit only by the lamp's soft glow, she didn't look much older than she had when we were in high school. "Hi," she said, smiling.

I walked into the room and sat on the edge of Phil's side of the bed, facing her. "How are you doing?"

"Did Phil tell you? He wasn't supposed to. It's bad enough we have to worry about it."

"That's what I'm here for, to worry with you."

"Mmm," she said and scooted across the bed, reaching out her arms. I pulled her close and hugged her tight. "How come I always feel so safe like this?" she asked.

I brushed my cheek against her hair. "Because I'm so big. It's just an illusion."

She laughed lightly and hugged me tighter. The electric toothbrush stopped and water ran briefly in the bathroom. Patsy scooted backward away from me. "Are you staying here tonight?"

The bathroom door opened and Phil said, "Not *my* bed. Jesus, you're as bad as the damn dog."

Patsy laughed. I stood up, then bent down and kissed her cheek. "Take care." I turned to Phil. "I have to go to my office. I'll sleep there."

"Okeydoke. Be sure the door's locked behind you. See you in the morning."

Chapter Twenty

I pulled into one of the diagonal parking spots on the small concrete apron in front of my building and went inside, leaving the lights off in the front office. If Eddie came by and saw the car, he'd pound on the door. I'd cruised Main Street on the way to the office and hadn't spotted him, but if he thought he had information that was worth money, he'd show up. In the back room, I turned on the lamp on the work table by the opaque window. I set up the cot, stretching out on it and staring at the ceiling where a hairy-legged brown spider about the size of a quarter was going about his spidery business.

I was half-asleep when I heard a loud *pop!* and, simultaneously, glass breaking. I got up in a hurry and ran into the front room, expecting to find the front window on the floor. It wasn't. I jerked the door open and stepped outside. The Cherokee's windshield was shattered, a sparkling, jagged rim of shattered safety glass surrounding a gaping black hole. I looked to the right just in time to see a slim figure with a baseball bat in one hand run around the corner. *"Hey!"* I shouted and took off after him, running past the front of Fanciful Flowers and around the corner, where I ran right into Eddie, who had apparently been bumped by the guy with the bat and was trying to regain his balance when I barreled into him. We did an awkward, stumbling dance, trying not to knock each other over.

"*Jesus*, Eddie, get out of my way." I pulled away from his clutching fingers and started running. Behind me Eddie shouted, "*Zack!* Zack, I been lookin' for you. I gotta tell you—"

"Wait in my office," I yelled and kept running. The man I was chasing darted across the street at the end of the block, heading west on Washington. I followed, running in the middle of the street so I'd avoid a baseball bat in the face if he was waiting for me around the corner.

He wasn't. He was also in the street now, where the footing was better than on the haphazardly shoveled sidewalks. The earlier traffic and the even earlier passage of the snowplow had left the road dry, with only an edging of dirty snow at the curbs. He was almost a block and a half ahead of me. I had lost some ground, but I kept going. I'm too damn big to be fast, but I can run forever. If I could keep him in sight, I'd catch him. The speed he was going, he'd be winded soon. On the next four blocks, the buildings were all block-long structures, broken only by dead-end driveways leading to parking areas or loading docks. The only way to get to the next street over in either direction was to follow the road. I figured he wouldn't turn on any of the cross streets until he was close to the center of town, where he had a better chance of losing me.

We kept the same distance between us for another block, but he showed no sign of tiring. My shoulder was aching and soon I was running with my left arm folded against my chest, which minimized the movement of my shoulder but also slowed me down. He was almost two blocks ahead of me when he ran into the intersection of Fourteenth and Washington and right into the path of a car heading south on Fourteenth. The driver swerved and hit the horn and the brakes, missing the runner, who had reacted by throwing up his arms as if the car was a gun pointed at him. He jumped backwards, stumbled, and fell, landing on his butt, the baseball bat rolling away from him. The driver rolled his window down and was shouting panicky questions and accusations. I covered half a block before the runner got to his feet and stooped to pick up the bat, facing me as he did so. The headlights were as effective as a spotlight. I knew who I was chasing now.

I could have stopped then, but the adrenaline was pumping and I was pissed. I kept going, reaching Fourteenth Street just as he got to Thirteenth. He maintained the same lead all the way to Tenth Street. I was running flat-out now, arms pumping, mind blocking out the pain, trying to close the gap because there were separate buildings on the block between Ninth and Eighth and all the blocks beyond, separate buildings with driveways and yards and low fences you could jump to make a short-cut to the Main Street side of the block. I'd never catch him once he had a choice of directions.

I was only three-quarters of a block behind him when he reached Ninth, but it was no good. He veered to the left, ran between two parked vans, and sprinted into the driveway between Miller's Hardware and Julianne's Junque and Antique Shoppe. By the time I reached the entrance to the driveway there was nothing to see but footprints in the snow between a set of tire tracks. The footprints ended at a six-foot-high chain link fence and no doubt continued on the other side, but I know when I'm beat. I leaned over, hands on my knees, head up, looking down the driveway and trying to catch my breath.

When I straightened up, a wave of dizziness hit me and I staggered back and leaned against the side of one of the vans parked at the curb, alternately drawing in deep breaths and swallowing hard to try to keep from throwing up. My shoulder suddenly caught fire, hot pain traveling down to my fingertips and across the nape of my neck. Don't run ten blocks four days after being shot: another of life's little lessons I had to learn the hard way.

I started walking slowly west, my legs wobbly, my whole body shaking like I was hooked up to an invisible vibrating belt. At Seventh Street I turned left and walked down to Main, then half a block farther west to the police station. When I got there, I stood at the bottom of the eight steps leading to the door, wondering if the wheelchair ramp at the side of the building would be easier. Probably not, since I didn't have wheels. I grabbed the railing and pulled myself up the stairs.

No one was in the lobby, although I could hear voices from the room behind the counter. I stood just inside the door, leaning over with my butt against the wall and my hands on my knees, head hanging down. After a moment I slid down the wall and sat on the floor, one knee bent, head resting on it. I looked up at the sound of footsteps.

Andy Riggs lifted the flap in the counter to come into the lobby. "Evening, Zachariah," he said as he pulled a navy blue parka on over his uniform. I nodded in response, wondering what it said about my life that a cop could find me sitting on the floor in the police building, breathing like a windbroken horse, and not even be curious about it.

Riggs walked to the door, the radio on his belt squawking as he went out. The door had closed behind him before the radio message penetrated my brain: Check on a report of gunshots in the vicinity of Eighteenth and Main. My office is at Nineteenth and Main. I got up and jerked the door open, but Riggs was already in his patrol car, pulling away from the curb, blue lights flashing but no siren.

Gunshots. It didn't necessarily mean anything. I'd responded to dozens of reports of gunshots when I was driving a patrol car. Lots of things sound like shots: trucks backfiring, firecrackers, trash cans falling over, baseball bats slamming into windshields. I went down the stairs and started walking east anyway.

As I watched Riggs's blue lights diminish in the distance, I suddenly thought of Eddie Paxton, waiting at my office. I was considering the implications of that when I heard a siren warbling, off to the south but coming this way. Riggs had called for a backup. No big deal; he probably saw the smashed windshield on the Cherokee and thought someone had shot it out.

A high shrill siren from the north made my heart jerk in my chest: Rescue One leaving the firehouse. I started running.

Chapter Twenty-One

A small crowd had gathered by the time I got there, fifteen or twenty hastily-dressed people milling around a street corner that had been deserted only minutes before. Rescue One's lights were flashing, splashes of red sweeping across the crowd of gawkers, flickering like flames on their faces, making them look like avid demons peering forth from hell.

Patrolman Dan Foley was providing crowd control, standing on the concrete apron ten feet in front of my office door, hands on his hips, looking like a belligerent ten-year-old daring anyone to cross a line he'd drawn.

Eddie Paxton was on his side in the open doorway, his bony face pale and slack. His jacket and all his shirts had been cut open; the thick white pads taped to his chest and back were splotched with blood.

One of the two paramedics crouching by him said, "Head 'em up, move 'em out," to his partner. Like practiced dancers running through a familiar routine, the two men loaded Eddie onto a gurney with a minimum of effort and wheeled him to the back of the rig. The doors slammed. The crowd moved back as Rescue One pulled out, siren shrieking. Andy Riggs was at my side, saying, "What happened here, Zack?"

I stepped over the blood in the doorway and walked across the office and went into the back room, closing the door. Someone tried the knob, then knocked, then went away.

I lay down on the cot, flat on my back, arms folded across my chest in a deathly pose, thinking about Patsy feeling safe with me. An illusion. Like a baby in its mother's arms. Christina Pauling hadn't died in Patsy's arms but in a cradle five feet away from her sleeping parents. Patsy's encompassing love couldn't prevent her daughter's death, any more than all her hoping now could prevent her womb from expelling the embryo within it. This was Patsy's seventh pregnancy and Philip the Second was an only child. Her first miscarriage was old history, the next two had occurred between Philip's birth and Christina's. The fourth was a year after Christina's death. Patsy filed for divorce soon after that. She and Phil were remarried in September. And she was trying again.

I closed my eyes and saw the bloody, ugly linoleum floor of the nurse's office at Mackie High fourteen years ago. *Too young to die, too young to die, too young to die.* The woman at Christina's funeral had said it over and over, a plaintive litany, powerless and dead wrong: From the moment of our birth, and even before, we're all old enough to die.

The spider was still on the ceiling, still going about his business, which seemed to be patrolling the northwest quadrant of a ceiling tile, an activity he pursued with admirable diligence but no apparent purpose. I arched my back and pulled the holstered gun off the back of my belt, realizing as I did it that I had been pretty uncomfortable lying on it. The gun slid silently from the holster. I extended my arm upward, sighting along the barrel, following the spider's movement across the corner of the tile.

Keys jangled at the door and the lock clicked. Phil came in, closing the door behind him and glancing up at the ceiling where the spider, unaware of any threat, continued his mindless patrol. I let my arm drop to my side, holding the gun loosely in my hand. Phil said, "What was Eddie doing here?"

"He stopped by the answering service and told Marilyn he was looking for me. I came down to wait for him. I heard the windshield break and went outside and saw the guy who did it running away. I ran into Eddie around the corner and told him to wait in the office. The door was open. I ended up down at the police station. I heard the call come in on Riggs's radio so I came back here."

"Who broke the windshield?"

"Nobody. Leave him alone. He didn't shoot Eddie."

"Don't fight me, Bucky. Maybe he smashed it to get you outside so his buddy could shoot you. Eddie's as tall as you are and looks about as heavy with all those clothes on. The shot was probably fired from the trees kitty-corner across the street. It's your office, your car's out front, you run out the door and around the corner and a few minutes later a man your height comes around the same corner and walks up to the door. In the dark, who'd know it wasn't you? More to the point, who would want to shoot Eddie?"

"Fuck!" I crossed my arms over my face, the thirty-eight in my hand. Phil took it away, maybe because it was pointing in his direction.

"Who broke the windshield?"

"Kevin Dale."

I heard Phil get up and go into the outer office. He seemed to be gone a long time. I had plenty of time to think about things I didn't want to think about. Like how coincidental it was that I'd been shot Monday morning and on Thursday night a man who could have been mistaken for me in the dark was shot. Nobody'd have any reason to kill Eddie Paxton, a harmless drunk, no threat to anyone. And what about Irene Sandhoff?

Maybe no one had any reason to shoot her, either. Maybe both shots were meant for me. In which case, Sandhoff was dead and Eddie was probably dying, while I, lucky devil, was lying on a cot in my office, alive and well, and guilty as hell.

But no one had any reason to shoot me, either, no one who was out and about and capable of doing it, anyway. Kevin Dale might hate me because I'd killed his brother when I was a cop, but his weapon of choice was a baseball bat, not a rifle. I got up and went into my office, the scene of the crime and, now, the Crime Scene. The county's high-tech boys had shown up and were doing pointless things like dusting the doorknob for prints. I raised an eyebrow at Phil, who winked at me. He tilted his head toward the door and I followed him outside, stepping carefully over Eddie's blood, which by now had been photographed from every angle.

Phil hitched himself up on the hood of his truck. I leaned my forearms on the fender, hands clasped together. "Run the times by me," Phil said.

"What time did I leave your house?"

He looked at his watch, to jog his memory, I assumed, since I doubted the answer was there. "Eleven-twenty. I turned the TV on when I got into bed and the sports was just coming on. Pretty close to eleven-twenty."

"I left your house, going the long way, past Carrie's house, and then I drove down Main looking for Eddie. I didn't stop anywhere. How long's that? Ten minutes tops, right? So it was about eleven-thirty when I got here. Christ, I don't know. I never looked at my watch. I was falling asleep when I heard the glass breaking. I don't think I was inside for more than ten minutes, though. Make it eleven-forty when Kevin showed up."

"Okay. You chased him downtown?"

"I lost him at Ninth Street. Three or four minutes. Then I walked to the police station, another couple minutes, and I was at the station when Riggs got the call. The dispatcher should have logged the time."

Phil nodded. "Citizen's call was logged at eleven-forty-eight and Riggs was dispatched immediately. That makes it seven or eight minutes between the time you left and Eddie got shot."

"That doesn't mean anything, Phil. You know Eddie. He probably spent eight minutes making up his mind whether to go in the office or stand outside watching for me to come back."

Phil nodded. "I don't think it's important, I just like to be thorough."

"Was Eddie conscious at all? Did he say anything?"

"Riggs says he was semiconscious and mumbled something about seeing ghosts. He probably didn't know where the hell he was or what he was saying."

"He looked pretty bad."

"If he lives, he'll probably be short one lung . . . This is really fucking things up. I thought I had it all worked out and you weren't in the picture at all. Now, unless someone was after Eddie—and who the hell would be?—it looks like someone was after you. Instead of Sandhoff."

"Do you have a solid suspect for Sandhoff? Because maybe he wants to throw you off by making it look like he was after me."

"Jesus. I hadn't thought of that."

"So do you?"

"Do I what?"

"Know who killed Sandhoff."

"I told you: I have a hunch. A hunch, a reasonable motive, and no evidence at all. The one thing I do know for sure is that my suspect wasn't anywhere near your office tonight."

"Shit. An accomplice, maybe?"

"I'm working on that. Why don't you go on home; we'll be here awhile. I'll lock everything up. Take my truck; I'll catch a ride."

"What about Kevin Dale?"

"I'll talk to him. I'm not going to hassle him, Bucky, but he might've seen someone in the area. Unless Mathilda wants to press charges, the little shit's all yours." He adjusted his glasses, then ran a hand through his curls. "He must've figured out why I wanted to know where he was Monday morning. I thought I was being real subtle, too. I wouldn't've thought he'd be able to put two and two together and come up with anything higher than three, but I guess he did. Probably figures you suggested him as a likely suspect and he decided to get even."

"What about tomorrow morning? Sandhoff's house, remember?"

"I got an appointment at eight. I sure would like to squeeze in a couple hours of sleep before then. How about later on tomorrow? I'll let you know. Here." He handed me my gun and the key to his truck. "Don't wander around any dark streets, okay?"

Chapter Twenty-Two

Resisting the temptation to hit the lights and siren and kick it up to a hundred and ten, I drove home like a law-abiding citizen, exceeding the speed limit by only ten miles per hour. I made a slow turn into my driveway, looking ahead. The house was there, just like always. I sighed at the sight of it, just like always. Irene Sandhoff had her *sanctum sanctorum*. This was my *ridiculum ridiculorum*.

Two years after April tossed her wedding rings on the kitchen counter and walked out of my life and apparently right off the face of the earth, I filed for divorce. The same day, I sat down and wrote an ad: *For sale by owner, custom-built English Tudor, four bedrooms, three and a half baths, family room, den, hardwood floors, central air, fireplace, patio, alarm system, two-car garage, detached work-shop and storage shed, on three wooded acres.*

I had planned to keep the other seven acres. I had also planned to run the ad, just as soon as I put a few finishing touches on the second floor, like paint and light fixtures and doors. It had been almost a year and a half since I wrote the ad, but it wasn't until two months ago that I finally got around to doing the work upstairs. The ad, handwritten in a slightly drunken scrawl, was still in a drawer in my desk. Sometime—

I had no idea when—I had added, in a different color ink and an even drunker scrawl, *Great place to raise kids.*

Because the upstairs wasn't finished when we moved into the house, April and I had used the den as a bedroom. I'd considered moving the bedroom furniture upstairs now that the rooms were finished, but why bother? The house was way too big for one person. It made a lot more sense to use only the downstairs.

So it was the den, my makeshift bedroom, that I went into once I'd put Phil's truck in the garage and gone inside. I stripped and lay down on the waterbed, feeling it moving slowly beneath me, willing sleep to come quickly. I might as well have willed the sun to rise.

I stared at the ceiling, where no spider appeared to distract me, and formed a mental bird's-eye view of my building and the block it sat on. Main Street on the south side, Washington on the north, Eighteenth and Nineteenth on the west and east respectively. The block was rectangular instead of square, the distance between the two numbered streets being only half that of a standard city block.

My building was a skinny L-shaped structure with its long leg running along Main, my front office being in the section where the two legs joined, the back room being the short leg of the L, Fanciful Flowers taking up the long leg. The outdoor space formed by the right angle of the building was a fenced, covered area used by the flower shop, empty now except for some birdbaths but full of plants and gardening supplies in the spring and summer. The rest of the block belonged to a lumber yard, its main building fronting on Washington Street.

Mackie's business district ends at Nineteenth Street. The east end of downtown isn't pictured in any of the brochures the Chamber of Commerce hands out. The businesses are too necessary to need flashy signs and decorated windows to entice customers. They provide unlovely but indispensable products and services: plumbers, electricians, appliance repairmen, septic tank cleaners, tile and carpet layers, air conditioning and heating services, roofers, pest control specialists. Fanciful Flowers is a bright spot in the midst of all the drabness. My office goes largely unnoticed.

In my mental picture, four figures converged on the block: me, Eddie Paxton, Kevin Dale, and a man with a rifle. All of us, all at once. A Portland cop once told me that coincidence sucks. I was inclined to agree with him.

So how did we all come to be there shortly after eleven-thirty on a Thursday night? I considered us one at a time. I was easy: I was there because I expected Eddie Paxton to show up with some information for me, probably something about Jordan Clausen.

Eddie was there because he was looking for me. He hadn't used a telephone since back when "It's your nickel" made sense. When he had something to tell me, he came by the office. If I wasn't around, he stopped by the answering service and told them he wanted to see me. He knew I checked in regularly and almost always at night before I went to bed. So, he had put out the word and then walked down to Nineteenth and Main to see if I'd gotten it. He might even have seen me when I drove through town looking for him. A blue Cherokee is a lot easier to spot than a drunk in a dark doorway.

Kevin Dale was there to break my windshield. Why then? Why not an hour later? Why not tomorrow? Or the day after? It had to be because he knew I was there. On the way to the office, I'd passed both the bowling alley and Sparky's Restaurant and I'd passed within a block of the Quick Shop, the only businesses open late at night except for bars Kevin was too young to go in. He was probably hanging out at one of the places and saw me drive by, heading toward my office. He hurried right over to continue his vandalism spree.

So there we were—me, Eddie, and Kevin Dale—coincidentally, but fairly logically, in the same place at the same time.
Which left the man with the rifle. How the hell did he get
there? By following me? I didn't think so. There isn't much
traffic in Mackie late at night. I'd driven from my office to
Sandhoff's house to the hotel to the convenience store to Phil's
house and back to my office, all in the space of an hour. No
one followed me. I was sure of that.

Maybe he'd been there earlier, before I went to Sandhoff's
house. Maybe he hadn't had a clear shot or there were people
in sight or cars driving by when I walked out to my car then.
But why would he hang around on the off-chance I'd come
back? Surely he'd assume I was leaving for the night.

If he hadn't followed me and he wasn't waiting for me,
that left pure coincidence. He just happened to decide to see
if I was at my office at eleven-thirty on a Thursday night and
I very coincidentally was and I came out of the building and
ran around the corner and Eddie Paxton very coincidentally
came around that same corner and Eddie very coincidentally
looked close enough to my size to pass for me in the dark, so
the man shot him. I wouldn't buy that story with someone
else's money.

I spent a few minutes trying to figure out who would want
me dead. The only motive that made sense was revenge. I ran
through the same list of people Phil had come up with. Only
Johnny Dale's family were the least bit likely to have both the
inclination and the opportunity and I trusted Phil to have eliminated them as suspects. Besides, why would they wait seven
years? Kevin Dale was a nuisance, not a murderer, and he hadn't
had time to go home and exchange his bat for a rifle and get
back to my office in time to kill Eddie by mistake.

I thought of Dickhead, my client's ex-husband. At least he
was someone I'd pissed off recently. I got up and got his home

phone number from my wallet and called it. He had an unmis-
takable whiny voice and I recognized it immediately when he
answered the phone. I hung up without saying anything. He
was in Redding, California. Unless he'd mastered astral-projec-
tion, he wasn't in eastern Oregon an hour ago shooting Eddie.

While I was up, I called the police station. Phil was there,
sounding tired. "Any word on Eddie?" I asked.

"He's not doing too good but he's not dead yet."

"Did you catch up with Kevin?"

"Yeah, and this is funny, Bucky: The little shit headed
home after he lost you and he heard the sirens so he went
back up by your office and saw all the commotion, only he
thought it was you they were loading into the rig and he
heard someone say you'd been shot and when I got to his
house he was puke-green, scared to death I was coming to
arrest him for shooting you. He was shaking so bad he could
hardly talk, but I guess he knew you got a look at him and he
figured your dying words were going to be 'Kevin Dale did it.'

"I thought about really throwing a scare into him but he
started blubbering so I went easy on him. He says he didn't
see anyone near your office. I told him you wanted to talk to
him about him trashing your car and your office and I didn't
know when you'd get around to coming by but he'd better be
right there waiting for you when you did. I also gave him a
rough estimate of how much it costs to get dirty words taken
off a Mercedes. And I told him if Mathilda presses charges,
I'm going to book his worthless ass myself."

"Did you happen to ask him why he picked tonight to go
to my office?"

"You been thinking about that, too, huh? Could've got up
a poker game with all the people showing up at your office
tonight. He saw you drive by while he was hanging out in the
parking lot at Sparky's. One of his buddies gave him a ride

home so he could pick up the bat, then dropped him off over by your office. I had a talk with Kevin's pal, too. Little bastard looked me right in the eye and said he didn't think there was anything strange about Kevin taking a baseball bat downtown at damn near midnight in the middle of fucking December. He doesn't remember seeing anyone else hanging around down there."

"Okay, see you tomorrow." I lay back down and pulled the sheet and comforter over me. After a while I got tired of trying to fall asleep so I formulated scenarios.

Number One: Irene Sandhoff and Eddie Paxton were both shot by mistake by someone who was after me. Logical, but I didn't like it.

Number Two: Sandhoff was shot on purpose and I was just in the way. Realizing the cops might not be sure which of us he was after, her killer decided to confuse the issue by taking another shot at me but got Eddie by mistake. Logical, but a little far-fetched. So far, he'd gotten away with murder. Why take a chance on getting caught pulling off a second one?

Number Three: Sandhoff was shot on purpose. Again trying to confuse the issue, her killer picked a second victim at random, by sheer coincidence choosing Eddie Paxton as a target and my office as the location. Scratch Number Three: coincidence sucks.

Number Four: There was no connection at all between the two shootings. Two victims, two perpetrators, two motives, two completely separate and distinct events. Bullshit.

Number Five: Eddie was the victim of a copycat killer who'd been inspired by Sandhoff's death. Again, bullshit. Why Eddie? Why at my office?

Number Six: Sandhoff was shot on purpose, then Eddie was shot by the same person but not because he was mistaken for me.

I worked on that one for a while, trying to come up with a connection between a reputable doctor and the town drunk. Eddie hadn't known Sandhoff. He'd only recognized her picture because he'd seen her jogging somewhere. Eddie spent most of his time outside, wandering all over town. He'd probably seen the entire population of Mackie at one time or another.

But if they were both shot deliberately by the same person, there had to be a connection. Maybe Irene Sandhoff was two-timing Fred Niles with Eddie Paxton and Niles shot them both in a jealous rage. I laughed aloud at the thought of Irene Sandhoff and Eddie Paxton locked in a passionate embrace.

Maybe Niles killed Sandhoff after a lovers' spat, Eddie found out, tried to blackmail Niles, and Niles shot him. I wondered if Niles had an alibi for Sandhoff's killing. Phil didn't seem particularly interested in him, so he probably did. Also, Phil said he had a suspect but no proof. A confession is pretty good proof and Niles struck me as the type who'd break down after one pointed question.

Knowing who Phil's suspect was might have helped, but this second shooting had apparently blown his theory all to hell and gone. There was no point in asking him anyway, because he wouldn't tell me. He'd been pretty close-mouthed about police business since August when a man was murdered at the Mackie Arms Hotel and I somehow forgot to mention that Allison Vanzetti, the prime suspect, was keeping me company in a motel room in Portland.

My thoughts wandered from the week's events in Mackie to those days in the motel room in Portland and from there to more recent days in a motel room in Connecticut and I fell asleep, probably with a smile on my face.

Chapter Twenty-Three

The phone rang at six-fifty the next morning. I answered it in my sleep and had to ask Dora to repeat what she had said. "I *said*, Baby Blue Eyes, that I got a girl on the line crying something awful."

I rolled over and sat up. "Who is she?"

"Well, I don't know, she won't tell me her name but she wants to know if you can meet her at your office in ten minutes."

"Only if I sprouted wings overnight. Can you put her through to me?"

"Sure, sweetie. Hang on."

The line went dead for a moment, then I heard a sniffling sound. "Hello? This is Zachariah Smith."

Words came out in a rush, in a sweet, girlish voice thickened by tears. "Oh, god, I have to talk to you. I'm so scared about Jordy. I don't know what happened to him. He was supposed to come back and he never did. I don't know what to do."

I rubbed my face hard. "Rachel?"

"Yes?"

Shit. Rachel Harroldson. My problem after all. "It'll take

me at least fifteen minutes to get to my office. Where are you now?"

"At home. Mom and Dad just left for work and Carlene—she's my cousin and she's eighteen—she's going to drive me to your office but if I don't get to school on time, they'll call Mom at work and tell her. They're treating me like I'm a criminal or something. I can't go to the *bathroom* without them asking me what I'm doing." Her tears seemed to have dried, indignation replacing anxiety in her voice.

"Can you just talk to me now?"

"On the phone? Oh, god, it's so *com*plicated." The tears were back.

"Okay, look, go to my office. I'll be there as soon as I can."

"But I'll be late for school. The late bell's at seven-twenty-five. I'll never make it in time."

"I'll take care of that. Don't worry about it."

"How—"

"Just go to my office. I'll take care of it. No one will call your mother."

"Well . . . okay."

I hung up and called the high school and asked for Ellen Finch. "I need a favor, Ellen. Two favors actually."

"What is it?"

"First, Rachel Harroldson's going to be late for school. Can you fix it so no one contacts her parents about it?"

"Yes, but what's going on?"

"Rachel's meeting me at my office in a few minutes. Which brings me to the second favor: Can you be there, too? I don't particularly want to talk to her alone."

"I'll come if you want me to, but I'm one of *them*, Zack. She might not talk in front of me."

"I know, but she's what? fourteen? and upset and probably very vulnerable." When Ellen didn't respond, I added, "If I were fifty, or married, I wouldn't worry about it, but I'm not. Can you picture her parents' reaction if they find out she was alone in my office with me when she's supposed to be at school? I don't need that kind of trouble."

"Ah. I see what you mean. I'll be there."

"If you get there before I do, try not to let her see you first. I don't want to scare her off."

"I understand. I'll see you soon."

I splashed some water on my face, brushed my teeth, and ran a comb through my hair, then dressed quickly in jeans and a pale blue sweater, grabbed a jacket and headed for town. I spent the drive thinking about the far-reaching ramifications of my friendship with Allison Vanzetti.

Before I met her, I'd never worried about being accused of misconduct with minor females. I'd chased down a fair number of runaway teenage girls without any problems. Then Allison came into my life. After we made the headlines together, a couple tabloids published titillating stories full of innuendo and insinuation and I endured a lot of sly winks and cradle-robbing comments. Before that, I wouldn't have doubted my ability to defend myself against any charges; I could trot out any number of people who'd swear that teenagers didn't appeal to me. My relationship with Allison tended to destroy my credibility and that galled the hell out of me. Allison's age wasn't what attracted me to her, but it was the reason we weren't together now.

As I approached my office, I spotted Ellen Finch in a blue Dynasty parked around the corner on Eighteenth. Rachel Harroldson was standing in front of the door to Fanciful Flowers. She was small and boyishly slender, with shoulder-length wavy hair, dark brown, the shorter section on top curled and stiffened with gel. Her little girl's face was too heavily made-up and the outfit she was wearing screamed *Look at me.* She looked like a child playing dress-up. Only this child was pregnant.

As I got out of the truck, she walked quickly to me and for a moment I thought she was going to throw herself into my arms. She stopped though and crossed her arms, hugging herself. "Let's go inside," I said and unlocked the door, holding it open as she walked into the office. All signs of last night's shooting had been removed. The Cherokee was also gone. "Have a seat, Rachel. I'll be right back."

I stepped outside. Ellen Finch was coming around the corner. When she walked into the office with me, Rachel stood up, then sat down again abruptly and started crying, knuckles pressed against her mouth.

"Rachel, I asked Miss Finch to come because I don't think your parents would approve of this meeting and I wanted . . ." I couldn't think of a way to explain my paranoia to this weeping child.

Ellen came to my rescue, saying, "I'm here to protect Mr. Smith's reputation, Rachel, not to interfere in your affairs. Your parents could cause him a great deal of trouble if they found out you were here. Unchaperoned," she added.

Rachel looked at her steadily for a moment, then wiped a hand across her eyes, leaving mascara smudges, and said, "God, that sounds like something out of some old novel."

Ellen smiled. "Yes, but it's a very modern problem for men. False accusations of sexual abuse may be rare, but it does happen. I know you wouldn't do anything unfair, but your parents certainly might overreact to the situation."

"They overreact to *everything.* They act like I'm some kind of . . . I don't know . . . like I did something really awful and ruined their life and . . . and . . ." She drew a deep, sobbing breath and said, "They're going to make me have an abortion and I don't want to."

I let Ellen handle that one while I went into the back room to put on a pot of coffee. Through the open door, I could hear Ellen explaining the procedures at abortion clinics: "You'll talk to a counselor alone, Rachel. All you have to do is tell her you don't want an abortion and they won't do it. It's not a decision your parents can make for you. They can't force you to have an abortion. No doctor will do it unless *you* agree to it."

"But . . . they're taking me to Portland *Monday.* If I tell them I won't do it . . . god, they'll be *furious.*"

"Yes, but you don't have to handle that alone. I'll help you."

"Do you think I should get an abortion?"

There was a long pause before Ellen answered. "My opinion shouldn't influence your decision, Rachel. I think you're very young to be a mother. Whether or not Jordan is involved, whether or not your parents help you, it won't be easy for you. But it would be better for you to have the baby than to do something you'll regret the rest of your life. The decision to have an abortion is never an easy one and unless you feel fairly certain that it's the best thing for you, I don't think you should do it.

"Remember, though, that the baby's birth won't be the *end* of anything, it will be the beginning. It's not like the movies. 'Happily ever after' won't come on the screen when you hold your newborn in your arms for the first time. That will be a very special moment, but afterward you'll have to face the responsibility of caring for that child. It's a big commitment, a lifetime commitment, in fact, and one that women far older than you can't always cope with. So . . . I don't know

what to tell you, except that the decision has to be yours—not
mine, not your parents', not a doctor's, *yours*."

I walked back into the room just as Rachel responded.
"And Jordy's," she said. "Shouldn't it be Jordy's decision, too?"

As I sat down behind my desk, Ellen ran a hand through
her hair, leaving it disarranged. It was the first time I'd ever
seen her at a loss for words. I heard Carrie's voice in my
mind: *Fuck men's rights. They don't have any rights until they learn
to accept the responsibility.* Sometimes I felt sorry for Tom.

Ellen said, "Yes, of course Jordy's feelings should be considered, but ultimately the decision has to be yours."

"Well, he said—" Rachel turned abruptly to me, leaning
forward in her chair. "He didn't come back. He promised he
would, he *promised.*"

I cleared my throat, avoiding Ellen's eyes, knowing I was
guilty by reason of sex. "When was the last time you saw
him?"

"Sunday night."

Stole him some gee-lettes, is what he stole.

"What time?"

"It was late, about midnight. I let him in the house. See,
Mom and Dad always go to bed early and watch television in
their room and it's way up on the third floor, so I let him in
the house and he slept in the basement. I didn't dare let him
come up to my room, but it was so cold outside and he left
early in the morning before anyone was up."

"Since Friday, is that it? After he ran away he spent the
nights at your house?"

"Yeah. During the day he just hung around town somewhere. It was the weekend, you know. He was kinda keeping
an eye out for his dad, but . . . I guess he didn't think he'd be
out looking for him anyway. He had a little money and I gave

him what I had, so he could eat. But I haven't seen him since Sunday night. He was gone when I got up the next morning. Sunday night . . . he was . . . he was talking kind of crazy. I mean he was really upset and he kept saying . . . well, he . . . "

"Was he talking about suicide?"

She nodded, head bowed, tears dropping onto her clenched hands. "He . . . he was going to . . ."

"I know about the razor blades."

Her head jerked up. "You do? I took them away from him. I told him . . . I don't know what I told him . . . that everything would be all right and . . . I don't know . . . things like that . . . and then he seemed okay and once we started making plans, well, he was okay then. He said he was okay, that he wouldn't really kill himself, it was just that everything was so mixed up and he didn't know what to do and I told him we . . . we had each other and . . . well, he seemed okay then."

"Do you know what happened at his house Friday?"

"Oh, they had a big fight. I mean, god, it was awful. My dad called Jordy's dad at work and told him I was pregnant and called Jordy names—like he'd raped me or something, you know—and then they dragged me over there, to Jordy's house, Friday afternoon—Jordy's dad went to school and got him, and Jordy and his dad and my dad all started screaming at each other and Jordy's mom could hardly stand up she was so drunk and Mom was hysterical and, god, it was really awful."

"Did Jordy's father hit him?"

"Oh, no, I didn't mean that kind of a fight. I just meant they were shouting and stuff. Actually, when we first got there it was all very . . . civilized. Like, these two stupid kids got themselves in a big mess and we're going to straighten it out because we're the *grown-ups. God.* Anyway, everything was okay until I said I didn't want to have an abortion. I mean, they were sitting there talking about how much it would *cost* and who was going to pay for it. Like Jordy gave me *warts* or something. Or *lice.* It's a baby and they were acting like it wasn't any big deal, like all they had to do was figure out who was going to pay for it.

"Actually, I think Jordy was kind of relieved at first, when Dad said they were taking me to Portland, but then I said I wanted the baby and I guess I started crying and Jordy stood up and started yelling at my dad, telling him we were going to get married and my dad called Jordy a bunch of really dirty names and Jordy's dad started shouting, too, saying I was a tramp and things like that and my mom went into her hysterical act and Jordy's mom was bawling and . . . god, it was awful. So anyway, Dad grabbed me and Mom and dragged us out of the house and we went home."

"You saw Jordy later that night?"

"Yeah, he came over—I knew he would—and I let him in the basement and he spent the night there. And Saturday and Sunday night, too, but he hasn't come back since Sunday."

"He didn't look like he'd been beat up?"

"No. Why do you keep asking that? His dad didn't hurt him. He would've told me."

"It was just an idea I had; I guess I was wrong. You said you and Jordy made some plans. What were they?"

"To go away, of course."

"The two of you."

"Well, of course. If we stay here they'll make me have an abortion."

"Where were you going?"

"Well, that was the problem, of course. If we had a car . . . but Jordy only has a learner's permit anyway. He said once he'd steal a car but I said no, the cops would catch us and then we'd really be in trouble. So, we decided if we could get a ride to Pendleton, we could take the train to Portland."

I didn't bother to ask what they planned to do in Portland. I was sure they hadn't thought it out, but I'd seen enough kids on the streets to know exactly how they'd end up. "When were you going to Pendleton?"

"We had to get some money first so we could pay for the train tickets. Jordy said he knew a guy who'd buy his rifle. He was going to do that Monday, sell the rifle, and then my cousin Carlene was going to drive us to Pendleton Monday afternoon when I got out of school. Jordy was supposed to meet me behind the school. But he never showed up. I kept thinking he'd call me or come to the house but . . . Anyway, last night I called his mom. She told me you were looking for him. She was nice, actually. She said she'd help us out if we wanted to have the baby."

"Jordy didn't take the rifle until Wednesday."

"What?"

"He went home Wednesday while his parents were visiting his grandmother at the nursing home. That's when he took the rifle."

"What?"

"He didn't have the rifle until Wednesday evening. He couldn't have planned to sell it before then."

"What? He had it with him."

"The rifle? When?"

"Everytime I saw him. He took it with him Friday. I didn't actually *see* it, he left it in the package. I mean, he couldn't carry a rifle around town but nobody would think anything about it if they saw him carrying a Christmas package since it's almost Christmas."

I rubbed my hand across the lower half of my face, feeling

rough stubble. That lying bastard Clausen. "Jordy was getting a rifle for Christmas."

"Yeah, he was real excited about it. I felt kind of bad for him, having to sell it, you know, but he said it didn't matter."

I looked at Ellen. "Will you take her to school?"

She stood up. "Yes, of course. Zachariah . . ."

"I'll talk to you later."

"All right. Let's go, Rachel. You'll only miss a few minutes of first period if we hurry."

Rachel got up and zipped her jacket. "But what about Jordy? Can you find him?"

Ellen was staring at me, the same question in her eyes. I looked at Rachel Harroldson, fourteen years old and pregnant, and said, "I'll try."

Chapter Twenty-Four

I was a block from Buddy's Auto Body Shop when I realized that if I wanted the truth, I'd be more likely to get it from Judy Clausen than from her husband. *In vino, veritas;* in eighty-proof whiskey, confession.

I made an illegal U-turn and headed back the way I'd come. It was not quite eight o'clock when I pulled up in front of Clausen's house. I wondered how early Judy started drinking. I got my answer when she opened the door, tall blue plastic glass in her hand. Without saying anything, she stepped aside for me to enter.

"Has something happened?" she asked when we were seated in the living room. A bottle of Early Times was on the coffee table next to her alarm clock, which was ticking off the seconds to oblivion, the alarm already set to bring her back.

"Your husband lied to me."

She stared into the tall glass, moving her hand slightly to set the contents swirling. "I don't know what you mean."

"Now *you're* lying to me. You know you bought Jordan a rifle for Christmas. You know he took it with him Friday. You know he didn't come home Wednesday evening to get your husband's rifle. He hasn't been home since Friday. What do you suppose the cops will think if I tell them that?"

"I don't know."

"They'll think you were setting up an alibi, making it look like Jordan was okay Wednesday. But I don't think he was. I think your husband—"

"No! You don't understand."

"Then explain it to me."

"I can't. I'm sorry, but you'll have to leave now. I don't want you here." When I didn't stand up, she said, "This is my house. You aren't welcome here. Get out."

I can take a hint if it's broad enough. I left her staring into her whiskey.

I pulled up in the back of the body shop just as Clausen came outside, heading for his pickup. When he saw me, he walked over, hands knotted into fists at his side. I got out of the truck, saying, "I need to talk to you."

"You leave Judy alone. She's not strong. She can't take much more. Just for Christ's sake, leave her alone."

"Listen, Clausen—"

He stepped close to me, face flushed with anger. "No, *you* listen and you listen good. I know you think you got it all figured out. Well, listen hard, pal. You're wrong. I didn't hurt my boy. I didn't beat him up and leave him for dead or kill him and bury his body in the woods or cut him up in little pieces and flush him down the toilet or whatever the fuck it is you think I did. You don't know what the fuck's going on so just stay the fuck out of it." He walked to his truck and got in and drove off.

I don't always recognize the truth when it's staring me in the face, but I can usually spot a lie a mile away. Clausen had me stumped, though. I knew he was right about one thing—I didn't know what the fuck was going on.

I got back in the truck and pulled out of the lot, resisting the urge to drive home and go back to bed. I was tired and hungry and unshaven and, damn it, I wasn't even getting paid.

I waited in Ellen's office while she went to get Rachel out of math class. When they arrived, I said, "Just a couple quick questions, Rachel. Do you know what happened after you left Jordan's house Friday night? Did he tell you anything?"

"*Nothing* happened. That's what got to him so bad. They didn't do anything. He said it was just like always. His dad watched TV and his mom was crocheting or something and no one said anything. It was like it wasn't important, you know. He said he just couldn't stand it, them acting like it wasn't any big deal. After they went to bed, he came over to my house."

"And he had the rifle then, right?" Rachel nodded and I asked, "Do you have any idea who he was going to sell it to?"

"Um . . . no. It was a funny name, I remember that. He called him up right then—we were down in the basement, you know, and there's an old phone down there, and he asked if he'd buy it, but I didn't pay any attention really."

"Try to remember. How was the name funny? Foreign? Or a nickname? Fats or Slim or something like that?"

"Yeah, a nickname, but it was something . . . I don't know . . . something that sounded like he was from the south. Alabama, or someplace like that."

"Bubba?"

"That's it! How'd you know?"

"Lucky guess."

I could tell Ellen had a lot of questions, but I didn't know the answers so I told her I'd talk to her later. I left the high school, headed for The Pits.

Bubba Fackler was a skinny, rat-faced man from Kentucky. When he wasn't in jail, he lived in a room over the most aptly named bar in town. I went in a door next to The Pits' entrance, climbed the narrow stairway and pounded on the door at the top, saying loudly, "It's not the cops, Bubba. Open up."

It took him a while and it sounded like he fell down a few times on the way, but he finally opened the door a crack, his thin, long-nosed face poking out at me. "Whatcha want? I got comp'ny."

I pushed the door open and walked past him. The tiny overheated room stank of armpits and crotches and every cigarette ever smoked in it. A naked woman a few decades past the age of consent was sprawled on her stomach across the twin-sized bed, a grayish sheet wrapped around one leg. Bubba was pulling on a pair of once-white undershorts, hopping around on one foot trying to keep his balance. "Whatcha want?" he asked again. "I ain't done nothin'."

I opened the closet door. A couple shirts were on hangers, the rest of Bubba's wardrobe was on the floor along with several unopened liquor bottles and twenty or so cartons of cigarettes, all different brands. A sealed carton containing a television was in the shower stall in the bathroom. I bent down to look under the bed, getting a good whiff of the woman's feet. There was nothing under the bed but a colony of dust bunnies and an ashtray stacked high with dead butts, some of them home-rolled joints. I picked a blanket up off the floor and tossed it over the woman. She rolled onto her side and started snoring.

Bubba had succeeded in getting his shorts on and was picking up beer cans from the floor, shaking each one, finally finding one that sloshed. He tipped it to his mouth and drained it, wiping his hand across his mouth afterward. "Whatcha lookin' for, Zack?"

"A rifle."

"I don't—Is this about that kid?"

"Did you buy his rifle?"

"He never showed."

"Was he supposed to come here?"

"Naw, I was gonna meet him in the woods, up at Haight and Ashbury. Monday afternoon. Two-thirty. Little shit never showed. I oughta know better'n to do business with kids, huh?"

"You should get into a different line of work altogether. You better do a little housecleaning. The cops might be around later."

"Aw, *jeez*, I don't need this shit, Zack. The kid said the gun was his. I wasn't doin' nothing wrong."

"Wake Sheryl up and get her out of here, too."

"Hell, she'll be out cold 'til sundown."

"There's a couple warrants out on her. She'll be pissed if she wakes up in a cell. You better get her up."

"Aw, *jeez*, what's she been doin' now?"

"Bad checks. Failure to appear."

"Lyin' bitch told me she took care of that."

As I left, he was leaning over the bed, saying, "Sheryl? Sheryl, honey?"

Back at my office, I checked for messages. Carrie wanted me to call her. Phil had left a message, saying he'd meet me at two o'clock. That gave me plenty of time to work on the Clausen problem before I had to think about the Sandhoff problem. I called Carrie, who tried hard not to sound panic-stricken about Eddie Paxton being shot at my office. I reassured her as much as I could, phoned the hospital to see how Eddie was doing—in Intensive Care, but still hanging in there—then left my office, planning to talk to Clausen again.

No one was at the house and Clausen hadn't returned to work. The young woman in the office at the body shop told me in a conspiratorial whisper that he left right after his wife called and a little while later he called and told the boss he wouldn't be back until Monday morning. "Because of a family problem," she said.

I cruised the hospital parking lot, thinking maybe Judy

had overdosed on Early Times, but Clausen's truck wasn't there. I stopped by my office and called the other two Clausens in the phone book, but they weren't related or weren't willing to admit they were. At the Willowhaven nursing home, I looked in the doorway of the room occupied by Judy's mother and decided against trying to talk to her. She was dying the hard way and didn't need any grief from me.

Feeling like I was running around in circles, which I was, I went back to Buddy's Auto Body, where the young woman behind the counter greeted me with a shy smile. Smiling back, I asked what her name was.

"Amy. Amy Tomlinson."

"I'm Zachariah Smith. I'm not sure I ever introduced myself."

"Oh, I already knew your name."

"Well, Amy, I hate to keep bothering you, but I need some help."

She glanced toward the manager's closed door and leaned across the counter, her voice dropping to a whisper. "Are you working on a case?"

"Sort of. Mostly I'm just trying to help someone out. Do you keep the payroll records?"

"Oh. No, I'm sorry. I'm not the bookkeeper. Mr. Reynolds handles things like that. He's the manager." She glanced again at the closed door.

"What about time cards? What I need to know is if Bob Clausen worked all day Monday."

"Oh, I can tell you that. He didn't. His wife called and he left. He came back later, though."

"Do you remember what time he left?"

"It was afternoon, between twelve and twelve-thirty, I think. He was eating lunch when his wife called."

"How long was he gone?"

"Oh, a couple hours. I think it was about three when he came back. Mr. Reynolds was kind of mad at him for leaving. He's pretty mad now, too. He told him he'd better get his personal problems straightened out or he'd find himself out of a job. I feel bad for him—Bob, I mean. He looked really upset Monday and today, too. Do you suppose his wife is real sick or something?"

"I don't really know, Amy. You've been a big help. I appreciate it."

"Oh. Well. It's nothing." She smiled and gave me a little wave as I left.

I drove back to the house in the Flats and jimmied the lock by sliding an expired credit card into the slit between the door and the jamb. Cheap locks are a burglar's best friend.

I only stayed inside a few minutes. In the master bedroom, there were obvious signs that someone had packed in haste, drawers half-open, clothes tossed on the bed, empty hangers on the bureau. All the clothes strewn about were Judy's and most of the clothes left in the closet were her husband's. I checked the bathroom, finding a single blue toothbrush hanging on a rack by the sink and shaving gear in the medicine cabinet. It looked like Clausen would be back, but Judy wouldn't.

Before I left, I stood in the living room for a minute, looking at the Christmas tree and the gaily wrapped presents beneath it. Jordan's name was on gift tags on four of them. Two were obviously clothes, wrapped without being placed in boxes first, and a third one had to be a CD. The fourth was a rectangular box, smaller than a breadbox, bigger than a Bible. The urge to open it and see what was inside passed after a moment.

Jordan's big present wasn't there, of course. He'd taken it with him: a rifle, just what he'd always wanted. But he was willing to sell it so he and his girl could go away together. A foolish plan made by children, but a plan anyway. But sometime between the time Jordan left Rachel's house early Monday morning and two-thirty that afternoon when he was supposed to meet Bubba Fackler, the plan fell apart. If it hadn't been for his father's behavior, I would have gone with the obvious explanation: just another scared kid running out on his pregnant girlfriend.

As I let myself out of the house, I thought I should probably dump the whole thing in Phil's lap. Maybe he could get the truth out of the man. I decided to give it one more shot myself. I wanted to see Clausen's reaction when I asked him to explain his sudden departure from work Monday afternoon.

Chapter Twenty-Five

Knowing it might be hours before Clausen returned, I went back to my office. Thinking I was probably wasting my time, I took a look at the photocopies of the three medical files Nancy Johanssen had found in her sister's *sanctum sanctorum*. I lined them up in a row on my desk. The most striking thing about them was their similarity:

R.S.	D.Y.	A.K.
11/2	10/22	4/27
MP3	MP7	MP4
1ST	1ST	1ST
AB?	AB?	AB?
CDL	CDL	CDL
XXX	XXX	XXX
VI	VI	VI
POS	POS	
SAB MG	SAB MG	
11/4	10/25	

The letters at the top of each page were in a space labeled PATIENT'S NAME. The numbers below that were in a space labeled DATE. In a stroke of pure genius, I deduced that the letters were patients' initials and the numbers indicated the date they had a doctor's appointment.

I didn't have much luck with the rest of it. MP followed by a number meant nothing to me. 1ST could be *first,* but first what? It could also be one ST, whatever an ST was. AB could be a blood type, but why the question mark after it? I couldn't make any sense out of the next three lines, except for XXX which meant dirty movies to me. POS: positive, maybe. SAB MG: MG could be Mackie General, but I couldn't come up with anything for SAB. The numbers at the end seemed to be another date, possibly for another appointment. A.K.'s shorter record seemed to indicate she hadn't had another appointment. Maybe she'd been NEG instead of POS, but wouldn't a doctor indicate that on the record?

I put the papers one on top of the other, tapped them neatly into alignment, and put them back in the drawer. They didn't look like any medical records I'd ever seen. They were probably just some notes Sandhoff had made, using the forms for scratch paper.

I considered getting something to eat, but I'd stopped feeling hungry awhile back. I went into the bathroom at the far end of the back room and showered and shaved. I dressed in clean jeans and a blue chambray shirt, noticing that they were almost the last clean clothes I had at the office. I threw my laundry bag in the passenger seat of Phil's truck, planning to stop by Carrie's and put a load in her machine. I was almost at her house when I decided to go to Sandhoff's office first. I could at least find out if the initials on the medical forms were patients. If not, the forms were probably nothing but insignificant notes.

Marla Twill had been crying. She was a small woman with a pixie face and a matching frosted-blond hairstyle. I knew hcr only slightly and had never been able to narrow her age down—somewhere between forty and fifty was my best guess. Today I'd have bet on fifty-five.

"I just can't believe it, Zachariah," she said as she led me into the office beyond the waiting room. "I know it happened. I know she's really gone, but I just can't *believe* it. I keep thinking I'll wake up and everything will be back to normal." She plucked a tissue from a dispenser on her desk and dabbed at her eyes as she sat down. "How can something like this happen?"

I didn't have an answer. She poised her hands above the computer keyboard for a moment, then spread her arms in a vague gesture of helplessness that seemed to encompass the entire office. Everything was as usual: the waiting room, tastefully decorated in soothing pastels; magazines fanned out on the low tables; frosted sliding window, open now, that allowed communication between the patients and Marla at her desk; appointment book; telephone; medical files lining shelves on the wall; examination rooms, the doors standing open, clean white paper pulled across the stirrup tables. Everything was in its place. But the doctor wasn't in.

"Can you think of any reason Dr. Sandhoff might have needed a private investigator?"

Her response was immediate and definite: "No." After a moment, she added, "Chief Pauling already asked me that."

"She called me that morning. She came outside when she saw me."

She nodded, dabbing at her reddened eyes again. "I don't know why. She didn't say anything. She came out of the exam room and looked out front and she said something—'I'll be right back' or something like that—and she went out. I was really surprised because she never went outside when the demonstrators were here. But I didn't have time to think about it because the phone rang and it was another bomb threat and I had just hung up when I heard the shot and after that . . ." She pulled another tissue from the box.

"I know you can't give me any information about patients. I don't expect you to tell me the names, but could you tell me if you have patients with these initials?"

"Initials? What do you mean? I don't understand."

"I'm just trying to figure out if something I came across is important."

"Well, I don't understand. I really can't tell you anything about the patients."

"I'm not asking you to. I just want to know if she had patients with these initials. You don't have to tell me their names."

"I . . . well, I suppose . . . What are they?"

"First one's R.S."

"R.S. Well, yes, more than one that I can think of right offhand."

"Pretty common initials, I guess. How about A.K.?"

"I don't know. I can't think of anyone."

"Can you check?"

"I don't really think . . . Oh, all right." She turned to the computer, swiveling the monitor so I couldn't see the screen. After a moment, she said, "Oh, yes. A.K."

"How about D.Y.?"

Marla was frowning at the screen, chewing on her lower lip. "What were the first initials you gave me?"

"R.S."

She looked up at me, an unreadable expression on her face. "Where did you get those names?"

"Is there a D.Y.?"

"I'm sorry, I really can't do this. Information about patients is confidential, you know that."

"I'm not asking—"

"I'm sorry, I'm not telling you anything else. I'm very busy, so if you don't mind . . ." She stood and gestured toward the doorway.

"If you think of any reason why she called—"

"I won't. Goodbye, Mr. Smith."

I'd been *Zachariah* only moments before. At the front door, I glanced back. Marla was picking up the phone. I went outside and closed the door. As I walked by the window, I looked inside and saw that she was already replacing the receiver. I went back inside. She was flipping through cards on a Rolodex and looked up at me, frowning.

"Sorry to bother you again. I was wondering if I could use the phone. I'm supposed to meet someone and I'm running late."

"Yes, of course."

She stood up and moved aside. I picked up the receiver and started coughing. "Damn, my throat's scratchy. Could I get a glass of water?"

"Sure, I'll get it."

"Thanks." As soon as she walked out of the room, I tapped the REDIAL button on the phone. I had already hung up before she returned with a paper cup of water. "No answer; he must have already left." I tossed down the water in a single gulp, wishing it were whiskey.

A few minutes later, I let myself into my sister's house. I pushed the MESSAGE button on the answering machine. Marla Twill's voice came over the speaker: "This is Marla . . . Oh, never mind, I just remembered you're working days this week. I'll call you at the hospital."

Tom, not Carrie. That should have been a relief, but somehow it seemed even more ominous.

Chapter Twenty-Six

Carrie and Tom's old farmhouse had been a warren of small rooms before the remodeling, which had been a group effort with Carrie providing the brains; Tom, the bankroll; and me, the brawn. The parlor and a downstairs bedroom had been combined to form a family room. A pantry located down the back hall from the kitchen was now Carrie's office, the command post for C and Z Paperhanging. The small room had been given the illusion of spaciousness by the installation of a big greenhouse window.

According to her desk calendar, Carrie had an eleven-thirty appointment at 1414 Appletree Lane. *Est/LR* was scrawled after the address. Carrie could work out an estimate for papering a living room in about thirty seconds, but Appletree Lane was on the far north end of town. It was only eleven-forty now. Plenty of time.

I went upstairs and entered the bedroom that had been converted into an office for Tom. As always, his desk was clear of everything but a telephone, a Rolodex, a notepad, a pen, and a small pewter replica of the Eiffel Tower he'd brought home in October after attending a medical conference in Paris. A clean desk may be a sign of a sick mind, but it's easy to search. I went through each of the drawers, finding nothing that seemed significant, then started on the file cabinet. Two of the four drawers were full of medical journals and I didn't have time to flip through each one looking for hidden papers. I didn't think I'd find any anyway. Tom wasn't the sneaky type. Discreet, but not sneaky.

The other drawers were full of neatly labeled, alphabetized file folders containing papers and clippings about various aspects of the medical profession. ABORTION was right up front. Nothing surprising about that; it's first in the Yellow Pages, too. I pulled the folder out and flipped through the contents.

Tom had clipped or photocopied articles from medical journals as well as from general interest magazines and newspapers. Most of them dealt with abortion as an ethical issue, rather than a medical procedure. Toward the back of the file, most of the papers were related to RU-486, also not surprising since the abortion-pill controversy was a relatively recent development. Tom didn't highlight passages or make notations in the margins. Since he had a near-photographic memory, I was surprised he bothered to keep the clippings at all. Maybe Carrie used the file. She was the one who was involved with the abortion issue.

I returned that file and read the labels on the others, finding nothing that interested me until I opened the second drawer. An unlabeled folder at the back caught my eye. Instead of papers, it contained a miniature manila envelope, its tab sealed shut. I shook it gently, lining the contents up along the side, then rubbed my fingertips across it. It seemed to contain four round pills, although Tom was such a fanatic about keeping drugs locked up and properly labeled that I doubted it. I couldn't think of a compelling enough reason to open the sealed envelope so I put it back.

I closed the file cabinet and looked around the office. Floor-to-ceiling bookshelves lined two walls. I rubbed my face with both hands and thought to hell with it, I wasn't looking behind all those books. I sat at the desk and flipped through the Rolodex, finding nothing I wouldn't have expected to find.

I took a good look around before I left, making sure nothing was out of place. Downstairs, I turned on the television in the family room, slouched down on the couch with my feet on the coffee table and stared at the screen, only vaguely aware of the images flickering there, the sound track as meaningless as white noise.

Was I reading too much into Marla's reaction to the initials? Maybe she just suddenly decided I was being a nuisance so she called Tom to ask him to tell me to stop. But it sure seemed to me that it was the specific patients I was asking about that upset her. And Marla wasn't a meek woman. She'd tell me to go to hell herself, she wouldn't call my brother-in-law and tattle on me.

When Carrie came home a while later, I was still there on the couch, my thought processes having had a soporific effect on me. She placed Matthew in my arms, saying, "Are you awake? Don't drop him."

I sat up straight and held Matthew in front of me, one hand supporting his head, the other his backside. He smiled and cooed and I smiled and cooed back. Carrie came back with Melissa who had, as usual, fallen asleep in the car. Carrie put her down beside me, where she curled into a ball. "God, it must be nice," Carrie said.

"What?"

"Being able to sleep like that. I wish I could do it."

Matthew was blowing spit bubbles, seeming quite pleased with his accomplishment. "Are you having trouble sleeping?"

"Not really. I just meant . . . only children sleep like that. Can you imagine staying sound asleep while someone takes you out of a car and carries you inside and lays you down?"

"I can't imagine anyone carrying me, period."

She smiled, then touched her forehead with the palm of her hand as if taking her own temperature. "Tom's been having trouble sleeping. I think Irene's death hit him harder than he wants to admit. He says it isn't that—he and Irene weren't close friends or anything, just colleagues. But still, he'd known her ever since she moved here and I think it bothers him more than he lets on. Anyway, no, I'm not actually having trouble sleeping, but Tom tosses and turns all night long and that keeps me awake."

"Did they have any of the same patients?"

"Tom and Irene? Some of his patients must have gone to her after he closed his practice. He handled obstetrical cases. And now, well, he sees all kinds of people in the emergency room, of course. I'm sure some of her patients show up there. And I suppose he refers patients to her. Why?"

"I don't know. Just wondering." I put Matthew on his stomach, stretched out lengthwise on my thigh, and patted his back gently. He chortled his approval.

"That didn't sound like a casual question, Zachariah."

"It's nothing, Carrie. I was just thinking that maybe they'd worked together on some cases. You said they were colleagues, not friends, but you don't have to socialize with someone to be friends. He probably cared about her more than he realized. Did you get the job?"

"Of course." She grinned. "The walls are at least two inches off plumb and she'd picked out the most godawful paper with vertical stripes. I had to hang a plumb line and practically draw her a picture before she got the message. Then she started ranting about suing the builder. God, the house is fifty years old at least. She wants it done right after the first of the year and if I don't find another paperhanger . . ." She gave me a meaningful look.

"I keep forgetting. I've been busy. I'll work on it."

"Soon, okay? I know it's almost Christmas . . ." She trailed off, knowing the holiday season was unlikely to distract me from finding a paperhanger once I decided to look for one. I ignored the entire second half of December as much as possible. All my shopping had been done weeks earlier, thanks in large part to high-priced mail order companies that provided gift wrapping and timely delivery right to the recipient's front door. I had no Christmas plans other than dropping by to watch Melissa unwrap presents.

The last Christmas I'd enjoyed was the last one with April. Late Christmas Eve, she'd put on a bright red teddy with jingle bells—but there was no point in thinking about that. Matthew was sucking on my pants leg, so I picked him up, holding him up in front of me. I thought of the first time I'd held him, when he was less than an hour old. I'd looked into his face, a face I'd never seen before but recognized from thirty-year-old photographs, and realized with aching clarity just what April had done: She'd stolen my children, children unborn, unconceived, but children we'd talked about, planned for, chosen names for, children for whom I'd built a big house on a large plot of land. Those children would never be. The day Matthew was born was the first time I'd felt real hatred for April. But I still searched for her in my dreams.

I looked at Carrie, aware that she was watching me. "You have plenty of time for children, Zachariah."

All the sisters in the world and I got stuck with a mindreader. I stood up, handing Matthew to her and dropping a kiss on her cheek. "I gotta go, things to do, people to see, all that shit."

As I was getting into the car, I thought, yeah, plenty of time for children, but they wouldn't be the same children, they wouldn't be mine and April's. Those children were gone forever.

I was backing out of the driveway when Carrie came out of the house, waving frantically. She signaled "telephone" in sign language—thumb at her ear, little finger at her mouth, middle fingers folded in.

When I picked up the phone in the family room, Dora, in a prissy voice, said, "Customers who wish to receive their messages in a timely fashion must keep the service informed of their whereabouts at all times."

"Sorry, Dora. What is it?"

"A message from the chief, which is why I was calling all over looking for you, but you just had another call, too. Dr. Harry wants you to call him."

Surprise, surprise. "Okay, what did Pauling want?"

Dora cleared her throat noisily, signaling that a direct quote was to follow. Phil rarely lost his temper, but none of the operators at the Main Street Answering Service were likely to forget the day he stopped by to talk to them after a message of his had suffered in the translation, resulting in my showing up to serve legal papers on a man just as the cops were moving in to make a drug bust. Recognizing me from my days on the police force, the suspect bolted.

Having ahem-ed sufficiently, Dora said, "'Two o'clock's a no-go. Sis decided to stick around.' End of quote. Sometimes I think he just makes these things up so we'll think you guys lead interesting lives."

"Don't tell him you figured that out, you'll spoil his fun." I made sure Carrie was out of earshot, then added, "If Dr. Harry calls back, tell him I got the message."

"Okay. Keep in touch."

Chapter Twenty-Seven

On the way back to my office I checked the parking lot at the police building. My Cherokee wasn't there. I called the Jeep dealership and was informed they'd installed a new windshield and the chief of police had picked the car up at noon. He'd left the bill for me. I considered trying to track him down to switch vehicles, but it seemed like too much effort. Besides, I didn't want to give him a chance to tell me to stay away from Sandhoff's house.

Nancy Johanssen's change of plans was convenient. I preferred searching her sister's house without Phil looking over my shoulder. Since Nancy was the sole heir, the house and everything in it was hers now. All I needed was her permission.

I thought at first that I wasn't going to get it. She answered the phone hesitantly, sounding nervous. I supposed she was bracing herself for a call for her sister from someone who hadn't heard the news. She explained that she had changed plans abruptly, arranging a leave of absence from her job by phone. "I felt a little silly," she said, "because I was ready to leave for the airport in Portland. Reverend Sloan had just arrived to take me there when I suddenly realized that it would be better to get everything taken care of as soon as possible. As long as I know

I still have to do it, I'll never stop thinking about her death. I just want to get this over with as soon as possible."

"I think that's a good idea. Would you mind if I came over? I'd like to talk to you."

After a long pause, she said, "Well . . . May I ask what it's about?"

"I've been trying to find out why your sister called me that morning. I might have a line on something, but I'm not sure. I'd like to look through her papers."

"I don't understand. Surely the police have checked into that."

"No one's attaching much significance to the phone call, but I'm beginning to think it's important. I'm sorry, but there's just no reason why she'd call me unless it was to consult me professionally."

"I see."

"I know this is hard on you. Maybe there's no connection at all between the shooting and the phone call, but I'd like to know for sure."

"Yes, I can understand that. I just don't know what you expect to find here. I've looked through most of her papers. Would you excuse me just a moment? I have something on the stove."

"Sure."

While I waited, I tried to think of a way to convince her to let me search the house. A wasted effort, as it turned out. When she came back on the line, she said, "Mr. Smith, I don't think you'll find any answers here, but I know you feel you have to try. I have no other plans if you want to come over now."

"Thanks, I really appreciate it."

My stomach had started rumbling when she mentioned cooking. I squelched its complaints with a bag of peanuts I found in a desk drawer. I needed to eat but I didn't want to give Nancy time to reconsider and change her mind. Maybe she would offer me some of whatever she had on the stove.

She must have been boiling water because no cooking smells greeted me at the door. She did offer coffee, leaving me alone in her sister's den while she went to the kitchen to make it. Sandhoff's desk reminded me of Tom's, neat and orderly, a place for everything and everything in its place. The desk was an old one, the kind secretaries used prior to the computer age, L-shaped to accommodate a typewriter, in this case an IBM Wheelwriter just like the one at my office that was collecting dust now that I was using the computer. Sandhoff's had a dust cover over it.

She used the desk drawers for storing stationery supplies. I turned to the two-drawer file next to the desk. The top file drawer contained household files in hanging folders, each with a label in a plastic tab. I checked through them quickly, barely glancing at the statements from utility companies and department stores and insurance companies. I pulled both the Visa and American Express files and set them aside to look at after the telephone file.

Telephone bills for the year were arranged in chronological order with the most recent at the front. She made few long distance calls. Most months, she'd called a San Francisco number three or four times, although the number didn't appear on either the October or November bill. "Is this your number?" I asked Nancy as she set a cup of coffee on the desk.

"Yes, it is."

"I'm surprised she didn't keep in touch with more people in San Francisco. She lived there a long time, didn't she?"

"All her adult life until she moved here. I think she still writes to a few old friends, but most of the people she knew in the City were friends of both her and her husband and she didn't keep in touch. His death was devastating to her and I think she didn't want to be constantly reminded of it."

"I suppose it's easier sometimes to make a complete break with the past."

I flipped quickly through the credit card statements. The Visa records covered two years but she'd only received six statements and had paid each bill in full. The charges were all from businesses in my neighborhood downtown for work she'd had done on the house. She'd used the American Express card frequently, twenty or more charges every month from restaurants, clothing stores, jewelry stores, gift shops. She apparently preferred to put all her routine purchases on the charge card and write a single check at the end of the month. Judging from the amounts, *Born To Shop* was her motto.

The bottom file drawer was full of old financial records, most of them from before she'd moved to Oregon. I found nothing at all that related to her medical practice. She'd taken her *sanctum sanctorum* seriously.

"I'd like to see what's on the computer," I said to Nancy.

"She didn't use it much. Just some kind of bookkeeping program. She preferred the typewriter. She said she thought at typewriter speed, not computer speed."

The computer had its own desk, against the one wall that wasn't lined with shelves. I sat down at the functional-looking work center and turned the machine on. It was an IBM clone, much like mine, and it turned out she used the same menu program I did. The menu offered me four choices: a word processing program; a utilities program; a record-keeping program, which was basically a computerized address book; and a financial program, which was basically a computerized checkbook. No games, no graphics. I noticed there was also no printer and mentioned that to Nancy, who said, "She never bothered to get one. She did all her writing on the typewriter. In fact, she offered to give me the computer once, but I have one of my own. She said the way she used it, it was just a very expensive adding machine."

I checked the financial program first, finding an electronic duplication of her checkbook, then I entered the word processing program and brought up the directory. There were forty-nine files. Glancing down the list, I realized she had named each file with a three-letter abbreviation of a month, followed by a number from one to four. Four entries each month. I smiled at the screen, willing to bet that this was her version of a diary. "How odd," Nancy said, "I was sure she never used it for writing."

I tried JAN1, JAN2, JAN3, and JAN4, then selected others at random. My attempts to retrieve the files were all met with a request for a password.

Nancy had been standing behind me, watching.

"You don't happen to know the password, do you?" I asked.

"No, I'm sorry. If each one has a password, there must be a list somewhere. She'd never be able to remember them all."

I shook my head. "She'd use the same password for all of them. What's her middle name?"

"Louise."

I chose DEC1 and entered LOUISE for the password. *Error.* I tried her birthday, telephone number, street name. *Error, Error, Error.* "What's your mother's maiden name?"

"Berry. With an E."

Error. "Any ideas?"

"Well . . . doctor?"

Error. We tried a few more wild guesses. "Is there some way to . . . I don't know . . . get around the password?" Nancy asked.

"I don't think so. I have the same program and I remember something in the instruction manual about the company that makes it not being able to help you out if you forget the password."

"So we have to . . . what's the expression? Crack the code?"

"Yeah. The cops didn't ask you about this?"

"No, but I don't know if they even turned the computer on. I told them she didn't really use it."

"People usually pick a password they're absolutely sure they won't forget. Middle name, birth date."

"That seems to defeat the purpose, doesn't it? It certainly makes it easier for someone else to figure it out."

"Yeah, but it isn't like national security is involved, just personal privacy." I grinned. "Sometimes people use passwords just because it's possible. My sister uses one on her records for the paperhanging company. Now what are the chances someone's going to want to break into her computer files to find out who had their bathroom wallpapered?"

Nancy laughed and said, "And you? You must use a computer since you seem to know how. Do you use a password?"

"I use good locks and an expensive alarm system. Well, I can't see spending a lot of time guessing. Let me know if anything occurs to you." I shut off the computer and stood up. "I'd like to look around the rest of the house if you don't mind."

"No, of course not. I've been working in her bedroom. I'm going to donate the clothing to a charity here in town. She has beautiful clothes and we're the same size, but . . . I just can't feel right about wearing her things."

"Why don't I start in there? It shouldn't take long and then I'll be out of your way."

She led me upstairs to a big bedroom decorated in pale green and white. Piles of clothes were folded neatly on the king-size bed. Nancy touched the top garment on one of the stacks, rubbing the fabric between her fingers. "She loved good fabric, wool, silk. I've always been more the cotton type." She grinned and gestured to the outfit she was wearing, an oversized pink sweatshirt, the sleeves pushed up, and tailored blue denim pants. "Irene was always . . . oh, *formal*, I suppose. I don't think she ever wore jeans in her entire life."

I nodded, saying something about preferring casual clothes myself.

"The suitcases are mine," Nancy said. "I haven't unpacked."

There were two suitcases and two carry-on bags by the closet. Nancy didn't travel light. I glanced again at the clothes on the bed: skirts and sweaters and wool pants mostly, with a pile of underwear at the foot of the bed, along with some leotards and tights. The closet was standing open, empty padded hangers on the rod, shoes in an over-the-door rack. I was thinking that Sandhoff didn't have a particularly big wardrobe when I realized these were all winter clothes. No doubt she had spring, summer, and fall clothing stored away.

I found the rest of her wardrobe eventually, in the third upstairs bedroom. That was as close as I came to detecting anything. I did find out that Irene Sandhoff had liked jazz and classic rock; that her taste in reading material ranged from Stephen Hawking to Stephen King; that she ate a lot of frozen low-calorie meals and didn't do much cooking from scratch; that a man—Fred Niles, I assumed—had left his shaving kit in the cupboard beneath the sink in the master bedroom bathroom; and that at the time of her death she'd been bicycling across the United States. A map on the wall by the exercise bike indicated she'd pedaled about ten miles a day and was halfway across Colorado. She apparently wasn't the sentimental type. She didn't keep old letters or photographs or mementos. Maybe that was all part of starting over after her husband died.

Two and a half hours older, but no wiser about Sandhoff's murder, I told Nancy I was finished.

"I'm sorry," she said, "I know you were hoping to find something that would explain why she called you, but I just really can't believe my sister had any kind of problem that would make her think of hiring a detective. Goodness, she wouldn't be involved in anything shady."

I smiled. "Not all my clients are shady characters."

"Oh, I'm sorry, I didn't mean to make it sound quite that way."

"Don't worry about it. Some of them *are* pretty damned shady." I put my jacket on.

Nancy opened the front door for me, saying, "Brrr. It's still snowing."

"They're forecasting six to eight inches." I pulled Phil's truck key from my pocket, then put my gloves on. "If you're not used to driving in snow, it'd be a good idea to stay off the streets."

"Oh, I will. I'd be scared to drive that little rental car in weather like this. A lot of people drive pickup trucks in this part of the country, don't they?" She was looking outside, at Phil's truck in the driveway.

"Yeah, they come in handy. That isn't mine, though. I borrowed it from a friend while mine's being worked on. In fact, I need to get it back to him before he decides I ran it off the road somewhere."

"Oh, that's right. You have one of those . . . Broncos?"

"Jeep Cherokee. Thanks again for letting me come."

Chapter Twenty-Eight

The more I thought about Sandhoff calling me Monday morning, the stranger it seemed. From what I'd heard, she wasn't the type to take care of personal business during working hours. I headed back to Belle Foret.

Marla Twill wasn't happy to see me and made no effort to conceal her feelings. In fact, she said, "Oh, god, go away."

I pulled a chair close to her desk and sat down. "It's good to see you again, too. Dr. Sandhoff called me at eleven twenty-five Monday morning. What was she doing then?"

"Doing? She was working. It was just like every other morning. She got here at seven, the first patient arrived at eight. We had a full schedule. I had to re-schedule some appointments because she was going to the luncheon for the Holiday Ball committee and I'd squeezed a couple extra patients in during the morning. We were busy. I don't know what you want."

"So she was busy with patients, busier than usual, and at eleven twenty-five, she suddenly decided to call a private detective. Doesn't that strike you as a little strange?"

"I don't know."

"Come on, Marla. She didn't take time out of a busy morning to make a social call."

"No, she wouldn't do that, but I don't know why she called you."

"Did she get any phone calls?"

"No. We had calls, of course, but I handled them all. Her private line never rang, I'm sure of that. She rarely got calls on it during working hours. Only a few people even know the number, although she always forwarded her home phone to it because a lot of times she'd stay here until seven or eight o'clock at night. But her home phone's unlisted, too, and everyone knows she wasn't there during the day. I know no one called that morning. And she didn't make any calls. She was with patients almost constantly."

"She called my office."

"I mean she didn't make any *other* calls. That was the only time she went into her office, I'm sure. I didn't know she used the phone. She was only in there a minute or so. I thought she'd just gone in to put the package down. After that, she was with a patient for a few minutes, then all of a sudden she went outside and—"

"What package?"

"What?"

"She took a package into her office?"

"Oh. Yes. Well, the mail had just come and I had to sign for it, Express Mail, or whatever they call it. Overnight delivery. It wasn't really a package, not a box, just one of those big envelopes."

"Who was it from?"

"I don't know. I didn't pay any attention to it. It was marked *Personal* so when it came I gave it to her."

"Did you tell the cops about it?"

"Well, no. Why would I? For god's sake, it was a piece of mail."

"Where is it now?"

"I . . . I don't know. Still in her office, I suppose."

I stood up. After a moment, Marla got up and led me into Sandhoff's private office. "Did the cops spend much time in here?"

"No, not really. They wanted to see her appointment book, desk calendar, things like that. And the telephone bill, to check on long distance calls, I suppose. I gave them everything they asked for." She moved a few papers around on Sandhoff's desk. "I don't see it."

"How big was this envelope?"

"Oh, just standard size, like a large manila envelope but colorful—blue and white and there's an eagle on the front, isn't there? It wasn't thick, it might have had a dozen sheets of paper in it, but nothing more. The bomb threats had made us pretty nervous about packages. It didn't have anything in it but papers." Marla had been opening drawers and cupboards while she talked. "It's not here."

"Has anybody taken anything out of here?"

"No. Of course not. No one's even been in here. Well, her sister was here Tuesday, but I don't think she took anything with her."

"Dr. Sandhoff might have thrown the envelope away. I suppose the trash has been emptied since then."

"Oh, yes. The cleaning people have been in and the garbage truck comes Wednesday."

"Would you mind if I searched a little more carefully? If she took the papers out of the envelope, they could be here someplace."

"This is her private office. I don't want . . . Oh, god. What difference does it make now? Do whatever you want." She walked out. I started searching the office systematically, clockwise from the door, skipping nothing, looking everywhere a few sheets of paper could be stashed.

I stayed less than an hour, finding nothing that seemed significant, then I returned to my office and took the three medical forms out of the desk drawer. I thought about just taking them to Tom and asking him what they were. But Marla's reaction to the three patients' initials had been more than a little strange. I was sure she called him because I'd specifically asked about the patients indicated on the files Sandhoff had unaccountably kept in her *sanctum sanctorum*. Something funny was going on. I placed the three sheets of paper side by side on the desk again.

R.S.	D.Y.	A.K.
11/2	10/22	4/27
MP3	MP7	MP4
1ST	1ST	1ST
AB?	AB?	AB?
CDL	CDL	CDL
XXX	XXX	XXX
VI	VI	VI
POS	POS	
SAB MG	SAB MG	
11/4	10/25	

I hadn't expected to make any more sense of them than I had before, but AB suddenly jumped out at me. First in Tom's file drawer, first in the Yellow Pages: AB for abortion. Why not? Sandhoff performed abortions. AB with a question mark. Meaning what? Maybe the patient had asked Sandhoff about an abortion. 1ST suddenly made sense: first trimester. MP . . . Wasn't there a word for the number of pregnancies a woman had? Multi-something. I checked the dictionary. Multipara. This was A.K.'s fourth pregnancy, D.Y.'s seventh, and R.S.'s third.

I worked on CDL for a while, getting nowhere, then moved

on to XXX: dirty movies; triple X; three times; kiss, kiss, kiss. Nothing with a medical context occurred to me. Damn it, I thought, I should be able to figure this out. It had taken me only a matter of seconds to figure out the five letters Allison put under her signature when she wrote to me. OLVIC: Oldest Living Virgin In Connecticut. I smiled at the thought. Allison was seventeen (and eight months, as she'd be quick to point out) and I thought she might be exaggerating the situation a bit. Connecticut had struck me as a fairly conservative place. Although, judging from the looks I'd gotten from her class-mates, I had little doubt that she was the oldest living virgin at the Fanhaven Academy for Poor Little Rich Girls. With the possible exception of the headmistress, Mrs. Mayhew, the *Mrs.* notwithstanding.

Hell, back to work. I worked on VI. Very Important. V, very, violent, valentine, victory, vespers, vestige, verisimilitude, Vaseline, Virgo, virgin, virginity, Vanzetti. Allison Vanzetti, Oldest Living Virgin in Connecticut. It was Friday and I still hadn't called her.

It took five or six minutes for her to come to the phone, during which time several different girls passed by the phone, noticed it was off the hook, and picked it up to see who was on it. They all giggled when I told them who I was and who I was waiting for.

Allison's voice was a relief: "Zachariah?"

"Yeah, hi, where were you?"

"In the pool. Are you all right?"

"I'm fine. I told you I was okay. I've been looking for a runaway."

"I suppose there weren't any telephones where you were looking."

"Ah. You're mad at me."

"Well . . . not mad really. I was worried and I kept waiting and waiting for you to call."

"There's no reason for you to worry about me, babe."

"Oh, no, of course not. People just shoot you and beat you up all the time."

"I've never been shot before and I can usually hold my own in a fight. You just happened to witness one of my rare defeats last summer. I don't want you worrying about me."

"I can't help it. I wish . . ."

"What?"

"I don't know. That you had some other kind of job, I guess."

"I think I'm stuck with this one. My job skills are pretty limited. It's either this, or a cop, or a paperhanger. Your girl-friends wouldn't be nearly as impressed with a paperhanger."

Allison laughed. "Your job isn't what impresses them."

"No?"

"Blythe asked me to see if you'd send a picture. Of your-self. In the nude."

"No way. Besides, who would I have take it? Blythe. That's the short brunette with the . . . um . . ."

"Size forty-two bra. You're not supposed to notice things like that."

"I'm not? Why not?"

"Because."

"Good enough reason for me. I won't notice in the future. I promise. Are you wearing a swimming suit?"

"Well, of *course*. You don't think they let us skinny-dip, do you?"

"I thought maybe you changed before you came to the phone. It took you long enough. What's it look like?"

"I'm not going to tell you."

"Why not?"

"Because you thought of asking when we were talking about Blythe's . . . "

"Actually I thought of asking when you said you'd been in the pool. One-piece or two-piece?"

"One. It's turquoise and very plain except that it laces together in the front. I have a white terry cloth robe over it. My hair's in a braid. Is this telephone sex? Like in those ads?"

"Not even close and where have you seen ads like that? Don't they have *any* supervision in that place? Laces up the front, huh? I wish I were there."

She sighed. "Me, too. Why aren't you?"

I didn't have a good answer so I changed the subject. We talked for a long time. Sometimes neither of us said anything for minutes at a time but the silences weren't awkward; it was as if we were in the same room, rather than separated by an entire continent, and had no need to fill every second with words. During one of the lulls in our conversation, I picked up D.Y.'s medical form and worked on CDL again. It had to have something to do with pregnancy. Cervix. Cervical disease? Cervical dilation. Cesarean delivery.

I heard Allison make a small impatient noise and knew she was sketching. I pictured her sitting in a big chair, long bare legs folded beneath her, drawing pad on her lap, head tilted to hold the telephone between her cheek and shoulder, long honey-colored hair flowing down her back—no, she had it braided: long, thick braid over one shoulder, white robe falling open . . . "What are you working on?" I asked.

"An old house I photographed a few days ago. I'm doing it in pencil right now but I can't get the porch right. It's real old and sort of sags, but when I draw it, it just looks like I can't draw a straight line. What are *you* doing?"

"Trying to figure something out."

"What is it? Can I help?"

I doubted it. On the other hand, I wasn't getting anywhere. Why not let Allison give it a try? Maybe these were standard medical abbreviations used only on women's records. Something to do with pelvic exams maybe. Would a seventeen-year-old virgin know anything about pelvic exams? "You can take a stab at it if you want to. Write these letters down: C, D, L."

"Wait a second . . . C . . . D . . . L . . . okay."

"Then X, X, X."

"Okay."

"Then V, I."

"V, I. Okay. You don't see C and D very often, do you? Actually you don't see any of them very often." I said "What?" but she was already talking again. "Let's see, five hundred minus one is four hundred . . . and then . . . um . . . " *What the hell was she talking about?* I looked at the paper in front of me as she continued, ". . . fifty and sixty, seventy, eighty . . . six. Four hundred and eighty-six."

In the silence of my office, my palm striking my forehead made a solid smacking sound. She'd written the letters in a single row. And had seen what I hadn't seen: Roman numerals. CDLXXXVI. Four hundred and eighty-six. Four eighty-six. *Four eighty-six!* Oh, *shit!* "Allison, you're a genius." *CDLXXXVI. SAB MG.* Shit, shit, *shit.*

Sounding a little puzzled, like maybe she was wondering if she'd overestimated my IQ by quite a few points, Allison said, "Well, they aren't all that hard, Zachariah. I can't imagine how they added or subtracted with them though. How could you do it when the numbers don't line up or anything?"

"I don't know. That's probably why the Empire fell. They couldn't keep the books straight. Listen, babe, I have to go. I'll call you again soon, okay?"

"Okay. I love you."

"I love you, too." And someday I was going to figure out what to do about that. But not right now. Right now I was going to go have a little talk with Thomas Ryan Harry, M.D. The fool.

Chapter Twenty-Nine

Tom wasn't home. Carrie told me he had just pulled in the driveway when the hospital called and asked him to come back. Eight kids had crammed themselves into a compact car and set off to celebrate the beginning of winter vacation, as well as the first good snowfall of the year. The driver lost control on a curve and sailed the car off a steep embankment.

I couldn't think of a plausible excuse for going into Tom's office. I went into the kitchen instead, feeling the need for caffeine, and found the coffeemaker's carafe half full. It had been empty last time I'd been in the house. Carrie had given up coffee when she was pregnant with Matthew.

"Did you fall off the wagon?" I asked her as I filled a mug and zapped it in the microwave.

"No, but I'm always tempted. It smells so good. Tom was here for a few minutes this afternoon. Right after you left." She sat down across from me at the glass-topped table by the window, hands clasped in front of her.

"He was? Things must be slow at the hospital. Dr. Dedication never leaves his post, does he?"

"He forgot something this morning, a report or something. I don't know." She sighed heavily.

I sat down across from her. Her hands were clenched so tightly her knuckles were white. "What's wrong?"

"Nothing really. It's just that he's tired and seems distracted all the time lately. He never forgets anything and besides why didn't he just call and ask me to bring it, whatever it was? I just . . ." Her voice wavered and broke. "I just wish he'd tell me what's bothering him. I know he's upset about Irene, but he doesn't want to talk about it and I don't know what to do."

"You want me to beat him up for you?" It was an offer I made every once in a while, whenever Tom seemed to forget how lucky he was. Usually Carrie laughed. This time she started crying. "Jesus, Carrie, just how much of an asshole is he being?"

She did laugh at that, a little bit at least, and she brushed the tears away and drew a deep breath. "I don't know what's wrong with me. Nothing's wrong, really. He just seems preoccupied and . . . Well, Irene's murder upset me, too, and . . . he doesn't seem to realize that and I try not to talk about it because it just makes it worse for him."

"He knows you're upset. He mentioned it to me."

"Did he? Well . . ."

"He thinks you're going to load your gun and shoot at shadows next week when he's working nights."

"Oh, for Pete's sake."

"You mentioned the gun to me, honey."

She waved that away with an impatient gesture. "Well, I won't. Has Phil said anything to you?"

"About the murder? I know what's in the paper, that's about it."

"But what about Eddie Paxton? Doesn't that make it seem like . . . Oh, never mind."

"I don't know why Eddie was shot. It seems like there has to be some connection but I don't know what it is. I don't think Sandhoff's killer was after me. Why do it there if he was? A hundred snipers could hide in the trees around my house and take potshots at me. If anyone wanted to kill me, that's where they'd do it."

Carrie shivered. "I wish you'd do something else."

I smiled. "You, too, huh? Allison thinks I should get a different job, too."

"I know where there's an opening for a paperhanger."

"Yeah, but I hear the boss is a real bitch to work for." I swallowed the last of my coffee, thinking that Tom would be exhausted and in no mood to talk to me when he got home from the hospital. I decided I'd go home, do my laundry, and come back into town later to see if Clausen had returned home. Tom would have to wait until tomorrow. I stood up. "I'm going to go on home. If you change your mind, let me know."

"About what?"

"Beating your husband up." I leaned down and kissed the top of her head, thinking that a beating from me was probably the least of Tom's worries right now.

Two inches of new snow had fallen, but the roads weren't too bad yet. When I got home, I checked with the answering service. Phil had called, wanting to know where his truck was. I called his house. Patsy told me he was sleeping. "I don't need to talk to him. Have him give me a call when he wakes up. I'm at home. School got out today, right?"

"Yes, thank god. Two weeks with no lesson plans. I think I look forward to the vacations more than Philip does. Teacher burn-out, I guess. All I have to do is make it through June, though, because I've decided I'll stay home with the baby for at least two years. You know how Phil feels about daycare and besides, I liked being home when Philip was little. We'll miss my income, but we'll manage. I can substitute, that'll help a little, and my mother can watch the baby whenever I work."

The forced cheerfulness in her voice made my throat ache. "That sounds like a good idea, Patsy."

She didn't say anything for a moment and I couldn't think of a way to fill the silence. Finally she said, "I can't . . . I can't just *assume* I'm going to lose it. I have to believe everything's going to work out this time."

"I know, honey. What does your doctor say?"

"Same as always: Everything seems perfectly normal."

"Well . . ."

"Mostly I'm worried about Phil, if something goes wrong, I mean. He's already practically a basketcase. I mentioned fixing up the little bedroom as a nursery again and he started . . . Wait a minute . . . He's awake. Hang on."

After a moment Phil came on the line. "You didn't wreck my truck, did you?"

"Only a couple small dents. You want me to bring it to you?"

"Where are you?"

"Home."

"I'll come out there. Patsy's folks are coming over in a little while and I'd just as soon have a good excuse for being gone. And now Patsy's giving me dirty looks, so I better get out of here before she starts throwing things. You gotta be crazy to marry a red-headed woman."

"And you did it twice. See you when you get here."

I put two steaks in the microwave to thaw, sliced some onions and mushrooms to sauté, and put some diced potatoes on to boil, thinking that if Phil wasn't hungry, I'd eat it all myself. Not that I'd ever known Phil not to be hungry.

I went into the garage and opened the door. I was getting into the truck when I heard Phil coming, still some distance down the road. Funny how you can always recognize the sound of your own car's engine. I backed the truck out of the garage so he could drive the Cherokee in. I could see the headlights through the trees by then and was standing by the back of the truck, shivering a little from the cold, when he turned into the driveway and kept on turning and headed off the driveway into the woods and drove right over a slender Douglas fir sapling and into its mammoth parent. Metal crunched, glass cracked, and I said "Jesus Christ!" and started running.

The Cherokee's engine was still running, revved up, whining with effort, tires kicking up dirt and pine needles in a futile effort to push through the huge tree. The back window was shattered, the cracked safety glass looking like a sheet of rock candy, a small hole like a black spot in the middle of it. Bullet hole. *Jesus, a bullet hole.* A second shot of adrenaline kicked in and I ran the last fifty feet without feeling the ground beneath my feet.

I jerked the driver's door open, the dome light coming on dazzlingly bright. Phil was slumped over the wheel, right foot jammed against the accelerator. I reached past him and turned off the ignition. The engine chugged for a moment, running on an overdose of fuel, then coughed out, the smell of gas mingling with the scent of pine in the air.

"Phil?" I pressed my fingertips against his larynx and found a pulse, strong and steady. Weak-kneed with relief, I went around to the passenger side and got in beside him. "Phil?" I checked for a pulse again, afraid I'd imagined it before. It was there, still strong and steady, and I could hear him drawing breaths. I wondered if he'd been knocked unconscious when he hit the tree, because I couldn't find a wound at first, not until I slid my hand down the outside of his left thigh and felt blood, warm and wet against my fingers.

I was afraid to move him in case he'd been hit in the spine. I checked his pulse again and then ran back to the house and called the sheriff's emergency line. Shot out of his jurisdiction: he'd really be pissed. I ran through the kitchen, turned off the burner under the potatoes, grabbed some towels and a first-aid kit and ran back to the Cherokee. Phil was standing by the open car door—more or less standing anyway. He mumbled something about Patsy and passed out. I caught him and lowered him to the ground. Far in the distance a siren wailed.

Chapter Thirty

The bullet had been removed in the emergency room and Phil was resting comfortably, meaning he was out cold, the only way to be really comfortable in a hospital. Patsy's parents had brought her to the hospital, so it was an awkward little group that had gathered around Phil's bed. Philip the Second had been picked up by a neighbor after seeing for himself that his father was doing all right. That left Patsy, her parents, Phil's second-in-command John Malcolm, and me. Patsy was clinging to Phil's limp hand and looked like she needed someone's arms around her. With her parents there, she was shit out of luck. Margaret Flynn forced herself to be civil to me, but her husband hadn't spoken to me in fourteen years, our last conversation having ended when he delivered a back-handed slap that split my lip and loosened a couple teeth. Even at sixteen, I could have taken him in a fair fight, but it wasn't a fair fight: he had righteous anger on his side and I had guilt on mine.

And now here I was, guilty again, because it hadn't es-caped anyone's attention that Phil had been in my car on the way to my house when he'd been shot. Put it together with Irene Sandhoff and I being hit with the same bullet and Eddie Paxton being shot outside my office and it didn't look good.

Phil had been conscious in the emergency room and had talked to John Malcolm for several minutes, but he hadn't been able to pinpoint where he'd been when the shot was fired. He knew he was on the stretch of road between my house and the nearest neighbor, over a mile of winding road cutting through dense forest. He'd been too busy trying not to pass out behind the wheel to pay much attention to details. All he could think about was staying on the road until he got to my place. The sheriff's department had made a perfunctory search of the area with little expectation of finding anything. Their expectations were fulfilled.

The bullet had gone through the rear window and plowed downward through the rear seat before hitting the floorboard and ricocheting upward, going through the bottom of the driver's seat and hitting Phil in the back of the left thigh. By that time, it had lost much of its momentum. It penetrated his flesh, but didn't have enough *oomph* left to travel far. In effect, he had a large puncture wound, as if the bullet had been hammered into his leg until its base was flush with the skin. Blood loss had been minimal, the bullet itself having exerted pressure against the veins and slowed down the bleeding.

Malcolm was hanging around waiting for an off-duty cop to show up to stand guard outside Phil's door, a precaution he felt obliged to take even if, as he said repeatedly, the son of a bitch was really after me. He said it enough times that I was tempted to suggest that maybe the cops should be protecting me instead, but I bit back my anger and kept my mouth shut. It was Patsy who finally said, "For god's sake, John, it isn't Zachariah's fault even if he is the one the guy's after."

Malcolm, reprimanded by the boss's wife, shot me an accusing look and went out into the corridor. A few minutes later Dan Fogel, in civilian clothes, poked his head into the room and said, "I'll be right out here, Mrs. Pauling. You just let me know if you need anything."

"Thanks, Dan." Patsy stood up, gently placing Phil's hand at his side. "Dad, why don't you and Mom go on back to the house. I'm going to stay here and I'd feel much better if you were with Philip."

Her mother said, "Now, Patricia Ann, there's no need for you to wear yourself out sitting up with him all night, especially in your condition. You heard the doctor say he was going to be fine."

I heard Patsy draw a long, shaky breath. Five minutes later, she finally convinced them to leave. Mr. Flynn raised an eyebrow at me on the way out just to let me know he hadn't failed to notice that his daughter hadn't asked me to leave.

I leaned against the closed door and Patsy came over and put her arms around me and leaned her head against my shoulder. I hugged her tight against me. We stood like that, not talking, and after a while she stopped shaking. Finally she raised her head to look at me. "I'm sorry Dad's so hateful to you. It's so stupid after all these years."

"Don't worry about it." I smoothed back her red curls. "Has Phil talked to you about Sandhoff's murder? He told me he had an idea who did it."

She shook her head. "You know he never tells me details. John Malcolm should know."

"He won't tell me."

Patsy sighed and rested her head against my shoulder again. "Neither will Phil." She lowered her voice and did a pretty good imitation of Phil's east Texas twang as she continued: "If he wants to be a cop, let him come back on the force."

"I think the last time I checked into that there was a condition involved, something about the mayor's dead body."

I felt Patsy jump a little as Phil said, "Me and His Honor kinda worked out a gentlemen's agreement awhile back. He doesn't tell me how to run the police department and I don't tell him how to suck up to his constituents."

Patsy had hurried to the bed at the sound of his voice. She leaned down and kissed him. "I love you. Don't ever scare me like this again." She kissed him again, for a bit longer this time, then straightened and said, "And don't eavesdrop when I think you're sleeping."

"I wasn't eavesdropping. I've been kinda floating in and out, couldn't tell for sure if I was awake or asleep. I'm kinda hoping I was asleep and dreaming: you and Bucky were looking mighty cozy over there." He paused to give one of us time to respond. When he got tired of waiting, he said, "That godawful accent of yours plumb woke me right up. Bucky?"

"Yeah?"

"Stay out of it, okay?"

I walked over to the bed. "I seem to be pretty much in it, Phil. It looks to me like he's tried to get me three times and someone else always manages to get in the way."

"I don't think so. I haven't figured Eddie out yet, but Sandhoff was shot deliberately. I know that, I just can't prove it yet."

"What about tonight?"

"I hate being flat on my back. Help me sit up."

"Just lie still," Patsy said and used the control to raise the head of the bed.

"What about tonight?" I asked again.

"Tonight doesn't make a goddam bit of sense." Phil slid over on the bed, wincing a little, and tugged on Patsy's hand, She got on the bed beside him, curling against him with her head on his shoulder. "Must've been after you, but . . . Jesus, I can't think of any reason. You haven't been sticking your nose in where it doesn't belong, have you?"

I hesitated too long before saying no.

"Aw, fuck, Bucky. What have you done?"

"Nothing really. I went on over to Sandhoff's house this afternoon. Her sister let me look around the house. I was just trying to find out why Sandhoff called me Monday morning."

"Goddammit, I told you that was canceled."

"Don't you two start fighting," Patsy said.

"You told me her sister was there. It's her house now, isn't it?"

Phil lay with his eyes closed for so long I thought he might have gone to sleep. Then he opened his eyes and said, "Did you find anything?"

On the drive into town behind the ambulance, I'd come to what seemed like an inescapable conclusion: I'd been the intended target of all three shootings. I had experienced a momentary sense of relief because it meant that whatever Tom was involved in, it had nothing to do with the murder. Now I wasn't so sure. I considered telling Phil what I thought Irene Sandhoff had been up to, with a little help from my brother-in-law, but it was all pure conjecture on my part and I wanted to give Tom an opportunity to explain first. I decided to let Phil draw his own conclusions.

"There's something on her computer, looks like she might have kept a diary but I couldn't get into it because she used a password."

"I already got that. Malcolm made a copy on a floppy disk and we printed it up at the station. You're right about it being a diary and it has some stuff that backs up my theory a little, but not enough to make an arrest."

"How'd you figure out the password? What is it?"

"Green."

"Green?"

"Her favorite color."

"I never would have thought of that."

"Neither would I. You don't really think we sat there guessing passwords, do you?"

"How'd you get it then? Her sister didn't know it."

"I asked the person she'd be most likely to confide in: her lover." Patsy raised her head at that. "Now see, if you'd come back on the force, you could just ask people straight out what you want to know instead of trying to figure it all out yourself."

"I like what I'm doing now." It was a pat answer and even as I said it, I wondered how true it was.

"You just like not having to play by the rules."

I couldn't argue with that.

"Is that all you found?" Phil asked.

"At her house, yeah, but Marla Twill told me—"

"Aw, shit, you've been pestering Marla, too?"

Patsy giggled a little.

"She told me an Express Mail envelope came for Sandhoff that morning and she took it into her private office. I'm pretty sure that's when she called me. It seems to me that something had to happen at the office that suddenly made her want to talk to me. I'm thinking maybe whatever was in the envelope upset her in some way. Only problem is, I couldn't find anything suspicious in her office."

"Express Mail, you gotta sign for that, right? Now why didn't Marla tell me about it? I asked her a hundred times if anything unusual happened at the office that morning."

"There's one other thing . . . those medical files I brought over to your house . . ."

"What about them?"

"Well . . . they were the only things in the entire house that had anything to do with her practice."

He nodded. I waited for him to say something else. I was

sure he hadn't returned the files to Sandhoff's office. If he kept them it was because he was curious about them. He'd be able to figure them out a lot faster than I did. All he had to do was match up the initials with the names of Sandhoff's patients and then question the patients themselves. Even if they didn't know Tom was involved, Phil would start giving some thought to just who'd been to France recently.

If he knew anything about it, he obviously wasn't going to tell me. He said, "Why don't you go away now, Bucky. If I can stay awake long enough, I'd like to check out all my body parts, be sure everything's still working, if you know what I mean. I don't suppose there's a lock on that door."

"No, but Fogel's standing guard. Phil, if this guy's after me now because he thinks I'm onto something, I'd sure like to know who he is. When I'm looking over my shoulder, it would help to know who I'm watching out for."

"I can't help you. I told you I'm working on a hunch. I think I know who's behind it and why. What I don't know is who's doing the shooting."

"You mean he's a hired gun?"

"More like an accomplice. Look, I'd assign someone to tag along with you, but, hell, you're better'n anyone I've got. The guy's been cautious so far. He likes easy shots with no chance of witnesses being around. Just try to use your head and don't give him the opportunity."

That sounded easier said than done. On the other hand, having a cop with me wouldn't stop a bullet. "Yeah, I will."

"And stay away from Sandhoff's house and her office and anything else even remotely connected with the case. Maybe they'll decide you're through snooping around."

"Yeah, sure."

Phil ran a hand through his sand-colored curls and said,

"Oh, hell. Look, I've got a good reason to think you're not in any danger now. I can't give you any guarantees. All I'm going to say is that the guy who shot me probably won't make another move until he contacts his partner, and when he does that, I'll know about it. Assuming everything works out right."

I nodded, thinking I'd prefer a guarantee. Phil added, "Besides, if I'd just shot a chief of police, I'd be inclined to lay low for a while, wouldn't you? Now go away, I'm feeling a little woozy. I think Patsy might have to give me mouth-to-mouth."

"I'll stop by tomorrow to see how you're doing. Patsy?"

"Hmm?"

"Unless he's feeling a whole lot better than I did Monday, he's all talk."

Chapter Thirty-One

Angry voices woke me the next morning. Myrna and Rosie had arrived at the flower shop and were engaged in one of their little lovers' quarrels. They never lasted long but were always conducted at top volume. I checked the clock, surprised to find I'd slept until eight-fifty. At least the fight would end soon. Fanciful Flowers opened at nine and Myrna and Rosie always called a truce before the customers arrived.

I rolled off the cot and checked the weather. It had stopped snowing sometime in the night, leaving a total of about five inches. The plow had already been down Main Street. I showered and shaved, put on a black sweat suit—the only clean clothes I still had at the office; I hadn't got around to doing my laundry yet—and made a pot of coffee. Last night, I'd driven by Clausen's house, but he hadn't returned. He had said that Judy had relatives in Malheur County. If he had taken her there, he probably ended up waiting until morning to head back because of the snow. Over my first cup of coffee, I decided I'd tackle Tom first, then see if Clausen was back.

Carrie sounded half asleep when she answered the phone. I had stopped to see her after I left the hospital last night. She'd been horrified when she heard about Phil being shot while he was driving my car. We talked about that for a moment, then I asked about the kids who'd been in the accident. One was still in serious condition, the others were doing all right. Tom had been at the hospital until after midnight.

"Is he awake? I need to ask him something."

"Hang on."

I heard the muffled sounds of the receiver changing hands. Tom sounded more awake than Carrie. I said, "We need to talk."

"Uh-huh."

"Do you want me to come there?"

"No."

"I'm at my office."

"Uh-huh."

Realizing he didn't want to have to explain anything to Carrie, I said, "I need some clothes. There should be some on the top shelf of the linen closet. Tell Carrie I didn't want to ask her to bring them down because the roads are bad. Will that work?"

"Yeah, sure. See you in a little while."

I zapped the three medical files through the fax machine, then locked my copies in a file and went next door to the flower shop, taking the snow shovel with me and clearing the sidewalk as I went. Myrna was standing by the fax machine, frowning at three sheets of paper. "They're mine," I said.

"What the hell are they?"

"Scrabble game. I play by mail." I folded the papers in fourths and stuck them in my jacket pocket.

Tom arrived fifteen minutes later, handing me a grocery bag full of folded clothes. "Thanks. I really do need them. You want some coffee?"

"Yeah." He took off his jacket and sat down in one of the captain's chairs in front of my desk. He was wearing a pale blue dress shirt and acid-washed jeans. Someone had commented at Carrie's wedding that the groom looked like a young Robert Redford. I'd never seen any real resemblance other than the pale blond hair and blue eyes. Tom's features were more defined than Redford's, almost aristocratic.

When I returned with the coffee, he said, "Well?"

"You're in deep shit, Tom."

"In what way?"

"Smuggling, for starters."

He regarded me steadily as he took a drink of his coffee. "No one can prove that."

"The pills are in the back of a file drawer in your office. They were, anyway. But that's why you went home yesterday afternoon, isn't it? To destroy the evidence."

"You son of a bitch." He drew a deep breath and set his cup down a little too hard; coffee slopped over the rim. "You've got a hell of a nerve, searching my office. How did you find out about this?"

"You're the nervy one, pal. Dr. Straight-Arrow sailing through customs with the abortion pill hidden in his luggage. *Why,* for Christ's sake? You were risking everything if you were caught."

"Well, I wasn't, was I? Look, I didn't deliberately set out to get the pills. I just went to Paris for the conference. They were given to me by another doctor there, an American. I didn't ask how he got them. Illegally, I'm sure. The manufacturer has strict security procedures."

"But why bring them back? You don't even perform abortions."

"Not now, but I have in the past and I can tell you the pill's a major improvement. Non-invasive, non-surgical, much easier on the patient for any number of reasons, medical as well as emotional. If the abortion pill were available in this country—"

"I know all that shit, Tom. I don't want a lecture. The fact is it isn't legal and bringing it in is a federal offense and *using* it, giving it to patients—Jesus, I can't even guess how many laws you broke."

"I didn't give it to anyone."

"But Sandhoff did, and you provided the pills. What did you think she'd do with them?"

He sighed. "You might not believe this but I brought the pills back as a joke. When I told Irene I was going to the conference and I'd be attending a couple lectures about RU-486, she said to bring her a sample. She was joking, of course. And I said I would, also joking. Then when I actually got hold of some . . . I know it sounds stupid, but I just thought it would be funny to actually bring her a sample."

"Jesus, Tom, what if you'd been caught?"

"Six little pills aren't hard to conceal. I showed them to her when I got back. Neither of us had any intention of using them. For one thing, the pills aren't used alone. A hormone injection has to be administered and it's not available here either, not in the correct dosage."

"But she did use them, right? On two women anyway."

"Let me explain the whole thing, okay? Irene talked to me late last spring about a patient she was concerned about, a married woman who got pregnant when her husband raped her while he was drunk. Irene tried to convince her to file charges but she wouldn't do it. And then, well, you know how it goes, they kissed and made up and everything was fine. But the woman didn't want to have another baby. She already had three children, her marriage was shaky, money was tight. The last thing she wanted was another baby. When she suggested abortion to her husband, he hit the ceiling. She was in a bad way, Zachariah. She didn't want the baby, and her husband told her he'd kill her if she had an abortion. He probably wouldn't, of course, but he would have put her through hell and the marriage would be over for sure and she had the other children to think about. She wanted Irene to tell her how she could make herself have a spontaneous abortion, a miscarriage. Irene refused, of course, and arranged for some counseling for her and . . . she's still pregnant, still married."

. . . kill me if I got rid of it and now he's hardly ever around and, god, I could just kill him. A.K.: Angela Knox, formerly Angela Billingsly, bouncy cheerleader of my adolescent fantasies.

Tom continued, "Irene told me then that if the abortion pill were available, it would be a solution to the woman's problem. The law doesn't require the husband's consent, but in reality a married woman needs her husband's approval to have an abortion, unless she wants to risk the marriage ending quickly. Not that married women don't have abortions without telling their husbands. As long as he never suspects she's pregnant in the first place, it can be done. Most of the time the marriage is in such bad shape he wouldn't notice if she had a finger amputated, let alone if she missed a period or two. Sometimes, well, she suddenly has to visit her mother, or her sister, or her best friend from college. Some of them just have it done on their lunch hour and have a headache every night until they can resume having sex.

"But the two women she administered the abortion pill to . . . the first thing they did when they realized they might be pregnant was to tell their husbands. And then it was too late, because neither husband would condone an abortion. But with the pill . . ." He spread his hands in an eloquent gesture that said the facts spoke for themselves.

I spoke them out loud anyway. "She takes the pill and in a day or two she has what appears to be a miscarriage, right? And her doctor falsifies medical records to back up her story. And her husband, the dumb bastard, feels so bad for her he goes out and buys her a dozen roses. Jesus Christ, Tom, you were a part of that?"

"I'm not going to argue ethics with you. Do you know who the women are? I don't understand how you found out about this."

I didn't enlighten him. "I don't know their names."

"Well, I'll tell you a little about them. Both cases are remarkably similar. Irene said it almost seemed as if it were meant to be—two women coming to her with almost identical problems, problems that could be solved with the abortion pill, just at the time that she was able to provide it. Irene had managed to get the hormone that's used with it in the correct dosage. I don't know how she got it, I didn't ask.

"Anyway, as I said, the women are both married. One's a Catholic, but she's moved away from the Church's teachings, not openly though, because her husband is very devout. She was pregnant for the seventh time in ten years. She simply couldn't handle another pregnancy, another baby, but she couldn't handle going against her husband's wishes, either. As far as he's concerned, abortion is murder. Irene gave her the pill."

"And what happens the next time she gets pregnant?"

"She won't. She's taking birth control pills now. Without her husband's knowledge."

"Jesus, what kind of marriage is that? She's lying to him every day."

Tom shrugged. "Either she deceives him or she leaves him or she continues to have children she doesn't want to have until she's so physically and emotionally exhausted she collapses. She's doing what she feels is best for herself and her children, and for her husband, too, believe it or not."

"What about the other one?"

"Basically the same situation. Her husband is vehemently opposed to abortion. He's active in the pro-life movement. She's in her mid-forties with grown children. Her first grandchild's due soon. She was using birth control, but ended up pregnant anyway. It happens."

"Carrie doesn't know anything about this, does she?"

"No."

"So you're lying to her."

"No, I'm not lying. I'm maintaining doctor-patient confidentiality. I discuss my work with Carrie but I don't go into detail about individual cases, I don't tell her about every person who walks into the emergency room. That would be unfair to my patients and Carrie knows it."

I slapped my hand down on the desk. "I'm not talking about your fucking doctor-patient confidentiality, Tom. I'm talking about committing crimes, violating laws, jeopardizing your career, putting Carrie's future at risk as well as Melissa's and Matthew's."

"You know how Carrie feels about abortion rights. She wants to see RU-486 approved for use in this country. I think she'd stand by me. If she didn't, well, she's capable of taking care of herself and the children without me."

"Would she stand by you if she knew your actions led to Sandhoff's murder?"

"They didn't."

"Damn it, Tom, think about it. How the hell many shady things could Sandhoff have been involved in? She was having an affair with a married man, that's one, but Phil would've made an arrest already if that's why she was killed. She was providing an illegal drug to patients, encouraging women to deceive their husbands, aborting babies the men wanted even if their wives didn't. Is there anything else you can think of? Was she selling secrets to enemy agents or dealing crack out of her office or embezzling funds from some charity? There has to be a motive for a murder and this shit with the abortion pill seems like a damn good motive to me."

Tom ran a hand through his hair and closed his eyes for a moment. "I've gone over it and over it. Nobody else knows about it. Irene knew and Marla Twill knows and I know. And now you know."

"And the two women she gave the abortion pill to. Maybe one of them confessed to her husband."

"No. They'll never tell anyone, not their husbands or their best friends or their mothers. For both of them, maintaining the fiction of a miscarriage is essential. If anyone found out what they'd done, their lives would be destroyed. Besides, I've been doing a little detecting of my own and neither of the husbands could have done it. As a matter of fact, they were both on the scene."

"Maybe one of the women did it. Maybe if it's so important for her to keep her little secret, she decided to get rid of the one person who could reveal it."

Tom shook his head. "They knew Irene would never tell anyone, partly because she was a doctor but also because she'd incriminate herself. Besides, why would she tell anyone? What would she gain by it? Both women are aware that Marla knows. Nobody's tried to kill her."

"Do they know that you're involved?"

"No. Only Marla knows that." He grinned. "If she tries to blackmail me, I'll hire you."

"This isn't a joking matter, Tom."

He sighed. "I know. But you're making more out of it than you should. It's done. It's over. I got rid of the remaining pills. For what it's worth, the first time Irene asked me for a pill, she didn't tell me she was going to use it. I should have asked why she wanted it, I suppose, but I didn't. The next time she asked for one, I did ask and she told me. I gave it to her anyway."

"I can't believe this. Christ, you don't even cheat on your taxes."

"Zachariah, what right does the government have to deny women access to a safer method for a legal medical procedure? Doctors should determine the best method of treatment, not politicians. It would be different if it were a questionable medical technique, but it isn't. Its effectiveness and safety are well-documented. It's only for political reasons that it isn't available here. What if someone found a cure for cancer or AIDS and doctors weren't allowed to use it for political reasons? Besides, it looks like it might be approved before long, anyway. The women needed it before it was approved—bad timing on their part, I guess."

"Come off it, Tom. It wasn't about patients' safety. Sandhoff had a new toy and saw an opportunity to try it out. Just another doctor playing God, and thumbing her nose at the government at the same time. The women weren't worried about safety either, they just wanted to get rid of their little problems without any social stigma and especially without pissing off their meal tickets."

"I'm not going to argue with you."

"Because I'm right and you know it."

"Because you're *convinced* you're right and nothing I say will change your mind."

"You ever read Hosea?"

"Who?"

"Hosea. The Book of Hosea. Old Testament. The Bible's got some great curses, but Hosea came up with the winner: 'Give them a miscarrying womb and dry breasts.'"

"For Christ's sake, don't start in with the Bible quotes. I haven't cursed anybody."

"Patsy's pregnant again and she'd sell her soul to have the baby but she's the one who ended up with a miscarrying womb."

"But there's no connection, Zachariah. I know how you feel about Patsy, but, damn it, there's no connection. Individual people, individual problems, individual choices. Sometimes one person's curse is another person's blessing."

Tom stood up and paced off the length of the room once. "What about Pauling being shot last night? It sure sounds as if someone's after you. What if—" He broke off abruptly.

"I know. What if Sandhoff wasn't the one he was after. There's Eddie Paxton, too." I drank the remainder of my coffee and set the cup down. "Phil seems to think Sandhoff was shot on purpose. The killer might have been after me last night because he thinks I'm onto something. I've been to Sandhoff's house and office. I was at her house Thursday night, not too long before Eddie was shot."

"I have to know how you found out about this."

"Her sister gave me the records."

"*Irene's* sister? What the hell does she have to do with it? You mean the patients' medical files? All they show is that the women miscarried."

"She found some medical records at the house and she gave them to me because she was planning to leave town and didn't have time to get them back to the office."

"That doesn't make any sense. There weren't any written records. Irene told me herself that keeping records was too risky. She was more concerned about protecting the patients' privacy than protecting herself, but she also didn't want anything around that would incriminate her. Do you still have them?"

"Copies. Here." I handed him the three fax pages. While he unfolded them and smoothed them out, I said, "Maybe she planned to use the rest of the pills and wanted to keep track of the cases for some reason. Maybe there are other doctors using the pills and they have some kind of secret research going on so they need to keep records."

He was frowning at the papers. "What the hell are these?"

"It's sort of a code. Patient's initials, MP is multipara, first trimester, AB's abortion, CDLXXXVI is four hundred and eight-six in Roman numerals. She must have thought that RU would be too obvious, so she left it out."

"You figured that out from this? Christ, I'd have never figured it out and I knew what was going on."

I shrugged modestly.

"You said these were at her house? That doesn't make sense. Irene had a hard and fast rule about never working at home. She didn't even read medical journals at home. She put in a lot of long hours at the office, but once she was home, she was off duty. Why would she have files at home?"

"They were evidence of a crime. Maybe she felt they were safer in her house. They were there, that's all I know."

"And you returned the originals to the office? Marla didn't mention that to me. She must not have any idea what they are. They don't look like anything important."

"I didn't take them to the office. I did just what I told Nancy Johanssen I'd do."

"What?"

"I gave them to the chief of police."

Chapter Thirty-Two

If I'd been hoping, just once, to see Tom lose his cool, I was disappointed. He sat quietly for a moment, apparently thinking over the situation, then said, "Maybe he won't figure it out. I'm surprised you did."

"He doesn't have to."

"What do you mean?"

"He's a cop investigating a homicide. If he thinks those records have anything to do with her murder, all he has to do is look at her files and he'll match the initials to patients and then he'll ask *them* what it's all about."

"They won't tell him."

"Sandhoff was murdered, Tom. It takes a pretty gutsy person to lie to a cop who's investigating a homicide. Even if they don't talk, there are records at the hospital." I pointed to the bottom of D.Y.'s record. "SAB MG and the date. Spontaneous abortion at Mackie General. Don't underestimate Phil. Once he finds out both those women had such nice convenient miscarriages, he'll figure it out. And guess what he'll figure out next?"

"What?"

"That you're the only doctor in town who's been to France recently."

"Marla would have told me if he'd asked to see the records."

"You keep forgetting it's a homicide investigation. Everyone's a suspect. No one who works in her office is going to know he looked at specific records. Not until he's ready to tell them."

"He still can't prove anything. I destroyed the pills. Irene's records and the hospital records show only that the women were treated for pregnancy and spontaneous abortion. These papers . . . they aren't proof. Who's going to be prosecuted anyway? Irene? She's dead. The patients? Historically, women who have illegal abortions haven't been prosecuted and in this case the abortions weren't illegal, only the method. I can't see any court opening that can of worms, especially since the doctor's dead. The women don't know how Irene got the pills. Marla and I could incriminate each other, but we won't."

"Tell me who the women are."

"No."

"Then I'll have to go to Phil. goddammit, Tom, someone murdered her."

"Not because of this."

"You can't know that for sure. Maybe you'll sleep nights if her killer is never caught, but I won't, not if I know I'm concealing evidence that might have some bearing on it. From what I hear, you're not sleeping too good anyway."

Tom's jaw clenched. I sympathized. He told me once that he hadn't realized he was getting a package deal when he married my sister. "If I tell you who they are . . ?"

I thought it over, but not for long. Rationalizations are my strong suit. "I started with nothing but these papers and figured it out. Phil's got copies of them. Let him do his own work. I won't say anything to him *unless* I come up with something directly linking these women or their husbands to the murder. Fair enough?"

"I don't have much choice, do I? All right. This one doesn't know anything about it." He handed me A.K.'s record.

"Angela Knox. I already figured that out."

"How . . . Oh, never mind." He handed me another paper: D.Y. "Diana Yates. I don't think you know her. They moved here from Pendleton a couple years ago. Her husband's name is Jeffrey. They were both at the demonstration. I saw them on the videotape that was shown on the news."

"Okay. How about R.S.?"

He hesitated. "You don't like her husband and you could destroy him with this information."

"I don't play that way and you know it."

"All right. Roberta Sloan."

The name didn't mean anything for a second. Then I felt my mouth drop open. Roberta, Bertie for short. "Reverend Willie's wife had an abortion?"

"Yes, and Sloan was at the demonstration, you know that. Bertie was at the Orange Mandarin. She was in charge of the luncheon for the Holiday Ball committee and went down early to be sure everything was set up."

"Willie Sloan's wife had an abortion. Jesus Christ."

Tom smiled. "Sloan was just a small town minister when she married him. He was fairly liberal, in fact. Then he saw the light and started thumping the Bible on the radio. His career took a real upswing. You can make a hell of a lot more money fighting the devil on the radio than you can taking up a collection from a small congregation. Bertie's got a nice life, plenty of money, social status, she likes being in the public eye. I don't know if she loves Sloan, but she definitely likes being his wife and doesn't want to do anything to jeopardize her marriage. So, publicly, she's the perfect wife for a right-wing radio evangelist. That doesn't necessarily mean she espouses his views privately."

"Jesus, if the pro-choicers knew about this . . ."

"They'd annihilate him. Zachariah, if you tell Carrie . . ."

"I won't tell her. But she wouldn't use this kind of information against him anyway. She isn't vicious. And besides, it's Bertie Sloan's right to choose what she's out there fighting for, isn't it? She couldn't hurt Sloan without violating his wife's privacy and she'd never do that. But I won't tell her, don't worry."

"All right. And you won't tell Pauling? None of them could have murdered Irene."

"Doesn't seem like it. I won't say anything to Phil, but you'd better be prepared for the worst because I don't think he returned those records to Marla and I can only think of one reason he'd keep them. If he was curious about them, trust me, he's already figured it out."

"What do you think he'll do?"

I'd given a lot of thought to that last night before I fell asleep. "If there's no connection with the murder, nothing. Phil's no glory-seeker. He's not going to bust this wide open just for publicity. And like you said, who's he going to prosecute since Sandhoff's dead? He's not going to go after the women and he'd have a tough time proving you're involved. He told me once that one of the things he hates about homicide cases is that the victim is victimized a second time when the investigation turns up all the dirty laundry. If this is nothing but Sandhoff's dirty laundry, he'll leave it alone."

"I hope you're right. Isn't he getting anywhere at all?"

"I don't know. He did say he had a suspect but I don't know who it is. There's also this business about her calling me just before she was killed. I'd sure like to know what that was about."

"I've been thinking about that. It can't have anything to do with the abortion pill. She would have told me if something was going wrong. I'm positive she'd talk to me before she contacted you, if only because we're related and she wouldn't want to create any family problems."

That had occurred to me, too. Which left me with that same nagging question: Why did Irene Sandhoff call me?

Chapter Thirty-Three

After Tom left, I went to the hospital to see Phil, staying only a couple minutes because John Malcolm was there and they were obviously busy, Phil having apparently decided to run the entire police department from the second floor of Mackie General. He really needed to learn to delegate.

Since I was at the hospital anyway, I stopped by the ICU to see how Eddie was doing. His condition, I was told, was guarded, an expression I had never understood. Guarded *by* something? *From* something? All I knew was that it sounded ominous, like you'd better hope what was guarding you was an angel. Since Eddie wasn't able to talk and couldn't have visitors anyway, except for family which as far as I knew he didn't have, I headed back down the corridor to the main entrance.

On the way I encountered Reverend William Sloan, looking dapper in a gray three-piece suit. He asked if I'd been to see Eddie.

"Just checking on his condition. He can't have visitors."

"One of the fringe benefits of my profession is that hospital rules don't apply." Sloan sighed. "There is a line in Ezekial: 'The land is full of bloody crimes, and the city is full of violence.'" He raised his eyebrows, perhaps waiting for a correction, but he had it right. He went on, "So true of our big cities, of course, but *here*, in Mackie . . . and now the chief's been shot, too. Unbelievable, simply unbelievable." He shook his head sadly. "I've known Eddie for years. We were in school together."

"Were you? He looks a lot older."

"No, he's my age, forty-nine. The years of drinking, of course, have taken their toll on him. I have tried many times to help him, but to no avail, I'm afraid. Such a waste of a life. And now this. I saw him Thursday, just a few hours before he was shot, and I remember thinking at the time that he probably wouldn't live to be very old. Now it seems almost like a premonition. He looked ill then. Although perhaps that was just because he suddenly found himself in a social situation he has long since forgotten how to handle." Sloan grinned, something he seldom did, at least in my presence.

"What happened? Did someone offer him a cup of tea?"

Sloan laughed, something else I'd seldom witnessed. "Oh, no, much worse. I introduced him to a woman."

I laughed, too, because Eddie's aversion to telephones was nothing compared to his aversion to women. "I'm sure she was charmed."

Chuckling, Sloan said, "Well, it was a bit awkward. I was at the Mackie Arms, picking up Dr. Sandhoff's sister. Bertie and I had invited her to dinner. The funeral was that morning, you know, and she really doesn't know anyone here. When I parked the car, Eddie was walking by and he stopped to say hello. Ms. Johanssen had been waiting for me in the lobby and she happened to see me arrive, so she came out and, oh, dear, I shouldn't laugh but it really was funny. You know what Eddie looks like and yet, what was I to do? Pretend he wasn't there? That would be an insult to him, wouldn't it? So I introduced them. I thought Eddie was going to faint. He mumbled something and scuttled off. Ms. Johanssen, needless to say, was also a bit taken aback. I'm sure she was never before introduced to a . . . well, a derelict."

I laughed again, picturing the scene, while Sloan grinned broadly, relishing the memory. I had never before shared a laugh with Willie Sloan. It occurred to me that I could destroy his marriage and his career with a few words.

"How's your wife?" I asked. "I haven't seen her in a while."

"Oh, Bertie is fine, just fine. A little anxious at the moment because Marlene is due any day now. Our first grandchild, you know. A very exciting event for us. Tinged with a bit of sadness, though."

"Oh? Is there a problem?"

"Oh, no. Marlene is doing just fine and she's had all the tests. The baby is fine. It's a boy, by the way. But Bertie . . . well, you wouldn't know this, but for a while it appeared that we were going to have another of our own. Quite a surprise at our age, I'll tell you. Bertie's only forty-three, but still . . . We would have had a child younger than our first grandchild. Still, children are such a blessing and if the Lord chose to give us another, we could only be thankful. Unfortunately, things did not go well and Bertie miscarried."

"I'm sorry."

"Thank you. Bertie was quite distraught, of course. We both were. However, one must accept the Lord's will. Still, it was a difficult time. I'm hoping Bertie will be solaced by the birth of her grandchild."

And when she held that baby in her arms would she think of the one whose life she had snuffed out? Christ, I was starting to sound like a pro-lifer. I'd better watch myself around Carrie.

Sloan checked his watch and said he'd better go on to Eddie's room. As we headed our separate ways, I wondered what I would have done if April had gotten pregnant and told me she wanted an abortion. Begged her not to, I was sure. And if she had done it anyway? I didn't know.

I drove by Clausen's house. The driveway and sidewalk were covered with unmarred snow. After a stop for lunch, I went to my office where I sat at my desk and tried to figure out what happened to Jordan Clausen.

The simplest explanation was that Jordan suddenly got cold feet about his impending fatherhood. He skipped his appointment with Bubba, no longer having any pressing need for cash for train tickets and probably feeling relieved that he could keep his brand-new rifle, and then he hid out somewhere until Wednesday evening, when he knew his parents would be out of the house for a while. He took some camping equipment and a second rifle, probably thinking he'd sell it later on, then he lit out for parts unknown, skipping out on his pregnant girlfriend in the time-honored fashion of the male of the species, as Carrie would have put it.

If I took Clausen at his word, his actions made sense. He called my office Monday wanting to hire me. By the time I called him back, he'd already reconsidered, knowing he couldn't afford to pay me and thinking the cops would probably find Jordan anyway. His lie about having money could be written off as pride. His attitude bothered me—it sure seemed to me that he was running scared—but I supposed a lot of people would consider his behavior a normal reaction to a private detective who wouldn't butt out when he was told to butt out.

The trouble was that I didn't believe Jordan went home Wednesday. I was sure it was a lie. Judy hadn't denied it, but had only insisted her husband hadn't hurt Jordan. I could only think of one reason for Clausen to lie: he was setting up an alibi. He wanted to make it appear that Jordan was still in the area, still up and about and moving around Wednesday evening. Why would he do that unless he knew it wasn't true? If the Wednesday evening story was a lie, the only explanation I could think of was that Clausen had hurt his son, probably pretty badly, possibly fatally, and he was trying to cover himself.

The fact that Clausen had left work Monday afternoon following a phone call from his wife had struck me as suspicious at first, but now I wasn't so sure. I'd been thinking that Judy might have called because Jordan had come home or phoned and told her where he was. Clausen might have left work to talk to Jordan and things might have got out of hand and Clausen might have killed Jordan and then called me to make himself look like a concerned father. But anyone who's ever watched a cop show on television knows about establishing the time of death. If he'd killed Jordan Monday, he'd have to be a complete fool to tell the cops the boy had been home Wednesday evening. His abrupt departure from work Monday could have been completely innocent: Judy'd been hitting the bottle a little too hard and he'd gone home to take care of her.

On the surface, the only thing Clausen could be faulted for was his failure to tell the cops Jordan had taken a rifle with him Friday. Maybe he just hadn't thought it was important. It was Jordan's own rifle, after all.

It suddenly struck me as odd that Clausen would tell the cops Jordan had taken a rifle Wednesday, if he was, in fact, lying about Jordan coming home that evening. Wouldn't that just inconvenience Clausen himself? What happened next Tuesday, his day to meet his buddies down at the rifle range? He could hardly show up with a rifle he'd claimed his son had stolen. Why not just say the boy had taken camping equipment? If it was all a lie anyway, why mention the rifle?

An answer occurred to me in the form of a scenario that formed full-blown in my mind: Jordan showed up at home Monday; Judy called her husband, who came home and beat the shit out of the kid; Clausen called me to give substance to his claim of being a concerned parent; Jordan, too badly hurt to run, was concealed in the house until Wednesday when his dad took him out in the country somewhere and shot him, staging it to look like an accident or suicide, which meant he'd have to leave his rifle at the scene. Then he told the cops Jordan had come home and taken the rifle.

An interesting scenario. It explained the call to me, Jordan's missed appointment with Bubba, the lie about Jordan being home Wednesday, the reason Clausen claimed Jordan took the rifle. It even provided a motive for murder—Clausen killed his son because he'd hurt him so badly that he would have been up on all kinds of charges if anyone found out. Many a murder has been committed in an attempt to conceal evidence of a previous, and usually lesser, crime.

It made sense. It could have happened like that. So why wasn't I doing anything about it? I'd been diddling around with the theory that Clausen hurt his son for days now and I hadn't done a damn thing about it. I hadn't even made an effort to convince Phil he should check it out. Why not? I believed Clausen had lied to me. I could easily see him losing his temper and belting his son during a confrontation. I could even see him losing control completely and killing him. The problem was that I couldn't see him plotting and scheming his way out of it.

I crossed my arms on the desk and rested my head on them, suddenly feeling tired. I had grown so accustomed to the ache in my shoulder that I was usually only subliminally aware of it, but now it seemed to flare into sharp pain, demanding my attention. I sat up, thinking a change of position would help. It didn't. The pain pills were long gone. I hadn't asked Tom for more because he'd know I double-dosed my way through them. A little youthful drug addiction and no one ever trusts you with dope again.

Jordan Clausen ran away. Why couldn't I just let it go? He ran away, period. The cops hadn't questioned Clausen's story. Why should I? I wasn't even getting paid, for Christ's sake. And I had other things to worry about: Irene Sandhoff calling me. And Tom and Carrie and Eddie Paxton and Phil. And whoever shot Phil, because he was probably after me.

I stood up, thinking, *Let it go, Jordan ran away.* I sat down again as a stray memory surfaced in my mind: Ellen Finch telling me where Rachel lived. On Elm Street, she'd said, in one of those ancient mansions. Elm Street curved along the eastern edge of Mackie Woods.

Jordan left Rachel's house early Monday morning, carrying an unusually long and skinny box wrapped in Christmas paper. Monday was a school day, Jordan was a fifteen-year-old boy who looked his age, and Mackie was a town where people actually reported suspected truants to the cops. He couldn't risk being seen and possibly picked up, so he went into the woods, just a quick jog across Elm. No one would see him. It was too cold for anyone else to be in the woods, except in the park area where neither rain nor snow nor temperatures low enough to freeze the balls off a brass monkey deterred the dedicated runners from their daily rounds on the jogging paths. Jordan had already arranged to meet Bubba in the woods, too. He'd go there early in the morning, wait until time to meet Bubba at two-thirty, then he'd head over to the high school after classes were dismissed to meet Rachel. But he never showed up.

Jordan went to Mackie Woods Monday morning. The implications of that were suddenly clear to me, and horrifying.

Clausen claimed his son took a rifle Wednesday evening. But Jordan already had a rifle.

And I was right: Clausen was setting up an alibi.

The truth is that sometimes you're better off not knowing what the fuck is going on. I sat with my head in my hands for a long time, wishing I'd figured it out sooner, wishing I'd never figured it out at all. Feeling tired, and old—Christ, I felt old, much older than thirty, eighty maybe, or a hundred and ten—I pulled my jacket on and left the office.

Chapter Thirty-Four

It was after three o'clock when I made my sixth or seventh trip out to Twenty-seventh Street and found Clausen's truck in the driveway, snow piled on the roof and hood, muddy clumps of ice hanging in the wheel wells behind the tires. He opened the door at my knock, left it open, and walked down a hallway leading to the back of the house. I followed him, closing the door behind me.

In the kitchen, Clausen sat down heavily at the table, wrapping his hand around a big mug of coffee. "Snowing like a son of a bitch down south," he said. "Couldn't get out at all last night. The drive took me damn near three times as long as it should've."

"Is Judy staying with relatives?"

"Her sister, yeah. Help yourself if you want some coffee."

I took a mug from the dish rack and filled it from an old electric percolator, then I sat down across the table from him. The kitchen doubled as a dining room, the table taking up most of the floor space. Judy's crafts were everywhere: straw flower arrangements in wicker baskets, macramé towel holders, crocheted pot holders. The table was covered with a cheerful yellow tablecloth with hand-crocheted trim added to the edges.

Clausen's eyes were red-rimmed and he hadn't shaved recently. "Nothing's happened, has it?" he asked.

"Jordan hasn't turned up, no."

He nodded. I wondered why I'd seen only the belligerence in his face before and not the desperation behind it.

We drank our coffee in silence for a few minutes. On the drive over I'd thought of taking the easy way out and going to Phil. The fact that it was way too late to make any difference had kept me from turning around and going to the hospital. I felt partly to blame, too. I'd made a half-assed attempt to find Jordan, letting myself be distracted by Irene Sandhoff's murder and Tom's departure from the straight and narrow. I set my mug down carefully, thinking that the only good that would come out of this was that Rachel would know Jordan didn't run out on her.

"I figured out why you called me Monday. Same reason a lot of people call me: you suddenly found yourself between a rock and a hard place."

Clausen made a harsh sound, half a laugh but half something not even close to a laugh. "You were in the paper a couple times. You sounded like a guy who didn't necessarily run to the cops with everything you knew. I guess I was thinking maybe you could help."

"Why'd you change your mind about talking to me? Because I was shot, too?"

Clausen sighed, loud and long. Mostly relief, I thought, letting go of the burden, giving up, maybe even glad that it was over. "Yeah, I figured you must've been feeling pretty pissed."

"Not really. I just thought I was in the way. Bad luck on my part."

Clausen nodded, his big hands gripping the mug hard enough to whiten his knuckles. The bruises on his right hand were fading, sickly yellows and greens now instead of purples and blues. I looked past him at the wall beside the door leading to the hall. A ragged hole gaped in the plasterboard.

"You shot the windows out at the high school, didn't you?"

"Yeah. Yeah, I did that." His big hands moved, fingers of the left hand kneading the bruised flesh of the right. "Funny, I'm not the type of guy who's good at . . . I guess you'd call it deception. If I'd gone bad, I'd be holding up convenience stores with a shotgun, I wouldn't be planning fancy bank robberies, you know what I mean?" I nodded and he continued, "Since Monday, it's funny, things just seemed to click, like I knew just what I had to do and how to do it. Can't believe I really did it, though. Seems like a dream. Nightmare, more like."

I nodded, took a sip of coffee, cleared my throat, wanting to get it over with, wanting to just tell him flat-out that he was wrong. But then the real nightmare would start. I kept quiet. After a moment, Clausen spoke again, his words quiet, unrushed, almost calm.

"See, all I could think was, I had to make it look like he didn't have a gun 'til later on. I went down to the rifle range Tuesday, just like always, so everybody'd see I had my Remington. Everybody down there knows me and Jordy share the one gun. Nobody knew he was getting his own for Christmas. We only got it last Thursday. He knew about it but we told him he had to wait 'til Christmas to open it. He took it with him Friday. You know that."

I nodded again.

"Shit, I didn't think Wednesday would ever come, but that's the day we always go to see Judy's mama and I kept thinking we had to do everything like normal, just go on like always so nobody'd think anything was wrong. Couldn't've gone Monday or Tuesday anyway because how would I explain how Jordy knew we were gone then, right? Had to be Wednesday, we're always gone Wednesday evening. So we went to the nursing home and then I told the cops Jordy'd come home and took the camping stuff and my rifle. And, well, shooting out the windows at the high school, I guess I figured that'd make it look more like he didn't have a rifle before that. Like he was pissed about school and soon as he got hold of a gun he went down there and shot out the windows. Scared the shit out of me when the chief asked me about them, though. I guess I didn't really think they'd suspect Jordy right off."

I felt like telling him he'd done a good job setting up an alibi for his son, congratulating him for fast thinking and clever planning. It seemed pretty damned stupid though, so I didn't.

"You told the cops yet?" he asked.

"I wanted to talk to you first."

"Yeah, well, I appreciate that. I reckon . . . I reckon I better go down to the police station myself, tell them myself. I already pretty much decided to, but I wanted to get Judy out of here first. Things keep getting worse. That guy at your office, and now the chief. I heard about it on the way up here. I guess he's gone plain crazy." His mouth twisted and he said, "Aw, shit, he's just a boy."

"Jordan didn't have anything to do with Eddie Paxton or the chief."

"You sure?" His voice was pathetically eager. What a straw to grasp at—that his son shot only one person, not three.

"Positive."

He sat back in his chair, slumping with relief. "Good. That's good. Better, anyway. I was thinking these last two shootings, they're my fault for not going to the cops. Hell, maybe he didn't stick around then, maybe he just cut and ran, could be far away somewhere, maybe down in California by now."

I studied his face while he stared into his coffee mug. He

was already hurting, had been hurting since Monday. The truth would hurt even more, but at least he'd be hurting for the right reason. "Listen . . . it's all too . . . abstract for a fifteen-year-old."

He frowned. "What do you mean?"

I cleared my throat. Christ, I didn't want to do this. Let him have some more time, I thought; let him believe his son was on the run, down in California, down where the sun was shining and the air was warm against his skin. Not where it was cold, not where it was freezing. I felt myself shiver. "What I mean is, if I were fifteen years old and mixed up and angry because my girl's parents were going to make her have an abortion and I had a gun and decided to use it . . ."

"Yeah?"

"I'd shoot her parents. Maybe I'd shoot my own parents, too, and maybe my girl and even myself. But I wouldn't shoot a doctor who performed abortions."

"No? Abstract, you said. Like the doctor wasn't even the one who's going to do it, right? They're taking her to some clinic in Portland."

"Yeah, that's right."

"Well. Well, I guess Jordy knew about all the trouble at her office, the demonstrations and stuff. Been in the paper for a couple weeks now. Guess he thought it was kinda like symbolic or something, you know what I mean?"

He wasn't getting it. "Yeah, it would be pretty symbolic. Clausen, listen—" I looked into his eyes, saw the exhaustion and desperation there and knew he couldn't face it. Even if, somewhere in the back of his mind, he understood what I was getting at, he couldn't face it. Not now, not while he could still believe Jordan was on the run, a boy in big trouble, sure, but even big trouble ends eventually. I decided to let it go, he'd have to face it soon enough. I said, "Judy called you Monday at work, right? She heard about it on the news, I guess."

"Yeah. Jesus, she was . . . I thought she'd gone crazy at first. Couldn't make any sense out of what she was saying. Kept telling me Jordy'd shot somebody. I headed home, heard the news on the way. I got Judy calmed down a little then I went up to the woods. Went twice, actually. First time there was cops around. Had to go back later on. I'm not sure why I went. I knew he wouldn't be there, not out in the open anyway. I guess maybe I was hoping he'd see me." He wiped the back of his hand across his eyes. "I found the wrapping paper in a trash can in the picnic area. Funny, I was just walking by, planning to go on into the woods and something made me glance down into that trash can and there it was, the damn wrapping paper from his gun. Red with snowmen all over. He was there all right, went up there and unwrapped his gun and took it into the woods and . . . and . . . did it."

Tell him, I thought. But he was already talking again. "I'd've taken him to the cops if I found him. See, it isn't that I don't want him to face up to what he did. It's mostly I don't want the cops going after him, gunning him down on sight. He's just a boy. I know how the cops work. Armed and dangerous, that's what they'll call him. I don't want them going after my boy with guns. I kept hoping he'd come home or call and we could help him, get a lawyer maybe, or just go with him to tell the cops." His sigh came from somewhere deep inside.

"You look tired," I said. "Did you get any sleep last night?"

"No, not much. Couple hours maybe. Judy was in bad shape, kept me awake most of the night and, Christ, the roads were solid ice this morning and goddamn snow blowing all over the place. It was like driving blind." He moved his shoulders, easing the tension.

I stood up. "Look, it's . . ." My mind went blank. What

day was it? Thursday was the funeral and Eddie was shot and Friday I found out about Tom and the abortion pill and Phil was shot. That was just last night. My days were too long and my nights were too short and I was tired. "It's Saturday already and a few more hours won't make any difference one way or the other. Why don't you get some sleep? If you want, I'll come back later and we can talk to the cops together."

He stood up, too, easing his shoulders again. "Yeah, maybe I will get some sleep. You're right, there's no rush now, is there? I reckon Jordy lit out Monday, don't you? I mean, if he didn't shoot the others, there's no reason to think he's still around here, is there?"

"No, there's no rush now. Get some sleep, I'll come by later on."

He nodded, already turning away, stumbling a little as he walked down the hall. I unplugged the percolator and put the two mugs in the sink, then I went into the living room and stood at the entrance to the short hall leading to the bedrooms. I could hear Clausen snoring already. I found a pad of Post-it notes by the phone and wrote him a note, telling him not to go to the police until I came back. I stuck the yellow square of paper on the television screen and left the house.

Chapter Thirty-Five

I drove home when I left Clausen's house. The streets in town had been cleared but the city's plow turned around at the city limits sign. Beyond it, the pavement was covered with six inches of snow. I had complained to the county every winter since I'd lived on Bunyard. They always told me the street was low priority because it had little traffic. I supposed they had a point, since it was almost three o'clock and a solitary vehicle had left tracks on the road between town and my house.

My driveway and the surrounding land were clear of tire tracks, footprints, ski tracks, snowshoe prints, or any other signs that anyone had been around, all very comforting although it didn't mean someone wasn't on foot in the woods. I ignored the sensation of crosshairs on the back of my neck as I parked in front of the house and walked to the door. Nobody shot me.

The light was blinking on the answering machine. I pushed the MESSAGE button. A high-pitched voice said: "Where are you? We don't know. Do you?"

I called the answering service, apologized to Marilyn for forgetting to check in, agreed for the thousandth time with her suggestion that I should get a pager or carry my cell phone all the time, and thanked her for the message, which was to call Nancy Johanssen. She answered immediately saying, "Mr. Smith?"

"Yeah, what can I do for you?"

"Oh . . . maybe I shouldn't bother you with this but I just don't know what to do."

I was inclined to agree. She shouldn't bother me with whatever it was. "What's wrong?"

"Oh, nothing, it's just that I figured out the password on Irene's computer. When I was packing her clothes, I was thinking about how so many of them are shades of green. It was always her favorite color and I remembered what you said about people picking passwords they wouldn't forget. So I turned on the computer and tried it and that was it—green. I started reading the files and it seems to be a diary. I only read a little of it. It's very personal and I felt like I was invading her privacy and, well, it's like having her voice on the answering machine—it's just so sad, reading her private thoughts and knowing she's gone. The thing is, I'm wondering whether I should tell the police about it. I just hate the thought of anyone reading her diary and, yet, suppose there's something on it that will help them find out who killed her? I thought you might be able to help me decide what to do."

Thinking it would upset her to know the cops had already read her sister's diary, I said, "It would probably be a good idea to let them know about it."

"Oh, dear. I just can't stand the thought of a policeman sitting here reading it. I wouldn't mind so much if Chief Pauling read it, he seems so nice, but with him in the hospital . . . and I'd feel better if you looked at it first anyway. If there's nothing on it that the police need to know about, I wouldn't have to tell them at all."

"Pauling takes a dim view of my interfering in police business. I'll call him if you want, see what he thinks. Maybe it can wait until he gets out. He'll probably be released tomorrow."

"Oh, would you do that? I'd appreciate it."

I told her I'd call back right away, then disconnected and called the hospital. The phone in Phil's room was busy and I was put on hold for five minutes before finally being connected.

"It's me. How are you doing?"

"Not too bad. I took a walk down the hall a while ago. You don't appreciate your legs until one of them won't hold you up. You want something?"

"Nancy Johanssen just called me. She figured out the password for the computer files. She wants to know if you want to see them. She didn't like the idea of cops reading her sister's diary, so I didn't tell her you already had. Maybe you can give her a call, tell her you'll stop by when you're out of the hospital or something."

"Well, now, I don't want her thinking I'm not doing everything I can to solve her sister's murder, so putting it off's not a good idea. No point in upsetting her by letting her know we already saw them, either. How about you go over there and make another copy. There were some blank floppies on the shelf by the computer. I'll call her later on and act like I just read them."

"I'm kinda busy, Phil."

"Doing what? It'll only take you a few minutes."

"Don't you have someone you can send over there?"

"Yeah, okay, I'll send a uniform over there in a patrol car and she'll get all upset. Seeing as how you went and got all chummy with her and she's calling you about stuff like this instead of me, why the hell shouldn't you do it?"

I could think of plenty of reasons, the main one being

that I wasn't on the city payroll. "Jesus, Phil, you're always telling me to stop interfering in police business and now when it's convenient for you, you want me to be your errand boy. I'm busy. You told me to stay away from there anyway."

"Yeah, well, I'd go do it myself but I got a bullet hole in my leg, which I might point out I probably wouldn't have if you'd learn to mind your own goddamn business."

"Maybe you better ask the doctor to increase your pain medication. You're in one hell of a shitty mood. You know how many hours I've put in this week, and nobody's paying me? I should just change Arrow Investigations to Dogsbody, Incorporated."

"What the fuck's a dead dog got to do with anything? You going over there or not?"

"*Dogsbody*. One word. It means a drudge. Everybody's always expecting me to do their drudge work for them."

"You going over there or not?"

"I'll go, but you owe me one, pal, and don't forget it." I hung up on whatever he started to say, probably something about me being deep in the hole when it came to favors owed. I called Nancy and told her I'd be there in thirty minutes.

I went into the bedroom and changed clothes, putting on long johns and thick wool socks, then jeans and a blue plaid flannel shirt. I added my warmest jacket, an olive drab military-style parka with a fur-lined hood, then stuffed a pair of fleece-lined leather gloves and a black ski mask in the pockets and pulled on snow boots.

At the end of the driveway, I stopped the truck. The Cherokee was still sitting with its nose against the Douglas fir. I trudged through the snow to it and got a flashlight and my cell phone. There weren't any phones where I was going and I was pretty sure I was going to need one.

I spent less than ten minutes at Sandhoff's house copying

the computer files. I wouldn't have bothered to actually copy them, since Phil already had them on another floppy disk, but Nancy was watching me. Impatient with the whole stupid charade, I turned down her offer of coffee, explaining that I was on my way to the woods to look for a runaway boy. "Goodness," she said, "I hope he's dressed warmly." I didn't think it made much difference what Jordan was wearing, but her words chilled me to the bone.

Downtown, I parked in a lot on the corner of Fourth Street and Jefferson and walked around a couple blocks, mingling with the Christmas shoppers and going in and out of stores that had front and back entrances. Certain no one was following me, I walked north on Sixth, which dead-ended at Monroe Street at the southern tip of the woods. Mackie Woods, where it all began and, for Jordan Clausen, at least, it all ended.

Chapter Thirty-Six

A hundred years ago, much of the land that's now within the city limits belonged to a man named John Henry Mackie. After the turn of the century, John Henry began selling off his holdings bit by bit. When he died in 1929, he had a few million in the bank, a small ranch outside of town, and a six-hundred-acre wedge-shaped piece of forest just north of downtown. His heirs got the millions and the ranch. He bequeathed the woods to the town with the stipulation that only one fourth of the land could be developed as a park; the rest was to remain in its natural state. If the city didn't want to comply with his wishes or decided it didn't want the land, ownership would revert to John Henry Mackie's descendants.

Over the years, a lot of developers had paid a lot of lawyers a lot of money to try to convince the city it could legally sell the property, but the city government had abided by John Henry's wishes. The hundred and fifty acres closest to downtown had been developed into a park, with jogging and biking paths, picnic tables, water fountains, public restrooms, and a playground.

The rest of the land remained undeveloped, but not undisturbed. Scout troops and assorted nature-lovers hiked through it and camped on it; Depression-era hobos and homeless families had found shelter in it; transients of all eras slept beneath the trees in spring and summer and occasionally froze to death in winter; children wandered into the woods, followed by search parties trampling the underbrush looking for them; kids carried six-packs and fifths into the woods for parties away from the prying eyes of parents; grudges were settled away from the prying eyes of the law; garbage was illegally dumped; bodies were buried in shallow, hastily dug graves; young lovers strolled through the acres in search of privacy, giving rise to an expression that was common in my grandparents' youth: young women who became pregnant out of wedlock were said to have stayed too late in Mackie Woods.

Only once had the town found it necessary to interfere with Mother Nature's management of the woods. That was in the late 'sixties, when flower children were in bloom. A small band of hippies moved into the north part of the woods where they smoked a little dope, sunbathed in the nude, and reportedly indulged in orgies. Mackie Woods had survived worse, so no one was particularly concerned until the day a local teenager was accosted in the woods by three long-haired men who were a little too high to be able to distinguish between Free Love and gang rape. Local police, sheriff's deputies, and a fair number of uninvited irate citizens hiked into the woods in search of the perpetrators.

Thinking they were about to be busted, the hippies set fire to their marijuana crop. It was a hot dry August; the fire scorched fifty acres of forest before it was brought under control. Two flower children died in the fire when a sudden shift in the wind caught them unaware; the rest soon moved on. The rapists, it turned out, were local bad boys.

The city of Mackie made its first, and so far only, official encroachment upon nature in Mackie Woods. Trees were felled to form two rough roads which served both as access roads for emergency vehicles and as fire breaks. One road cuts almost dead center through the woods from north to south, the other runs east to west, a little north of center. In an aerial view, the two roads form a cross. Given that and the deaths that had precipitated their construction, it was probably inevitable that the roads would be dubbed Haight and Ashbury.

I walked quickly across the playground area to the beginning of Haight. A few hardy souls had sledded down the slopes and made angels in the snow earlier in the day, but the park was empty now. It was four-thirty in the afternoon on one of the shortest days of the year. A heavy cloud cover promised more snow and a frigid wind was blowing.

The surface of Haight was a combination of loose gravel and dirt, frozen now and covered with half a foot of snow. Suggestions to pave Haight and Ashbury had always been vetoed. A smooth surface would be an open invitation to bikers and four-wheel-drive enthusiasts, the steel bar blocking the entrance to a paved access road that led through the park to the beginning of Haight being more a symbolic barricade than a functional one.

By the time I'd crossed the park and headed north on Haight, the wind was blowing snow, not soft fat flakes, but tiny icy crystals that stung my face. I remembered the ski mask in my pocket and put it on, pulling my jacket hood over it.

I had the cell phone in one of the jacket's voluminous pockets and now I took my gun out of my hip holster and put it in the right-hand pocket where I could get to it easier, thinking as I did it that it would have made more sense to bring a rifle. Not that I was particularly worried. Mackie Woods teems with small wildlife but larger animals are rarely seen anymore because of the proximity to town. But there are reports of bobcats and cougars being spotted now and then, although I suspected overactive imaginations accounted for most of the sightings. Except for deer, the only large animal I'd ever encountered in Mackie Woods was an enormous elk that must have wandered over from the Umatilla National Forest. He had reacted to my puny presence with a disdainful look before moving majestically away.

Mackie Woods covers less than a square mile, but once you're past the park area, the impression is of endless forest in all directions, the trees dense, blocking any view of the horizon. The larch and maple trees were stark skeletons now, their snow-laden branches a study in black and white. The dark green boughs of the evergreens were frosted with snow. It was all very picturesque, beautiful in fact, but I spent the first fifteen years of my life in southern California where snow was something you traveled to see and when you tired of it you went back home and hit the beach. After fifteen years in eastern Oregon I was used to the winters, but that didn't mean I liked them.

The snow crunched beneath my boots, its surface a glittering blanket of ice crystals. Just before I left the park and entered the woods themselves, I turned and looked back. Unless there was a sudden thaw, I didn't have to worry about getting lost. The footprints I was leaving in the snow beat the hell out of Hansel and Gretel's trail of bread crumbs.

I planned to stay on Haight until it intersected with Ashbury, then head west. I was operating on a number of assumptions. The first was the fairly sweeping assumption that I was right, something that hadn't always panned out in the past, but what the hell. The second was that Jordan Clausen was a young man of his word who fully intended to sell his rifle to Bubba Fackler and run away with Rachel Harroldson.

The third was that Jordan had been in Mackie Woods Monday morning while Irene Sandhoff's killer was lying in wait at the top of the hill overlooking Belle Foret. With hours to wait until his meeting with Bubba, Jordan would have wandered westward, drawn by curiosity to the sounds of the demonstration, which would have carried clearly on the cold winter air.

My fourth assumption was that whatever happened, happened fast. A shot was fired; a killer fled; a fifteen-year-old boy suddenly appeared, attracted to or startled by the gunshot and the sudden sounds of chaos on the street below. The killer must have panicked—a clean kill, an easy getaway, and suddenly a boy coming out of nowhere, a witness who had to be disposed of in a hurry.

The cops hadn't made a thorough search of the woods, and Phil would kick himself for that and wish he'd asked the sheriff to bring the dogs out, but his judgment had been sound. The killer would have been a fool to hide in the woods, when an easy jog could get him out and into a car in under ten minutes. He could pretty much count on having enough time before any kind of search could be organized. If, as Phil thought, there were two people involved, the second would have simply listened for the shot, then driven by and picked up the killer as he came out of the woods at a predetermined spot.

But the boy was in the way, an eyewitness to murder. No second shot had been fired, which meant they had come face to face. The outcome of their encounter was sure to have been swift, and inevitable: Jordan wouldn't have had a chance.

When I reached Ashbury I turned left, heading west toward the edge of the woods where the land dropped away and Belle Foret lay below. It was fully dark now, but the stark contrast between the snow and the trees and rocks made the flashlight unnecessary. I knew I was getting close when I spotted a yellowish shimmer ahead: the glow of a streetlight on Belle Foret.

I left Ashbury then, heading northwest, walking between trees. The going was rougher, the ground uneven, pine cones and fallen branches hidden beneath the deceptively smooth surface of the snow. I turned the flashlight on, angling the beam toward the ground ahead of me. At one point I stepped onto a seemingly solid piece of ground and was suddenly knee-deep in snow. I hauled myself out of the hollow I'd stepped into and continued on, picking my way more slowly and testing the ground carefully with each step.

The glow of another streetlight was ahead of me. I walked to the edge of the cliff and looked down on Belle Foret. I'd miscalculated by less than fifty feet. Sandhoff's office was slightly north. Moving back from the drop, I continued on until I was directly across from the building. A ponderosa pine loomed just behind me. Closer to the edge, the ground was covered with bushes, soft and formless with their covering of snow.

I turned my back to Belle Foret and looked around. Which way would he go? Southeast, I thought, toward town, because the roads on the east and north sides of the woods were country lanes, where a lone car was more likely to be remembered than it would be on Monroe, where traffic was light but steady. Monroe was tree-lined and curving, with houses on the south side, but in the age of double-incomes, houses are seldom occupied on a weekday morning. A car moving slowly down the street, stopping briefly near the park to pick up a man, probably innocently dressed in jogging clothes, would go unnoticed or at least unremembered.

Southeast, then, and Jordan would have been somewhere in that direction, too; otherwise he wouldn't have been seen by a man in a hurry to get away from the scene of the crime. I walked southeast, looking for a place of concealment.

In the end, it was easy. I was no more than fifty yards from the cliff edge when I spotted a fallen tree. The underbrush in the forest wasn't dense, the big trees blocking out the sunlight needed by smaller plants. But the fallen tree, felled years ago, probably by lightning in a summer storm, had left a gap in the forest's canopy. Smaller plants had flourished in the open space where the sun was no longer filtered through thick branches.

I found Jordan Clausen beneath a tangled growth of bushes on the far side of the fallen tree.

Chapter Thirty-Seven

I know a lot of prayers. None of them ever seem sufficient in the presence of violent death. In the end, all I could manage was a fleeting thought of gratitude that it had been below freezing all week and the animals had left him alone.

I left him alone, too, holding aside the thick branches of a bush only long enough for the beam of the flashlight to touch his face briefly. I crouched beside him for a moment, then stood up and pulled the telephone from my jacket pocket.

I called the hospital twice. The first time I was brusquely informed the line to Room 206 was busy and I was placed on hold before I could say a word. I listened to an insipid instrumental rendition of "White Christmas," then disconnected and tried again. This time I tried to interrupt the operator, to explain that the call was urgent, but she trampled my words like a human bulldozer and placed me on hold. "Jingle Bells" played tinnily in my ear until I disconnected again.

I started to call the police department, decided I didn't want to talk to anyone but Phil, and settled for as close as I could get: I called Patsy. "I've been trying to get Phil," I told her, "but his line's busy and the bitch at the switchboard keeps putting me on hold. Can you try to get through to him and give him a message?"

"Sure, I'll call the nurses' station on his floor. What is it, Zachariah? You sound funny."

"I'm on a cell phone. Tell him I'm in Mackie Woods and I found the boy I was looking for. He's dead. Tell him to send someone to Haight and Ashbury and I'll lead them in."

"Oh, god. Okay, I'll do it right away. I'm sorry, Zachariah. I'll get through to him, don't worry."

"Thanks, Patsy." I put the phone back in my pocket and checked my watch, feeling disoriented when I saw it was only five-fifteen. It was dark as midnight in the woods. It seemed impossible that not much more than half a mile south, downtown Mackie was brightly lit, the Christmas decorations on the light poles were flashing gaily, temporary Santa Clauses were ringing bells on street corners, and shoppers were making their way from store to store in search of the perfect gift.

The thought of gifts reminded me of Jordan's rifle. I crouched down again, curious whether his killer had taken it. By his legs, I spotted a long squared-off shape that might have been a box, but it was too dark for me to be sure and I didn't want to splash the flashlight's beam over him again. I looked up, over the fallen tree, toward Belle Foret, hoping the glow of a streetlight was visible, feeling a need for light, for some sense of connectedness with a world less dark than this bleak forest.

A movement caught my eye. I watched and in a moment I saw it again, on the path I'd taken through the trees, an erect shadow moving in the darker shadow of a pine. A man.

Under any other circumstances, the sight of another person in the woods wouldn't have bothered me. I considered it too damned cold for a walk in the woods but some people like winter. The fact that we were in the same area might only mean that he'd come across my tracks and was curious. Even if he were up to no good, thinking a lone walker in the woods was an easy mark, there was no reason for me to be worried.

He'd have second thoughts about hassling me once he got a look at me. And if my size didn't do it, my thirty-eight would.

But these weren't ordinary circumstances. There was a dead boy at my feet and I'd been living for days with the knowledge that a killer might be after me. I stayed still, peering over the fallen tree, hoping my jacket and ski mask would camouflage me from the man's sight until he was closer. And he was coming closer, making his way slowly from tree to tree, following my footprints in the snow.

There was something stealthy about his movements that sent shivers across my scalp and made my heart beat a little faster. Running in a low crouch, I moved away from the fallen tree and took shelter behind a big pine. I squatted and peered through the snow-laden branches. He was still coming, still following my trail, heading for the fallen tree.

I checked behind me, planning a route, then moved from tree to tree in as straight a line as I could, hoping the thick trunks and the spreading branches would block me from his sight. The crunch of snow beneath my feet and the whisper of clothing as I moved seemed enormously loud to me, but I couldn't hear a sound from the other man. The rushing noise of the wind blowing through the pines was so constant I had stopped hearing it, but it was covering the sounds of movement.

I stopped and crouched behind the low-hanging, snow-covered boughs of a pine, looking back the way I'd come. He was almost to the toppled tree now. As he moved around some small obstacle on the ground, I saw him in profile for just a moment. He was too far away and it was too dark for me make out his features, but I had no trouble identifying the long, slender object resting in the crook of his arm. A rifle. All of a sudden the weight of the thirty-eight in my pocket wasn't nearly as comforting as it had been before.

I checked my watch, surprised to find that it was only five minutes since I called Patsy. She'd have talked to Phil by now and he'd be setting things in motion, but he'd handle it as quietly as possible to avoid drawing throngs of curiosity-seekers to the woods. No cop cars with lights flashing and sirens screaming were going to come barreling down Haight.

The man had reached the fallen tree. I had walked around it, passing by the gnarled roots, but he scrambled over it. He stood for a moment, looking in my direction, looking, I was sure, at my tracks in the snow, leading away from the tree, marking the path I'd taken as surely as neon arrows pointing the way. He turned back toward the tree and pushed aside some tangled branches. A narrow beam of light suddenly appeared, a bright shaft from the man's hand to the ground. Even from my distant vantage point, I could see the light flit quickly across Jordan's pale face before disappearing as quickly as it had appeared.

My mouth went dry. He had known Jordan was there. This was the killer. This was the man who put a bullet through Irene Sandhoff's brown eye and snapped Jordan Clausen's neck, the man who shot Eddie Paxton in the back and fired at Phil in my Cherokee. This was the man who was gunning for me.

I didn't even wonder who he was. It didn't matter right then. What I did wonder was how he'd known where to find me. Nobody followed me from downtown, I was sure of that. I hadn't told anyone I was coming to the woods.

As the killer turned and started walking again, following in my footsteps, I realized I was wrong. I had told someone. Cruelly mocking now, her words echoed in my mind: *Goodness, I hope he's dressed warmly.*

Chapter Thirty-Eight

I considered and discarded some plans in rapid succession. *Run like hell* had a certain appeal, but a bullet in the back didn't. Heading for Haight and hoping I came across a cop or two also had its charms, but I hadn't heard any cars laboring up Haight yet. Firing a few rounds to attract attention occurred to me, but I hadn't brought extra shells. A single shot wasn't enough and more than one would leave me short of ammunition. Staying where I was and waiting for him was too risky. He was already a lot closer than I wanted a killer with a rifle to be.

I thought of the telephone in my pocket—a quick call to the cops, but it wouldn't be quick. I could see myself engaged in endless explanation, my voice carrying, the man with the rifle knowing I was summoning help, deciding to stop the cat-and-mouse game and get it over with in a hurry. If I could get past the operator at the hospital and get through to Phil, he'd get the picture immediately, but again the killer might hear my voice and no matter how fast Phil acted, it wouldn't be fast enough.

I started working my way back toward Belle Foret, moving from tree to tree, checking behind me each time I reached a sheltering trunk. He was still following my prints, moving slowly, not making any attempt to get closer. My tracks marked an erratic path of flight, from tree to tree to tree. He had to know I'd seen him. He was probably hoping I'd appear in an open space between trees so he'd have a clear shot. He wouldn't want to fire more than once if he could help it, not this close to town. One shot was all he'd need anyway. He was good with a rifle. He could easily drop me from a hundred feet away, not nearly close enough for my gun to be much of a threat to him. Modified to fit the circumstances, the punch line of an old joke flitted through my mind: I showed up at a rifle match with a revolver.

While one part of my mind was busy choosing a route through the trees, checking the ground for solid footing, listening for sounds of pursuit, another part of my mind had gone into overdrive, putting all the pieces together.

Nancy Johanssen, the original old maid librarian, sole heir to her sister's estate. Her phone number appeared regularly on her sister's phone bill until October, when the calls ceased. They had a falling out of some kind and were no longer speaking. What could happen between two sisters that would drive one of them to murder the other? I couldn't believe it was just the money, although I knew Sandhoff was well-off.

When I searched Sandhoff's house, Nancy had pointed out her luggage to me. But nobody packs two suitcases and two carry-on bags when there's a sudden death in the family. She packed leisurely, probably well in advance. Or maybe she had her partner's luggage, too, stashed in her murdered sister's bedroom. It was her partner's, I thought, because there was also a shaving kit in the bathroom, with a razor and shaving cream. Fred Niles had a full beard and mustache, the kind you trim with scissors.

A good actress, Nancy Johanssen. She must have been horrified when I discovered that her sister, with her preference for typewriters, had kept some kind of dated journal on her computer. Luckily for her, I ran up against the password. I thought of the floppy disk I'd tossed carelessly on the seat of Phil's truck. I'd have bet my entire ten acres that the files I copied didn't match the ones Phil already had. Nancy would have erased anything that supported his suspicion of her. I wondered if she'd spent hours in front of the terminal, desperately trying passwords. More likely, she'd known her sister well enough to guess it immediately and had played along with me, suggesting words for me to try.

The computer files were an excuse to get me back to her sister's house so her buddy with the rifle could try again. Yesterday she had stood in the open doorway of her sister's house, taking note of what vehicle I was driving so she could pass the information on to her partner. But I'd told her the truck was borrowed and mentioned I was returning it. I hadn't though and Phil had been driving my car. Today, she hadn't needed to know what I was driving. I told her exactly where I was going. They must have had a good laugh about it: The fool of a private eye was going alone to the woods, taking a walk in the snow, leaving a trail anyone could follow.

But I had declined Nancy's request to stop by the house and read the files. Phil sent me anyway. *Son of a bitch!* He set me up, the bastard, and when I had more time to think about it I was going to be pissed as hell. I almost laughed aloud, realizing he probably had someone tailing me when I left Sandhoff's house. Instead of losing the killer downtown, I'd lost the cops.

I had made my way westward until I was less than fifty feet from the drop to Belle Foret. The cover was lighter near the edge and I'd have to step into the open to get there. I peered through branches, trying to spot my pursuer. I didn't see him. I crouched against the trunk of a pine, watching, waiting. Sweat was making the ski mask prickly against my face. I pulled it off and dropped it. I'd already taken off my right glove and had my thirty-eight in my hand. I was no longer aware of the cold, fear and adrenaline providing their own kind of heat, but now I suddenly realized my right hand was numb. I transferred the gun to my gloved left hand for a moment, flexing my frozen fingers a few times.

Where was he? He was always easy to spot before. All I had to do was follow the line of my footprints. Long seconds passed with no sign of him. My heart started beating in dull heavy thuds. Was he circling around? He must have figured out that I was trying to get to the edge, hoping to make it to one of the sections where the drop-off wasn't so sheer, where I could slide down a steep incline to the street below.

I turned slowly, checking behind me and to both sides. No sign of him. A drop of sweat ran down the side of my face, hot at first against my chilled skin, then ice cold. Afraid to move until I knew where he was, I stayed hunkered down by the tree, watching for him. As the seconds passed, I thought of Eddie Paxton.

Fast woman, he'd said. Irene Sandhoff's clothes, her winter wardrobe, had been sorted into stacks on her bed: skirts and sweaters and wool pants, underwear, and leotards and tights. Leotards and tights and an exercise bicycle. She had cycled from eastern Oregon to Colorado in the comfort of her spare bedroom. She didn't jog and she didn't own any jogging outfits. She didn't wear casual clothes. But Eddie Paxton had seen her jogging.

Fast woman, he'd said, not because she was running, but because he'd seen her Monday morning dressed in jogging clothes, probably near the park, waiting for the sound of a gunshot, the signal for her to get the car and be ready to pick up her partner. Eddie heard the shot, too, and then he heard cop cars and an ambulance streaking toward Belle Foret. With his memory jogged by Irene Sandhoff's picture in the newspaper, Eddie managed to make a fuzzy connection: The woman he'd seen had to have gotten to Belle Foret in a hell of a big hurry to be there when the shot was fired. Eddie's concept of time was foggy at best, his brain too burned by alcohol for clear thinking. *Fast woman,* he'd said, not realizing it would have been impossible for her to get to Belle Foret, not realizing he hadn't seen Irene Sandhoff at all, he'd seen her look-alike sister.

But then he saw her again, when Willie Sloan introduced him to Nancy Johanssen in front of the Mackie Arms. Nancy recognized him, the old derelict she'd seen Monday morning and probably dismissed as a threat. But Eddie had reacted by scurrying away. Willie Sloan thought it was because he was embarrassed at being thrust into a social situation, but Nancy knew the truth—Eddie Paxton had just come face to face with a ghost.

Later, when he was either sober enough or drunk enough to think it through, he decided to tell me, maybe because he was afraid she'd come after him, more likely because he thought the information might be worth a few bucks. He stopped by the answering service, then walked over to my office, not knowing Nancy had already sent her pet killer after him, not knowing he was being stalked through the streets of Mackie. Poor Eddie, he'd tried to tell Andy Riggs, mumbling something about seeing a ghost while he lay bleeding in my doorway.

Nancy must have panicked Thursday night, because it was all falling apart, her best-laid plans were in ruins, first the boy in the woods, then the drunken bum, then along came a snoopy private eye with some unsettling information that could mean her sister had become suspicious. Probably scared to death that there was some evidence somewhere that would implicate her, Nancy suddenly changed her plans and stayed in Mackie.

I still couldn't see him. The jagged line of my tracks trailed crookedly through the woods. Single tracks back as far as I could see. Where was he? And where were the cops? I checked my watch, using my gun hand to push my jacket sleeve up a bit, squinting at the luminous digits. Fifteen minutes? Was that all? It seemed like hours since I talked to Patsy. Surely I'd been creeping through the trees for much longer than that. Fifteen minutes was plenty of time, though. Phil should have done something by now, but I still hadn't heard a car on Haight.

I checked all around once again and this time I saw him, rifle still in the crook of his arm. He was too close, a couple hundred feet at the most, not walking in my tracks any more, but off to the south, moving from tree to tree, circling around, trying to get to the drop-off before I did. He didn't even have to be close. All he had to do was spot me going over the edge and pick me off when I made it to the street below, where the closest shelter was the row of cottonwood trees on the other side of the street. A change of plans seemed in order. I decided to head in the opposite direction, away from Belle Foret. If I could move quietly and quickly enough to put some distance between us, I could make it back to Haight, and with luck, I'd run right into the cops.

I was moving away from the tree, walking backward, checking each step carefully before I put my weight down, watching for any sign that he'd spotted me, when the phone in my pocket rang.

Chapter Thirty-Nine

I fumbled for the phone in my left pocket, thinking *Why the hell didn't I turn it off?* I yanked it out as it rang a second time. Feeling like I had fallen into a nightmare, I flipped it open, put it to my ear, and, barely breathing the word, said "Hello?"

"Hi. I thought you might be lonely. I got hold of—"

"Patsy, I need help fast. The Belle Foret side of the woods, north of Ashbury."

"Oh, god."

I dropped the phone. He was coming for me. In a straight line this time. The cat-and-mouse game was over. I used my teeth to pull the glove off my left hand and dropped to one knee in the snow, the gun steadied in both hands, a tree trunk at my left shoulder. He was coming fast, two hundred feet . . . one fifty . . . a hundred . . . eighty feet. I raised the gun and aimed.

Hitting what you're aiming at from seventy-five feet away with a handgun doesn't take skill, or talent, or practice, or a good eye and a steady hand, or even luck. All it takes is a miracle. I got off three rounds, fanning them out a bit, adjusting my aim automatically as he dropped to one knee—jerkily, it seemed to me, but he brought the rifle to his shoulder in a smooth and practiced movement.

I dived into the snow, rolling behind the tree as the rifle cracked, and kept on rolling, coming up hard against another tree trunk. I got to my knees, suddenly aware of sounds coming from behind me, confusing me. Had I got turned around somehow? I jerked around toward the noise and a bright light hit me in the eyes, blinding me.

"Police! Everybody freeze!"

The light spun away from me and I turned my head to follow its path. The man with the rifle was on his knees, bent forward, his arms wrapped around himself. The rifle lay in the snow at his side. Two men ran past me, beams of light wavering ahead of them.

A hand clapped down on my shoulder and I looked up at John Malcolm. "Talk about the nick of time," he said. "Were you hit?"

"No." My voice came out in a weak croak.

Malcolm pulled his radio off his belt and turned it on, the air filling with the most beautiful sound in the world, the static squeal of a police radio with the squelch too high. He adjusted it, then spoke into it, saying, "Adam One, this is Adam Two."

Phil responded, his voice tense: "Go ahead, Adam Two."

"We got 'em both. Smith's okay."

"Ten-four. I'm en route."

While Malcolm was telling Phil where we were, I got to my feet, holstered my gun, and pulled my hood up. Then I walked to the tree where I'd dropped the phone. I brushed the snow off it and called Patsy, telling her quickly that everything was okay, then I dropped the phone in my pocket, put on my gloves, and rejoined Malcolm, who said, "Who the hell called you? I almost shit when the phone rang. I thought we must be getting close, but we hadn't spotted you yet."

"Wrong number."

Malcolm laughed and walked away. I followed him over to where Dan Foley and Bill Jackson were kneeling beside the man who had stalked me through the forest. I'd never seen him before. An average-sized man, in his forties, dark-haired. He looked pretty ordinary, not the stuff of nightmares at all. He was on his back on the ground, his face pale and contorted with pain.

"Looks like you bounced one off his hipbone, Zack," Dan Foley said.

I looked toward Haight. Vehicles, two or three from the sound, were on the way. Red lights suddenly flickered across the trees in front of me. I turned around and walked to the edge of the woods, looking down on Belle Foret where Engine Two, the fire department's aerial ladder truck, was just pulling up. The turntable at the rear spun, then the ladder extended upward, its top coming to a rest on the cliff edge. As Rescue One arrived, lights spinning, siren shrieking, Phil started climbing the ladder, favoring his left leg.

When he got to the top, I took his hand to help him. Once he was on solid ground, I grabbed a handful of his jacket and pulled him forward until his face was close to mine. "You set me up, you bastard."

Prying my fingers off his jacket, he said, "Yeah, I did, and, damn, it was such a good plan. It just didn't work out the way I thought it would. Which is all your fault, goddammit. Jackson and Foley were following you when you left Sandhoff's house and what did you go and do? You lost them, you jackass. They were still sitting downtown waiting for you to come back to the truck when Patsy called and told me you were up here. Jesus, don't you have any sense? Coming up here by yourself when you knew someone was gunning for you." He shook his head, at my stupidity, I assumed.

I wasn't about to be distracted. "You set me up. You sent me over to her house so she could send him after me."

"Well, yeah, that was the idea." We moved aside, making way for two paramedics who had just reached the top of the ladder. "But I figured we'd get him long before he got to you. All I needed was for them to make contact so I could figure out where the hell he was. See, I spent most of yesterday talking myself blue in the face and I came damn close to bustin' a judge's nose, but I finally got what I wanted."

"You had her phone tapped."

"Yeah, it was set up yesterday just before I headed out to your place. I knew they had to be getting together somehow and it was too risky for him to go to the house. I had it under surveillance after dark anyway. I figured they had to be using the phone. But, dammit, the phone never rang. First call she made was to your office. Then you called her back and I couldn't believe it when you turned her down when she asked you to come over. First time you ever did what I told you to and you screwed it up. But it worked out okay, since you called me so I could send you over there. I figured she'd get on the phone right away to tell her pal you were coming. But she didn't, so I figured she'd call as soon as you left. She didn't do that, either. Jackson and Foley were in position by the house, waiting to move in, so I told them to follow you. Damn, for a few minutes there, I thought I had it all wrong. Then Patsy called and told me you called her from the woods. From the *woods*. That's when the light finally dawned. Shit, I had the damn phone tapped and they were using cell phones. All this goddam technology is sure making life complicated. I sent Jackson and Foley to the park and Malcolm met them there. They found two sets of prints, so I sent them in on foot, thinking a lot of commotion might just force his hand and fuck things up worse."

"You *set me up*, Phil. Goddammit—"

"Oh, shut up, Bucky. You sound like a broken record. Who shot him?"

"I did."

"Good. Less paperwork. I guess they didn't get here in time, huh?"

"They almost did. But my phone rang and he decided to quit playing games and get it over with."

"Your *phone* rang? Oh, Jesus. Who was it, the answering service trying to track you down?"

"Patsy. She thought I might be lonely."

"Oh, *shit*. I should've told her what was going on, I guess. Actually, my first thought was to call and tell you to get the hell out of the woods, but I figured it wasn't a good idea."

Jackson and Foley had the prisoner on his feet. The paramedics from Rescue One followed as they led him to the ladder and started down it.

"What's his name?" I asked Phil.

"Beats the hell out of me. The San Francisco cops got a description from a neighbor who'd seen them together a time or two, but it fit about half the men in the state. Pretty cagey lady, Ms. Nancy Johanssen. She came damn close to pulling it off. Jesus, I forgot: What happened to Jordan?"

"He was up here Monday morning and he saw the guy shoot Sandhoff."

"Christ. Where is he?"

I took him to the fallen tree, walking slowly because Phil was hanging on my arm to keep some of the weight off his wounded leg. On the way, I told him everything I knew about Jordan and his parents.

"That's gonna hurt," he said. "They left him up here for six days because they thought he was a killer."

"Yeah. I also figured out why Eddie was shot." By the time

I finished explaining it to him, we were at the fallen tree. I moved the branches aside for just a moment. Phil used his radio to give instructions to his men. We waited without talking until they arrived, then walked back toward Belle Foret.

"For money?" I asked Phil. "Was that it? She killed her own sister for her money?"

"Yeah, in a way. That was what first made me take a good long look at her. Sandhoff was no Rockefeller, but she and her husband were pulling down big bucks in San Francisco and they made some investments, real estate mostly, and then she got a cool million in insurance when he died. That much money involved, I figure it doesn't hurt to take a look at whoever's getting it.

"What happened is, Johanssen thought she was about to lose the money. She had a lock on the inheritance, no other relatives or anything and she was looking forward to getting it pretty soon, too. Sandhoff had cancer. It was diagnosed right after her husband died and she had some surgery then and again right before she moved out here. She was doing okay, I guess, but didn't have a hope in hell of living to a ripe old age. Johanssen's almost ten years younger, too, so she musta figured she'd be sitting pretty long before she was retirement age."

"Was Sandhoff changing her will for some reason?"

"She probably would have, but I don't think she'd cut her sister out completely. Sandhoff and Niles were planning to get married as soon as his divorce was final. The only way Edie Niles would agree to a quick divorce was if he gave her everything they owned plus a big chunk of his future earnings to finish putting the kids through college and they're all going for Ph.D.'s. Since no one knew for sure how much time Sandhoff had left, he agreed to everything Edie wanted, which meant Sandhoff would've been pretty much supporting him. I figure she told her sister about it and good old Nancy decided she didn't much like the idea of Fred Niles cutting into her inheritance."

"Sandhoff stopped calling her in October. They must have fought about it. Jesus, for money. I can't believe it."

"Yeah, there's some stuff about the big fight on the computer files. Johanssen isn't exactly what she seems. That prissy librarian act of hers is bullshit. She actually does have a degree but her employment history is pretty spotty. Right now she's working for a library all right, but she's doing low-paid clerical work. She's got a history of being mixed up with real low-life types, even has a record—a couple of drug busts, some domestic disputes with live-in boyfriends. I don't know who this guy is, but it looks to me like she recruited him for the job."

"He got more than he bargained for. Two homicides, two attempted homicides, three if you count me tonight."

"The best-laid plans and all that shit. I bet you got a Bible quote to cover it."

But I didn't. Phil went to talk to his men and I walked out of the woods by myself, going back down Haight to the park, and then walking downtown to Phil's truck. I drove over to Clausen's house. I had a quote to cover that: . . . *make thee mourning, as for an only son, most bitter lamentation . . .*

Chapter Forty

It was almost seven o'clock when I left Clausen's house. Judy's brother-in-law was driving her home from Malheur County. Clausen was sitting in the dark, waiting for his wife, mourning for his son.

At the police station, Phil filled me in as much as he could. Nancy Johanssen wasn't talking and neither was her partner, who was at Mackie General in good condition. He had been carrying identification in the name of William Parks, but it was phony and Phil was waiting for fingerprint identification.

"The way I got it figured is, Johanssen flew to Portland Sunday. Sunday and Monday are her days off at work. Her pal drove up earlier and met her at the airport and they drove out here. I don't think there's any way they could have known about the abortion demonstrations before they got here, but they must've already planned to do it at her office. They were probably tickled pink when they saw the demonstrators. It would look like an anti-abortionist did it, so maybe we wouldn't look too hard for another motive.

"I'm waiting for a copy of the charges on the cellular phones. I'm betting he had a phone in the woods with him and made the bomb threats, hoping the building would be evacuated and Sandhoff would come out. I reckon he would've waited all day until she left for home if he had to.

"After the shooting, Johanssen got her pal away from the scene of the crime, then drove back to Portland and caught a flight back to San Francisco. He probably stuck around since she was coming back the next day. Johanssen was counting on no one questioning her whereabouts on Sunday and Monday. She was off work, she'd just claim she was at home by herself and didn't see anyone. Marla Twill offered to call her Monday to break the news. She didn't get an answer so she left a message on the answering machine and Johanssen called back within an hour. I'm not ever telling anyone how long it was before it dawned on me that she didn't have to be in San Francisco to get the message off her answering machine. When I talked to her, I just assumed that's where she was. She probably wasn't more than a hundred miles from here by then. She even mentioned it was real foggy there and she was worried about whether she could get a flight out. She flew back here early Tuesday, buying a ticket in her real name for a change, and did her grief-stricken-sister act."

"What made you start thinking about her? Just the money?"

"Mostly that. Also because I couldn't come up with any other suspect. I had a little trouble with the abortion issue as a motive right from the start. Just didn't ring true somehow. Her alibi for Monday morning was flimsy, but it's pretty hard to prove someone wasn't home alone, so I couldn't break it unless I could find someone who remembered seeing her here or at one of the airports. The closest thing to evidence I had was that she didn't make a call to Oregon from her home phone Monday, but she could tap-dance her way around that, claim her phone wasn't working or something so she used a pay phone and forgot her phone card number so she pumped coins into it.

"I knew she had to have a partner—for one thing, as far as I can find out she's never fired a gun in her life—and that's where I ran into a brick wall. The San Francisco cops couldn't get a line on him at all, except for a vague description from neighbors who saw a man going into her apartment a couple times recently. Hell, I didn't even know for sure if that was him."

"She should have worn a disguise when she was here. A wig and dark glasses or something. At least Eddie wouldn't have been a problem for her."

Phil shrugged. "What were the chances she'd be seen? All she had to do was drive him into town, drop him off at the park, then hang around to pick him up again. She probably spent most of the time sitting in the car, keeping in touch with him with those damned phones. She was only here once before, for a couple days last summer. She wouldn't expect to run into anyone who'd recognize her and she probably didn't even think about how much she looks like her sister. Back in Texas I used to be mistaken for one of my brothers every once in a while and it always surprised the hell out of me. I don't think we look anything alike."

"I wish I knew why Sandhoff called me. That's going to drive me crazy for the rest of my life."

"I got an idea on that." He pulled a paper from his in-basket and handed it to me. It was a photocopy of a receipt for an Express Mail package. The name on the return address was J. N. Lashinsky, with an address in San Francisco.

"Who's he?"

"One of your fellow gumshoes. The post office got the receipt to me about an hour ago and I called him. Sandhoff got hold of him early last week. Must've called him from Niles's house or something, because the call wasn't on her phone records. She wanted him to check out any men her sister was seeing. She had an appointment with her attorney next month and I think maybe she was going to change her will then. She had to know her sister had a history of picking the wrong men. Maybe Johanssen even said something to her, like when Sandhoff told her she was going to marry Niles, she claimed she was getting married, too. Kind of a sibling-rivalry thing. Anyway, Lashinsky did his best, but he couldn't get much on this Parks or whatever his name is. So, just to let Sandhoff know he was earning his pay, he tailed the guy for two days. He faxed me a copy of his report. It's not too interesting except for the last paragraph. Saturday morning he watched Parks pack up his car. He put a rifle and some camping gear in the trunk and he had a map of Oregon on the front seat. Lashinsky's last line is, 'He appears to be going to Oregon on a hunting trip.'"

"Oh, Jesus, she must have panicked."

"Yeah, I think maybe she did, but I bet she also thought, no way, her sister wouldn't do anything like that. But she must've been scared enough to decide it would be a good idea to find out just what was going on, so she called you. She wouldn't want to go to the police with some wild story about her sister plotting to murder her. Too bad we didn't come across the report. It must have been in her office somewhere and Johanssen found it when she was there the next morning. We probably didn't miss it by more than an hour or two. My mistake. It wasn't until Tuesday afternoon that I started thinking about her as a suspect and I went back over to the office and searched it thoroughly. It might have been enough to book her for suspicion and at least I would've known who she was working with. It wouldn't have helped Jordan Clausen any, but Eddie wouldn't've been shot. They're moving him out of intensive care tomorrow, by the way. Looks like he's gonna make it."

"That's good."

Phil nodded. "He's a tough old guy. Oh, yeah, almost forgot: Kevin Dale wants to know how long he has to hang around the house waiting for you."

"I forgot all about it."

"Well, go see him soon, okay?"

I said I would. Phil said, "One more thing. You can deliver a message for me. Tell Dr. Shit-For-Brains that if there was any way I could go after him without putting two women through hell, I'd do it."

I considered pretending I didn't know what he was talking about, but knew he'd never fall for it. Besides, a potential problem had occurred to me and I was hoping Phil could clear it up. "I'll tell him. Do you think Nancy gave me those files deliberately in an attempt to steer the investigation off course? If she knows about it, she might decide to make an issue of it, just to tarnish her sister's reputation."

"Fred Niles planted the files in the house Tuesday, after we already searched it. Sandhoff gave them to him for safekeeping and he started thinking maybe it was her using the abortion pill that got her killed. He didn't want to come right out and tell me about it so he took the papers to her house, thinking if we came across them and figured it out on our own, he wouldn't be so much to blame for spilling the beans. Giving them to you was probably the only innocent thing Johanssen did."

"Good. Anything else you want to say to me?"

"What's the use? You never listen."

I left soon after that. I spent a few minutes at Carrie's house, then left there, planning to go home, but I drove to Kevin Dale's house instead. Barbara Dale invited me in, which shocked the hell out of me. Seven years ago she called the cops whenever I knocked on her door, the fact that I was a cop then myself not bothering her at all.

All the furniture in the living room was pulled away from the walls, dropcloths draped over it. "Kevin just finished this room," Mrs. Dale said as we walked through. The wallpaper was brand new, the smell of the paste still noticeable. I checked the seams automatically: nice job. My cop friend in Portland said coincidence sucks, but I suddenly thought of something someone else had said—G.K. Chesterton, if I remembered correctly: "Coincidences are spiritual puns."

Kevin was in the kitchen, where the smell of fresh paint was strong. His jeans and white T-shirt were both liberally dotted with several different colors of paint. Kevin was tall and skinny, with dark hair and dark eyes and a perpetually sulky expression.

His mother left us alone. I sat down across the table from him. I considered trying to explain it once again. I was a cop doing my job when I shot his brother. I didn't kill Johnny because of who he was or what he was or even what he had done. The middle-aged couple who owned the drugstore Johnny had tried to rob were already dead. Killing him wasn't going to bring them back to life. I shot him because of what he had the potential to do and that was to kill his other three hostages. But what was the point of trying to explain it again?

"Looks good," I said, gesturing toward the freshly painted walls.

"They're making me do the whole fucking house. I finished hanging the wallpaper but I still gotta paint the hallway and both bathrooms. If it wasn't so cold, they'd make me do the outside, too, I bet. Jeez, I'm eighteen and they're treating me like a kid. I wouldn't mind so much if they just grounded me, but why do I have to re-do the whole fucking house? And I have to get it done before Christmas Eve, too, 'cause they're having some kind of stupid party."

"Well. It looks good."

He gave me a one-shouldered shrug in response. "I guess I owe you some money, huh? I gotta get a job before I can pay you. My dad says he won't do it."

I looked around the kitchen again, checking the paint job. "You know where my sister lives, don't you?"

"Well, yeah. That big old farmhouse out on Franklin. Why? I didn't do anything to her house."

"I know. I was wondering why you didn't."

He shrugged again. "She didn't do anything to me. She can't help it if she's your sister."

Mattie hadn't done anything to him either, but I supposed there was some logic at work. Mattie chose to sleep with me; Carrie was stuck with me. "Can I use your phone?"

"Uh, yeah, sure." He politely left the room, but I suspected he eavesdropped because when he came back the sulky expression had been replaced by one that might have been hopeful. Carrie had said "Are you crazy?" first, then "Absolutely not," followed by *"No,* Zachariah," then by "Oh, *shit!"* and I knew I'd succeeded in wrapping her around my little finger once again.

"You want a job?" I asked Kevin.

I left a few minutes later. Carrie had a new paperhanger, starting the day after Christmas. A small accomplishment, but I felt better than I had in days.

I went home and went to bed. Every time I closed my eyes, I saw Irene Sandhoff's eye turning to blood, or Jordan Clausen's pale, cold face. I got up, paced the room for a few minutes, then got back into bed after setting the alarm for four in the morning, when it would be seven in Connecticut and Allison would be awake. I closed my eyes again, holding the images at bay with the memory of Allison's voice on my answering machine: *I wish you were here, or I were there, or we were somewhere in the middle together.* As sleep overtook me, I was trying to figure out where the middle was. Nebraska? Iowa? Well, maybe somewhere south of the middle . . . somewhere warm, with sandy beaches . . . Allison's hair gleaming gold in the sunlight . . . turquoise with laces up the front . . .